CORYDON
AND THE ISLAND OF
MONSTERS

CΩRYDΩN

AND THE ISLAND OF

MΩNSTERS

TOBIAS DRUITT

SIMON AND SCHUSTER

SIMON AND SCHUSTER

First published in Great Britain in 2005 by
Simon and Schuster UK Ltd, A CBS COMPANY.
This paperback edition first published in 2006.

Simon & Schuster UK Ltd
Africa House, 64–78 Kingsway, London WC2B 6AH.

A CIP catalogue record for this book is available from the British Library.

ISBN 978-0-68987-538-0

5 7 9 10 8 6 4

Printed and bound in Great Britain.
www.simonsays.co.uk

To the True and Ancient Order

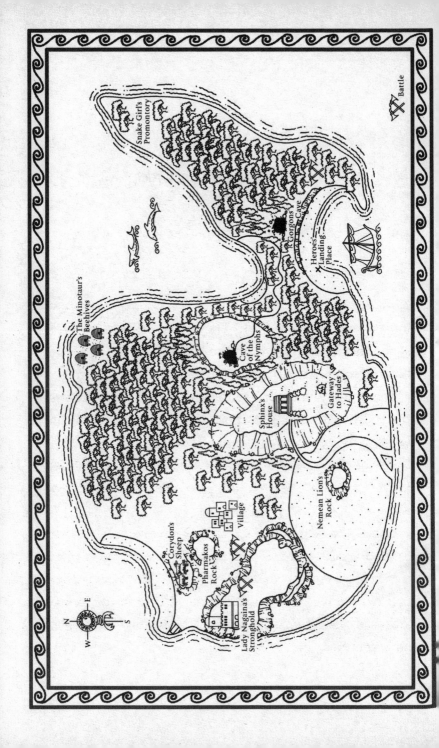

#

ONE

High up in the island's mountains, a shepherd boy looked out over his flock. They were resting in what shade they could find from the heavy heat of noon. The boy rested too, on dry grass under a rustling olive tree.

Below him, he could see the whole valley. Cypresses pierced the sky like spearpoints. The hillside he sat on was tawny, parched like an old lionskin.

The boy's name was Corydon. He had been an outcast for almost as long as he could remember. He was always alone.

There was something about his body, something that made him different. It was lucky, for a shepherd, but it had always been bad luck to him. His own mother had helped to chase him from the village, to the desolation of the Pharmakos Rock. 'You belong there!' she had screamed.

His mother's fury was part of the boy's flickering memories of a past different from his present. They mostly came in dreams. When he was awake, he tried not to remember.

When he dreamed of the time of pharmakos, what he remembered was the food. Figs, the dry crisp husks of barley embedded in the good bread, and the soft white tang of cheese, as good as the cheeses he now made himself. He remembered the peppery green, glistening streams of olive oil. The sweetness of the honey and how it overpowered his mouth, making his teeth hurt. It was the only time he'd had enough to eat in his whole life.

Months of food. But with the food came a sly kindness that he felt was all wrong. It was like when boys trick one of themselves into being the butt of a joke.

Then the terrible moment had come.

He pushed the memory away. He forced himself to think about something else.

Kleptis, for instance. Or sheep-stealing, really. No one called it that, though.

Kleptis was the only thing Corydon had ever been good at.

The boys of his village – the older ones – liked to go out and take a sheep or a lamb from someone they didn't much care for. Someone who had shouted at them for playing noisily during a sacrifice, for instance. Corydon had loved to go with them. He loved the cool walk through the moonless night, the excitement of creeping up to the flock, the stealthy and dangerous business of grabbing one sheep without disturbing the whole flock and alerting the shepherd. Corydon had often been the one doing the grabbing. Somehow, the sheep seemed to treat him almost as one of themselves. He'd even taken goats, the hardest animal of all to steal. And once he'd been on a daytime raid, deadly dangerous, because the shepherd being victimised would beat any boy he caught. Corydon remembered how he'd managed to snag twin lambs, and to carry them to the koumos, a scrabbled hole of stones in the hillside. He had dumped the lambs in the hole and covered them with pine branches, working frantically, hearing the belling of the shepherd's dog . . . He had been terrified. But the older boys had clapped him on the back and had given him the best pieces of the stolen meat. Later, the village headman had forced them all to make it up with the man whose sheep they'd stolen; they'd all gone off to the altar of Zeus and sworn an oath of friendship, between clenched teeth.

It had been this man who had said, first, that Corydon should be the pharmakos. The scapegoat.

And the boys who had helped him become an adept kleptis had been among the first to throw things at him on the day of the pharmakos.

But they had also been his salvation. Kleptis had kept him alive, given him a life.

It had taken him a while to build up his small flock of sheep. But after the pharmakos time, he had been left bare on the hillside, with nothing between him and death but the knowledge he had. And because of his days as kleptis – or perhaps because of something in himself – he had a way with the grazing beasts of the hills. He could scramble and clamber down cliffs and along ledges and down sinkholes, nimble as a goat, to places where other shepherds had been forced to abandon sheep because they were not so agile as he was.

And often, gloriously, he stole his animals. Lambs, ewes. Revenge on those who had cast him out was sweeter even than the meat he devoured.

Now he prized his animals fiercely. They were his livelihood and his friends.

As he looked them over, he saw that the sheep furthest down the mountain were startled by something moving below them, something that was itself climbing, something they feared. As the frightened sheep moved faster, he noticed that the panic was spreading, so that the whole flock began hurrying over the rocks, slithering in the light, dry grass, heading uphill.

Whatever it was moved below the hazel thicket.

As his favourite ewe rushed past, her heavy belly full of lambs, Corydon scrambled to his feet and ran after her. He wondered what had scared them so – wolves? bear? He fumbled for his only weapon, a small slingshot he

4

had made himself. The leather had dried a little, but it still held one neat stone. He ran, stumbling a little, and turned around, ready to hurl his stone at whatever was menacing his sheep far below.

He saw that there were many of the menacing things. They were half-hidden in the hazel thicket, making it rustle and tremble.

Wolves, then. Bears did not hunt in packs.

As he looked down, he saw that one of the attackers was larger than the others. Perhaps it was the leader. He decided to aim at it. Whirling the sling around his head, he flung the stone towards the shadowy figure. As it came out of the shade of the trees, he gave a great start. This was no wolf, but something huge, something metallic that caught the light. Surrounding it were men, more men than he had ever seen together on the hillside, at least six of them, and a whole train of carts, each cart burdened with what looked to the boy like giant metal houses. His stone had bounced off the largest of these.

To his horror, he realised that one of the men had noticed the stone he had thrown, and was scanning the hillside. Instantly Corydon dropped into the warm dust, flat on his belly. He lay as still as a rock, rigid with terror. His hands gripped the hard, baked earth in front of him. Now he couldn't see the men or their strange houses, but he could still hear, and what he heard increased his dread, for one of them was speaking:

'Hmm. This rock. Don't think the sheep dislodged it. Maybe we have a local here, someone who could tell us what we want to know.'

The boy crouched still lower. But a movement behind him made him look up.

It was his own favourite ewe, in lamb. She was gazing down at him, bleating. The silly beast had given him away. He heard the man cry, 'Hey, look!' and begin scrambling hastily up over the rocks towards him. Instinctively, he remained crouched in the dust. The next thing he knew, a huge hand seized him by the hair, and another hand went over his mouth. He was hauled into the air, struggling, and he heard the voice of the man who had captured him. 'Who do you think you're throwing stones at, you little wretch? Oy, what's this?' he said, grabbing Corydon by one leg, still holding him by the hair. 'Look what I've found here, captain!' he called eagerly. 'A new attraction! Just look at his leg! He's a right funny one and no mistake.'

The captain clambered up the slope. 'I've never seen this before,' he said. 'One of his legs is shaped like a goat's leg. Great gods! Add him to the other freaks.'

Corydon writhed desperately. He had no idea what 'freaks' were, but he knew that the man had noticed his leg. Now would come the beating, and perhaps this big angry man might even kill him. But instead of feeling a hard whip across his back or a knife in his belly, he found

6

himself slung over the man's shoulder and carried down the mountain.

Behind him he heard one of the pirates muttering, 'Mormoluke, mormoluke.' To Hellene villagers, the mormoluke was a goat-footed demon who stole and ate children. This man, at least, was like the people of Corydon's village.

But the others were puzzling. They touched him willingly; they seemed not to fear him, and they even met his eyes. After all the men had looked at him, a kind of metal house was brought out. He was shoved into it, and the metal house was loaded onto a cart, like the others.

The slow procession continued all the long afternoon. As the sun set, everyone stopped – for the night, Corydon thought.

Looking out, he saw that the men were bringing tents. He felt his cage being lifted into the air and placed in a small circle of cages. Some of the pirates disappeared, to look for water. It was almost dark now, and it was hard to see what the other cages contained. From the one directly opposite him he heard a faint bellowing, low and deep like the waves crashing in a sea cave. Corydon peered towards the sound, and gave a start backwards. He saw the heavy torso of a man, but it had the head of a bull. His head was thrown back, and he was making that deep bellowing sound. Very loudly, from the cage next to him, he heard a hissing. He strained his eyes towards the cage on his right. He saw the body of a lizard, and the long neck and head of a snake, but there was not merely one of these heads. There were five. He could see ten eyes surveying him, lit from within, like cats' eyes, but these were all different colours. Then they shut.

Corydon felt rising panic. Anxiously, he struggled to see into the remaining five cages. It was by now too dark to make out much, but he could see that one held a vast beast of some kind, crammed into the tiny space, and he heard a high, sharp laugh from another cage.

'Oh, Zeus, help me!' he breathed. 'Great God Pan, come to my aid!'

Nothing happened, but he began to feel a little better. Slowly, steadily, Pan kindled courage in his heart, and he felt it burning with a steady flame. 'After all,' he thought, 'they did not kill me. I am alive, and perhaps tomorrow I can escape from this horrible place, and go back to my gentle sheep.'

A voice broke into his thoughts. 'Why are you praying?' it enquired. It sounded like a woman, but somehow different – thinner and sharper and harder. It was a voice like a knife blade. He knew at once that whoever was speaking was also the one who had laughed.

Corydon's mouth was dry with fear. He swallowed desperately, mustering his courage. Then he spoke up boldly, inspired by Pan. 'I was praying for a way to escape from here,' he said. This was not quite the truth, but Corydon had no intention of confiding his fears to whatever had spoken to him out of the darkness.

The shrill laugh came again. 'Escape!' said the high, sharp voice. 'No chance of that. I have tried and tried. And if *I* cannot escape, how can a puny child like *you* expect to get away?'

Corydon had not made a plan yet, but he began to try to think. None of these monsters had got away – how could he? 'Perhaps a miracle of the gods?' he suggested tentatively, expecting to be laughed at.

But there was a cold, hard silence. Then the voice came again, full of hate. 'Gods! Gods are the ones who did this to me. If you still have faith in their goodness, then you're doubly caged, my little one.'

Corydon wondered why the creature had said this. Finally, he said, 'Why am I doubly caged if I believe in their goodness?'

The simplicity of the question might have startled the creature, for it answered at once, with equal simplicity: 'Because faith in them keeps you passive. If you expect them to do the rescuing, you'll sit here till you die. And if you do get out, you'll think it's their doing and not yours.'

Corydon didn't really understand what the creature was talking about, but he was frightened by the bleakness of its voice. 'I think I'll go to sleep now,' he said shakily.

'Goodnight, little boy,' said the creature. It was mocking him, but there was something comforting about it too. Corydon lay down on his straw, looking forward to morning when he would see the creature in daylight and know what it was that had – yes – befriended him.

He slept deeply, but woke as the stars were growing pale. The dream had come again, the dream that made his heart ache.

It was always the same dream.

The small village of his birth shone white under the heavy, bright sun.

Down its main street, a procession wound slowly. Men and women beat drums and sounded cymbals. Children ran about in the dust.

They were all laughing, and pointing at him; he was somehow at the centre of it all. He walked with his hands bound behind him; the ropes hurt, dragged at his arms.

He saw the white painted houses with their pots of herbs, the women in their black headscarves, the other children.

He knew he was saying goodbye to everything he knew. Even in the dream, he could sometimes feel his eyes fill with tears.

'Pharmakos! Pharmakos!' shouted the people.

That was him. He was the pharmakos, the scapegoat whose death would heal the village. Every few years, the village purified itself by sending out a pharmakos, someone who was blighted in some way, as he was. That person was never seen again. They died somehow in the wilderness beyond the villagers' fields.

This year, he knew, the cleansing was badly needed, because plague had come on the wings of summer. All over the village, babies had flushed scarlet, felt hotter and hotter, cried and cried, and finally stopped crying in the stillness of death. The villagers had begun to look for the plague's cause, and their search had led them to the boy.

In the dream, he always walked passively, while his mind hunted frantically for an escape.

The procession drifted on in the thirsty dust, straggling out of the village and through the parched, empty fields.

At last they reached the Pharmakos Rock, where the scapegoat was usually tied in place.

The boy was tied tighter. But his arms didn't ache as much as his heart. Would no one speak for him?

He looked around at a sea of hostile faces.

Heard his own mother cast him out.

Then the dream changed.

Some of the villagers were looking anxiously at the sky.

A huge storm cloud was rolling up from the west, livid and green. A cold wind blew from it, and on the wind came a harsh sound, a heavy clashing of metal.

The villagers heard the sound, and were alarmed. 'Hurry, hurry!' they cried to the men. Then they could wait no longer; they began to run back down the dusty track to the village, looking over their shoulders.

The clashing sound grew louder, the sound of a soldier's spear, clanging on his shield. It mixed with the first clap of thunder from the storm cloud. The sun had disappeared behind the cloud now, and the cold wind grew stronger, whipping hair into his eyes.

He had no idea what was coming, but knowing it was near made his belly tighten on itself, as if he were going to be sick.

He shut his eyes; he didn't want to see what was coming. Already he could smell the metallic stench of fresh blood. Something enormous stooped over him; he felt heavy metal brush his cheek, stinging him.

He heard a voice like the harsh grating of bronze on bronze. It was like the cry of a hunting hawk.

He waited for the owner of the voice to kill him. Yet nothing happened.

Except – suddenly his bonds were gone. He fell forward, onto his hands and knees. As the first drops of rain struck his parched body, he found the courage to look up at the sky.

He saw them flying into the heart of the storm: two of them, brazen-winged, enormous, calling to each other in their high, harsh voices. The lightning played about them, and their heavy bodies shimmered.

That was when he always woke. And sometimes cried.

He wanted to know what it meant; it must mean something. Was it a true dream?

'Great Pan,' he sighed. 'Tell me who I am.'

But the hills and forests were silent in the cold grey of early dawn.

βήτα
Two

Sitting on her rock in the cave's entrance, the gorgon Sthenno watched the stars grow pale, and noticed that the North Star was farther west than usual. 'Strange,' she thought.

A few moments later, her sister, Euryale, clattered into the cavern, claws rasping on the hard rock. She spoke impatiently: 'Sthenno, I know that some star or other is in an unusual position, but I *am* rather hungry.'

'We ate only five minutes ago,' Sthenno replied, not taking her eyes off the North Star.

'Look, Sthenno, why don't you at least try to rest?'

'I can't *rest*. You're an immortal too. You know how it is for us. Anyway, I like looking at the stars.'

'Well, I'm going to try to rest,' said Euryale. She disappeared into the darkness of the cavern. Sthenno heard a crunching noise, then silence.

Left alone, Sthenno scrabbled about and retrieved a bundle of fragments from under another rock. Sitting down on her own rock, she began to leaf through the old, crumbling scrolls, trying to find out about the different phases of the North Star. Finally, on a yellow parchment stained with age, she found something. When the North Star was west of its normal position, it usually meant that a god or a goddess was happy – and sometimes, that a god or goddess was angry. 'Hmmm,' thought Sthenno, 'but which god or goddess? And happy or angry?' Carefully, trying not to tear the fragile parchment, she turned it over, hoping to find some more information, but all she found were examples of the gods' wrath. She sat on her rock all night, thinking about it, wondering. Who could have angered a god?

As full morning broke the greyness with clear pink and gold, Sthenno's meditations were disturbed by the clash of Euryale's metal wings. She clashed them every morning at dawn, and it never failed to annoy Sthenno.

'I had just found out something and was pondering it when you came along and clashed your bronze wings.'

'Sorry,' said Euryale. She didn't sound it. 'Now can we go and have breakfast?' she asked hopefully.

Sthenno thought for a moment. 'Oh, all right,' she said irritably. 'What do you want today? I suppose you'd like a chunk of cow's liver?'

'Actually, I was thinking of a change,' said Euryale with dignity. 'I was thinking of duck's head.'

Euryale would never eat just the head, Sthenno thought. She would eat the whole bird. 'If you want,' said Sthenno. 'But remember it's a bit unhygienic.' Her thin body rippled with a delicate shudder.

The two gorgons went into the main cavern and looked at the enormous rock which served as their table. Euryale rushed to a space in the cavern wall where the food was stored and seized five large ducks. Hurling one onto the table in front of her sister, she immediately began to eat, tearing off great chunks of the duck and cramming them into her mouth.

Sthenno watched with distaste as Euryale devoured the duck. Her sister was always either hungry or hunting for food. Her only other pleasure was to make small pictures with her claws on the walls of the cavern. The pictures were always of huge slabs of meat, fresh and bleeding, or of animals stuck with spears or arrows. It was all part of her sister's primitive nature, Sthenno thought. Euryale was just primitive enough to believe in magic, and she seemed to think the food pictures magicked the food into her waiting claws, that they gave her success as a huntress.

Euryale had no ideas at all, Sthenno thought. She might be an immortal, but she was all belly and no brains. She nibbled her own duck's head without appetite. Euryale had already finished her first head and was starting on her second. Sthenno looked up and watched her sister, partly in amazement and partly with horror. By the time her sister began on her fourth, Sthenno had had enough. The sound of crunching bones disturbed her thoughts, and she wanted to concentrate on the odd activities of the North Star. She got up and went outside, and gazed out to sea, hearing the familiar sound of waves breaking slowly on the shingle.

Stealthily, Euryale began eating Sthenno's unfinished breakfast.

There was a screeching noise of claws on rock. Sthenno knew Euryale had finally finished eating and was now drawing one of her tiny pictures of food.

Sthenno began to walk back towards the cave. Because it wasn't fed by a spring, their cave was surrounded by dust, pale and gritty, that stuck in claws and wings. Parched furze struggled to grow in the grey heat. The entrance cave had a hole in its high ceiling that let in sunlight, so it was fringed with ferns; thyme drooped into the hole from above, its purple flowers a bright dry splash of colour.

But none of this meant anything to Sthenno. She wasn't interested in things, but in ideas and patterns.

Without her beloved stars to study, Sthenno was at a loss. She hated the daylight hours. Still, there were always her scrolls. She resolved to complete her logbook of star movements. She knew that if she kept very meticulous records, never neglecting a single tiny trembling star, she could find out how they moved, and why – and unlock the secrets the Olympians were keeping from the rest of the immortals. Yet she kept losing the records she made so carefully. Sometimes, Sthenno wondered if Euryale ate them.

Euryale completed a careful, delicate picture of a deer lying on her side, bleeding from gashes in her flesh. She knew she'd have to go hunting again soon. No matter how much she ate, she couldn't eat enough to fill the great aching gap inside her. She didn't know where the hole inside came from. Sometimes she thought it had been with her from birth. Sometimes she was bored with the daily round of their lives – Sthenno's obsessions, her own appetite – that she wanted to throw back her head and howl. But she could never do that, just as she could never get away from Sthenno, from this cave, from this island. Centuries of the same old thing. But how could she go when she couldn't even imagine it? Go where?

So she went hunting again. 'She always leaves me to get the food,' Euryale thought, resentfully, watching as her sister crouched over some fragments of papyrus in the cave entrance. 'If she gets any thinner she'll blow off the island.'

She frightened herself, thinking even that. The only thing worse than living with Sthenno would be living alone.

Euryale set off, and began to wander among the thickly wooded slopes of the island's mountains. Heavy with the scent of cypresses, thick with a springy mattress of fallen needles, they were her favourite hunting grounds. Pigeons and doves had been calling from the trees, but fell silent as Euryale approached them.

Deep in the woods, she saw not a deer but a small quail. Euryale felt a moment of self-doubt. 'My picture might not have been good enough to enchant the deer, to make them come to me,' she thought. She crawled on for a bit longer, looking for something bigger than a bird. Finally, she saw the deer of her dreams, a soft brown doe, and leaning against her warm body was her dappled fawn. Euryale rushed forward, talons outstretched to seize, yet utterly silent. The deer watched her come as if fascinated, unable to run. Then she bent her head to nuzzle her fawn one last time, and Euryale suddenly stopped dead. The soft nose of the mother deer, the delicate legs of her tiny baby; why should these make her unable to strike? Furious, with herself, with the deer, she leaped forward again and plunged her bronze talons into the deer's soft neck. The beast gave up her life with a gentle sigh. The terrified fawn pressed his head against his dead mother's flank, refusing to leave her, and giving small bleats. Again, the sight maddened Euryale, and she struck again, killing it with one quick slash of her claws. As blood poured from her victims, Euryale let out a long brazen cry of pleasure.

From afar, Sthenno heard Euryale's shriek of happiness. She knew that Euryale had found her prey. Sthenno smiled. Even though Euryale was sometimes annoying, she was nice in her own way. Sthenno could enjoy her gusto, though only from a distance. Close up, Euryale was far too noisy.

Sthenno watched the edge of the trees, waiting for Euryale to return. While she waited, she looked up at the sky. It was almost midday; Helios stood directly above the earth, and his beams scorched the dry grass brown and baked the soil into hard cracks. Sthenno knew it was time to seek the shade; noontide was unlucky, for baby lambs and for careless shepherds.

Suddenly, as she formed these thoughts, she remembered the boy. The mormoluke. The special boy.

His black hair. His thin brown face. His eyes, big and dark.

She and Euryale had saved him. Perhaps it was the most important thing they had ever done. For he was important. Sthenno knew that.

His village had thought him unlucky. Sthenno knew why. She still remembered his thin arms and legs, the bony feel of them in her claws. One of his legs had been different. Not wrong, but different: furred and goat-footed.

But she had known him at once and her heart had leaped with joy. He was the mormoluke. The one the stars foretold. She had the scrolls which revealed his importance. She and Euryale had saved him, though she didn't know where he had gone since then. She had known it was not yet the right time.

He would come when he was needed.

She knew this, but still she worried. Had he survived, out there on the mountainside? Was he lonely?

He must return soon, she thought. The stars were never wrong.

It was time for one of Sthenno's prayers to the stars. Absorbed in her thoughts, she had almost missed the exact moment. Anxiously, she rushed towards her study, where she knew her special praying circle was waiting. The floor was reddish, with green coppery markings. Sthenno had made a crude circle on the red rock with a charcoal stick. She looked up at the blazing blue sky of noon through the hole in the ceiling. She began her first prayer. She decided that she would say it to one of the stars in Scorpio's tail. She had picked Scorpio because she knew it was directly overhead, beyond the blueness.

As she looked up, she prayed to Artemis. Though not a huntress, like Euryale, Sthenno was warmly devoted to the virgin huntress: she who lived alone amidst wild beasts, on the wild mountainside. Sometimes Sthenno thought that roaming the mountain was like roaming the heavens with your eyes.

20

She wandered out of the cave again, and stood staring out at the sea. A happy Euryale called up to her. 'My picture helped me!' she cried, presenting the deer and fawn. She dived past Sthenno, into the cave, and Sthenno could hear her clattering about, her claws rasping on the bare rock of the dining alcove.

Though Euryale had just hunted, she had enjoyed it so much that she wanted to go hunting again as soon as possible, and she bounded off before lunch to see if she could find something bigger.

As she walked, she suddenly remembered the boy.

The thin, dark boy they had saved.

Where was he now?

Euryale shrugged. There was no way to know. He was somewhere. Alive. That was all that mattered. One day he would turn up.

As she returned, this time carrying a dead boar, Sthenno came to meet her.

Just then both sisters heard an astonishing sound. It was the shingle rattling under the tramp of feet. Human feet.

Euryale stood alone. Sthenno began to creep timidly back towards the entrance to the cave.

'Sthenno,' said Euryale, 'it might be an adventure.'

The sound of feet got louder.

'I'll stay,' said Sthenno at last, after a long pause.

The footsteps stopped. The sisters heard a mutter

of voices and the beginning of what sounded like an argument.

The biggest voice boomed out: 'It was a mistake to leave the creatures down by the shore just to go and look for a settlement. Especially Her. For all we know, She might have escaped. And now She might be creeping up behind us to turn us all to stone. And – there's that new one, the morm—'

'Don't say the word, for Zeus's sake!' screamed one of the smaller men. He was already wearing a blue bead, to ward off ill luck.

There was an uneasy silence.

'I vote,' said a smaller, slyer voice, 'that we should go back and bring the monsters with us. Then if there are any people on the island, they might pay us money to see them.'

'Money, on this island?' scoffed the first voice. 'Some hope! The only people you'll find here are villagers. There's nothing else here but bones.' A kicking noise showed that a booted foot was stepping on what might well be an old discarded bone of Euryale's. 'And no wonder,' the voice added, 'considering what we've found here today.' Again there was an uneasy silence.

'I agree with Belshazzar,' said a third voice. 'Let's not try to haul them very much further today. Get the skins out, Belasmir. Let's get the fresh water. I thought I saw lights to the west.'

'All right, captain,' said the first voice. 'But I don't like

22

it here. There's something about this place that gives me the creeps.'

'You're an old woman,' came the captain's voice. 'What do we have to fear?'

The voices began to fade into the distance. A crunch of shingle told that a small boat was being put back to sea.

'Did you hear that?' said Euryale in a whisper. 'There are monsters, and they're on their ship.'

'I'm afraid,' said Sthenno softly. 'They said one of them might turn people to stone.'

'But we're not people, silly. We're immortal. I bet if those pirates saw us, *they'd* be scared.'

Sthenno brightened a little. 'I think,' she said, 'that the monster might be an enormous bright light with patterns of the stars on it that only an immortal could see. And when a human looks at it, because of the bright light, they shrivel into stone, like a flower in the sunlight.'

'I think,' said Euryale, 'that it would look like a vast boar, with two crimson eyes, and long white tusks, so long they look like snakes. And its anger would scorch the hunter until he withered like a dry leaf.'

Both sisters were silent for a moment. Then, 'I'd better prepare,' said Euryale. She went into the cave, got her sharpening stone, and began to sharpen her claws.

Sthenno followed her. She was wondering what the pirates had found on the island.

*

Medusa, too, had seen the dawn break. In its faint light, she couldn't help seeing herself in the mirrors all around her. The cage she was in was made of mirrors. Everywhere she looked, there was another copy of herself. She hated seeing herself. Most of all she hated her face. It was mauve, with a few darker purple spots and a greenish tint. Like a bruise. Medusa herself nearly threw up at the sight. And now she had deep purple eyes, eyes like the poisonous plants near what had once been her home.

The pirates had built her cage of mirrors so that they could show her off and make money from her. People couldn't look at her directly; if she met their eyes, they died, and died terribly – in fact, they turned to stone.

She remembered the first time it happened. An ancient priestess of the goddess had blundered upon her, and Medusa had looked up, angry, ashamed. The woman had slowly hardened, her mouth freezing just as it opened to scream. Others froze instantly, the greyness of rock rippling down their bodies as fast as water.

She had been to many little towns now, and the children had fled from her, crying.

She remembered how the small hands of children felt; a friend's small daughter had loved to brush her shining golden hair.

She looked out at the landscape reflected in the mirrors around her, hating it for being so beautiful.

As she looked, she noticed a cave. In it something

caught the sun, a glint of something – gold? bronze? Perhaps it was a sword she could use to kill her captors. Then she could escape.

She saw Belshazzar and realised he'd noticed it too. No hope, then. She hated him even more than the others. He was the one who beat her. If she turned someone to stone, he beat her, not because he cared, but because it might reduce ticket sales. She felt sure putting her on show had been his idea, largely because the others never had any ideas, good or bad.

'Um – I'm just going for a bit of a walk in these lovely woods, captain. Might pick up something for dinner if I take my bow.'

She heard his oily voice. Anyone brighter than the captain would know he was lying. He was going after the metal gleam, hoping it was gold. From inside her cage, she laughed, a mad screech like the ragged cry of a bird.

'Shut up!' all the men shouted. Belshazzar slipped away in the confusion.

γάμμα

THREE

Sthenno and Euryale had noticed Belshazzar almost at once. The pirate may have thought himself sneaky and cautious, but he was no match for Sthenno's eagle eyes, or Euryale's hunter's instincts. As he approached the cave, crawling through the undergrowth, Sthenno and Euryale remained still and hidden behind rocky pillars in the cave entrance. So Belshazzar felt it was safe to straighten up and to begin to look about for the gold he was sure he had seen. He had equipped himself with an oil lamp, and as he moved deeper into the cavern, noticing strange drawings on the walls as he went, the hairs on the back of his neck stood on end; he felt he was being watched, studied. Swiftly he put down the lamp and turned, fitting an arrow to the string. No one. Nothing. He lowered his bow slowly, then slung it over his shoulder and began cautiously moving down the passageway again, his eyes seeking gold. Behind him, Sthenno and Euryale followed his tracks, swiftly, silently, Euryale a little in front. As Belshazzar entered the dining room, his eye was caught by the pictures on the ceiling, the food stored on shelves, the hearth glowing with the last embers of a fire. Someone lived here. Who? Or rather, what? He took out a small roll of papyrus and began to make a careful map of where he had been, noting down every detail.

Euryale and Sthenno watched, silent, remorseless.

Belshazzar rolled up the scroll and carefully chose to go straight ahead, ignoring the forks to left and right. He moved cautiously down a passage which was damp and cool; the rock shone slightly in the flame of his lamp. Suddenly the passageway opened out into a cavern; he lifted his lamp high, and was amazed to see that he was in a cave the size of a ship, huge, thick with red stone formations that shone glowing in the lamplight, as if the walls were daubed with fresh blood. Gigantic pillars of rock, also stained red, and shining columns like the colonnade of a temple were everywhere. It was beautiful, but somehow terrifying. He gazed, and then a noise behind him made him suddenly turn round.

His mouth dropped open. The lamp fell from his slack hand. The bow fell with a sharp clatter. He had seen them, two of them, ten feet tall, with bronze wings, with eyes that shone with amber light, with gleaming talons outstretched . . .

Belshazzar screamed: 'Gorgo! Gorgo!'

Mad with terror, he plunged away into the darkness, tripped, and fell heavily onto slick stone. He lost his footing completely. Slowly he began to slide down, like a new lamb on a damp hillside, then faster and faster, down, down, down into the darkness. Then he felt a great burst of pain in his head. Darkness enveloped him.

Sthenno watched the man slide screaming, into blackness. She noticed his terror, but it did not move her. She was simply glad that he was going, glad that she didn't have to see him or smell his strange alien smell.

Euryale watched with a mixture of contempt and horror.

'There are more of these men, we know. We heard them talking. They may come after him. He probably left footmarks.'

'I hadn't thought of that,' said Sthenno. Her stomach writhed with fear at the thought of more of these creatures invading her cave. Perhaps if they reached her scrolls, they might even destroy all her hard work, destroy her great project.

Euryale was calmer. To her, the man was simply prey, though not very exciting or even edible prey. 'Don't worry too much,' she said kindly. 'If they do come I can deal with them. They're only about the size of a doe. They don't seem good at running or hiding, and they're

29

very clumsy too. Did you see him drop all his weapons as soon as he saw us?' She paused, and then added thoughtfully, 'And after all, the villagers have always been pretty easy to manage, and they're the same kind of creature, I think.'

Sthenno nodded. 'Yes, but the point is, what should we do with this one?'

'It's obvious. Leave him here.'

Sthenno felt an unwanted worming of sympathy for the man. To die so slowly, of thirst or starvation . . . Perhaps, too, he would scream again . . . 'We'll have to feed him,' she said firmly.

Euryale looked up, surprised. 'Why?' she said wonderingly.

'We can't let him die of slow starvation. If you want him dead, go down to the pit and kill him yourself.'

Euryale shrugged. 'If you want. Whatever you like. The fall probably killed him anyway.' But a faint moan from the pit proved her wrong even as she spoke. 'All right,' she said. 'He's your pet.'

Bright morning light woke Corydon. He was used to sleeping on the hard earth of his hut, so it took him a minute to realise that he was somewhere else; then the memory rushed over him – the pirates, his dream – and the voice in the night! He looked in the direction from which the voice had come.

Instead of seeing the creature, he could see only a circle of polished bronze mirrors reflecting his own dirty face.

Why mirrors? Where was the creature?

A thought came to him. Were the mirrors protecting it? No. The mirrors were protecting the pirates from the creature. But why?

'Because it's death to look me in the face,' said the shrill, high voice, the same voice he had heard in the night.

Corydon jumped.

'What are you?' he gasped.

'I was once a woman. Now I am something else entirely.'

'What?' asked Corydon, though a shiver was prickling down his spine.

'They don't have a name yet for what I am,' said the voice, 'but my own name used to be Medusa. You can call me that, if you like. That's what they call me in the show.'

'What show?'

'That's what we're all here for, you know. The show. The big striptease. Where the pirates put us on display and charge people money to see it.'

Corydon thought. If seeing Medusa killed people, how could she be in a show?

Medusa seemed to guess his question. 'That's why they built me this cage. It's death to look upon me, but it's not death to look at something that reflects me. If you saw me in water, or polished bronze, anything, you'd be safe.' She laughed that bird-laugh again. 'Or fairly safe.'

Corydon thought again. 'You used to be a woman,' he said. 'What happened to you? How did you change?'

'Your story first,' said the voice sharply. 'How did you come to be a monster?'

Corydon had never been told before that he was a monster. Not as such. People had run away and screamed, but he'd never thought of himself as something worth screaming at. He knew he had no special powers, and it certainly wasn't death to look upon him.

'I don't think I am one,' he said at last.

'Of course you are. Why else would they have brought you here?'

Corydon was silent. Then he said, slowly, 'Well, I shot a stone at them. I thought they might want to punish me for that.'

'Maybe they do. But you're a monster. I can tell, and do you know how? Because no one has come looking for you. No one is wondering where you've gone. No mother, no father. You're alone in the world, just like me. All monsters are.'

Corydon was silent again. Then he said, slowly again, 'Maybe I am alone. But that's because I'm a shepherd. And we're always alone.' With that, he turned his back, deliberately, on the gleaming cage. He began shakily to sing a little song he had made up on the hillside, about a nymph-girl who lived in an ocean cave.

He sang to block out the harsh bird-voice that had called him a monster, but as he did so he knew that the thing they were keeping in the cage was listening. Listening hard. Corydon had never sung for anyone before. He was surprised to find that he rather liked it. At the end the voice, gentler now, said softly, 'Oh, well done, little shepherd-monster. One day, I will sing you some of my songs.'

Corydon had been too intent on their exchanges to notice the other cages, but as he looked around he became aware of them. The many-eyed thing was a hydra. The bellowing creature was a minotaur, and there was also an enormous lion whose breath was sharp flames, a woman with the body of a serpent, a woman with the wings of a great bird, and the claws, too, and a lion with the head of a woman, wearing a tall jewelled hat. They were all astounding, powerful. Just glancing at the crowned, winged one made Corydon's belly turn to water and his knees to jelly. For the first time, he began to wonder how the scruffy pirates could possibly be keeping all this power leashed. Every nightmare in the world was here, and some that the world had not yet even begun to dream. He thought slowly, but with great concentration. The key to escape must be the same as the answer to his question. He decided to spend the day watching and waiting.

The long, dreary day began. His grimy pirate jailer tossed a few hunks of stale barley bread into the cage, but Corydon was used to worse and fell hungrily on it. Then there was nothing to do but sit on the straw and think until the first straggling villagers came to peer and shriek. As two children stared into the cage of the Minotaur, their mother, who had come to guide them, looked into Corydon's cage. After a few seconds of open-mouthed shock, she cried in a high voice of terror, 'Mormoluke! Mormoluke!', and ran, her hands over her face, not even gathering up her children.

Her words awoke his most powerful memories: he smelled the dust again, heard the voices of his friends and family calling him the same terrible name, and again recalled the storm, the harsh cries, the bronze wings of his rescuers. What was he? Boy or *mormoluke*?

He had once been a boy, he knew that. He remembered his mother's arms around him once, on his name-day, though usually, he recalled, she did not like to touch him.

'You see,' said the high, terrible voice beside him, 'there is nothing between us.'

Corydon was trying not to cry.

Perhaps the person inside the mirrors sensed this. 'I have a song,' she said, almost shyly, 'a song that ends like that. Would you like me to sing it?'

Corydon gulped. She took it for yes, though, and

began singing in a voice surprisingly sweet, almost hon-eyed, but the song was as terrible as she was, and he didn't understand it. Afterwards he remembered only fragments, pieces of what she had sung: something about a fat red placenta, and an eely tentacle, and he knew it did end with those frightening words, 'there is nothing between us'.

But somehow, though he had no idea what the song meant, he *did* understand it; it was a song about hatred and misery and being frightened of yourself. He was impressed that she could sing a song that made so little sense and that nevertheless made so much.

She was waiting, and he also knew because he was a singer, that she really did want to know if he liked it.

'I'm not clever enough for it,' he said in his blunt way, 'but it's about monsters, isn't it? About being one?'

'About becoming one,' she corrected softly, and the venom had come back to her voice.

'Oy! You there! Shut your stupid mouths, would you?' The pirate voice cut across the moment they had shared.

'Don't worry,' she said softly. 'We can't expect them to appreciate poetry. Just look at them.'

The venom in her voice must have reached the pirate, for he turned angrily about. 'I heard that!' he roared (it was the black-bearded pirate, the one the others called captain). 'So I'm a clod, am I? And what are you – Sappho, or something? Just you learn a bit of respect.'

With that he drew a strange rod or staff out of his boot. The staff was only about as long as a man's arm, and four long tassels hung down from its tip. It was covered in some kind of writing – or was it pictures? – dense and thick with it, as if whoever had done the writing had too much to say for the space. At its tip was a red stone the size of Corydon's fist. It was smooth and round, like an eye. The pirate ran towards Medusa's cage, brandishing this curious weapon. Corydon heard a scraping noise, as if Medusa was trying to get away. But there was no escape. Leaning in, cautiously looking in the mirror, the pirate landed a heavy blow on her – Corydon heard the thud, heard her cry out in pain. 'That'll teach you!' snarled the pirate. And then Corydon heard nothing for a long time, though he called often to her, anxiously, fearfully.

δέλτα

Four

'But where's Belshazzar?' asked the pirate captain, exasperatedly. He eyed his sullen crew. Despite the takings, they were fed up with all the work, and fed up, too, with fear; fed up with being afraid day and night that something would slip, that a monster would get loose and kill the lot of them. Now they were beginning to mutter again, and the word they were saying was 'mormoluke'. Everyone knew the child was a bad-luck token if ever they'd seen one. Staff or no Staff, you couldn't tame luck. One of the crew was wearing so many blue beads as charms against the evil eye that he looked like a walking shrine. He had confided yesterday that he had 1,020 in all. This also made him very slow when it came to carrying water. Belshazzar had more sense than that, the captain thought. Only where had the man got to? He'd been gone for almost three days.

'Er – captain, sir – I just thought I'd say – he was last seen near Her cage, sir.' The cringing voice alerted him to trouble. Of course Belshazzar's disappearance had made them extra jumpy. 'Her' was what they called Medusa.

'Try not to be more stupid than you are,' he snapped. 'If She'd got him, we'd have found a nice little statue, you complete imbecile.'

'Oh – yes. I suppose – but then what about – you know – old Bully?'

They feared the Minotaur too. Something about his smell. The captain swept ruthlessly on. 'Last time he got someone we found the bits all over his cage. And the same goes for Lady Nagaina, too.' This was the hydra. She was his pet.

'What about – It – captain?' They would never even dare to nickname the Sphinx.

'We've never known It to take anyone. Though a man in Korinth did say how they do it. Something about their eyes – they can just burn you up when they feel like it. Luckily they only feel like it once every hundred years or so.'

'Well – captain – maybe It felt like it yesterday.'

'Instead of sitting here jawing like a bunch of old women,' the captain snarled, 'why don't we start a search for our mate? I'll stay here, and you lot can go and look.' The others immediately set up a wail about the dangers, the monsters and the horrors, but the captain ignored them and took out the Staff again. 'Like a touch of this, would you, Nikos?' Nikos and everyone else got up hastily and sped off up the track.

Sthenno was getting worried about the man they had caught. He wasn't eating anything, and every time she came into the cave where his prison lay, he would scream and fall backwards, injuring himself. She decided to consult the stars again. She felt certain she had seen a portent in a conjunction between the Great Red Star and the Lion's Tail. She thought it might mean a death, and she did not want to be a killer.

Euryale rested after a long, wearying hunt. She heard the man's cries, his desperate scrabblings, but they didn't interest her very much.

Belshazzar was trying to escape again. He wasn't thinking very much, or listening, or planning. He was simply scrabbling desperately at the cave walls. The very smells – the mix of blood and oil and herbs and some other strange, sharp scent he couldn't name – terrified him. Yesterday, in a desperate bid, he'd nearly made it out, but as he peered over the rim of the hole that was trapping him, he'd seen his worst nightmare peering down – the gorgon, the skinny one with the bluish hands and the livid eyes. He was equally terrified of the other, stockier one, the one who smelled like blood. Their images haunted his brief snatches of sleep.

Every day they held out raw meat to him. He imagined it was some kind of threat, that they were showing him what they planned to do with him. It had never occurred to him that they might be offering him food.

He managed to scrabble to the top of the hole, only to meet the absent glare of the bloodstained gorgon. Belshazzar was so frightened that he lost his grip at once, the slick mud sliding through his fingers as he slithered bumpingly, painfully, back to the very bottom. He burst into tears of fury and fear and frustration. His only hope – and he knew it was a tiny chance – was that the other pirates might, just might, rescue him.

The Staff! It might work, even on fiends like these. At the thought, he suddenly felt almost hopeful. Until he remembered the gorgon's livid eyes, and began sobbing with fear once more.

Nikos and his party pushed on through the spiky furze. One of them began to think he could see Belshazzar's tracks here and there in the dust. He was a pirate who had once been a hunter, and he was noticing other signs, signs that made him nervous.

'There's been something big along here,' he said, 'something almost giant-size. Look how this furze bush is all pressed down. And this thyme plant. If we—'

'If I had the Staff, you'd be for it,' Nikos snarled. 'Trying to scare us, aren't you?'

'Well I am scared,' said a third man. 'I've been scared every minute we've been on this barren rock.'

Belasmir laughed harshly. 'Poor little baby!' he sneered.

'Shhh!' said one of them. 'Listen!' They all heard it – the soft rustle of metal. It sounded like a warrior readying himself for battle, drawing his bronze sword softly from its sheath, picking up his heavy round shield. All the men instinctively lay flat on the ground. But the noise had really been made by Sthenno, slowly moving out to the rock to examine her star charts.

The men's sudden movement caught her eye. She saw them instantly, and without making another sound, she shot back into the cave at top speed, her wings spread wide, to warn her sister. Euryale slid out of the cave at once, with Sthenno following her, reluctantly. Silent, fierce, they flew towards the new menace. The pirates got to their feet and drew their swords, just as Sthenno and Euryale landed in front of them.

All the pirates turned green with terror. They thought of running, but they were trapped between the monsters and the sea. They decided to attack. Perhaps working with monsters made them foolhardy. For at once they could see that it would have been better to jump into the sea. Their swords glanced off the gorgons' bronze wings and metal claws, but they went on, trying to find some gap in the creatures' armour. It was their only hope, and it wasn't much of a hope; they all knew it.

Belshazzar heard the clash of metal, heard what he thought were gorgonish screams of triumph. He decided it was now or never. Desperate, sweating, he wormed his way to the top of his pit again, and this time he managed not to slip in the wet clay. He hung onto the top ledge, and with a frantic wriggle pulled himself up and off and away and out of the cave. He saw his shipmates fighting a losing battle with the terror that had kept him penned, but he never even thought of rescuing them. He left them to their fate, and ran, full tilt, in the direction of the camp. He knew his only chance lay in the Staff. 'And that way I'll get that gold too,' he thought as he ran, 'if there's any gold to get.'

Corydon kicked at the straw. The heat haze shimmered. He wasn't used to being so inactive, and he missed the warmth of his ewes, their chalky milk, their soft sounds. He began to put his loneliness into a little song that sounded like their funny bleating. Trying a few bars aloud, then playing his pipes, he wasn't surprised to feel Medusa listening.

'That's good,' she said, as he finished. 'You must really miss them.'

'How do you know what I'm thinking, just from music?' he asked.

'Well, you're not that hard to understand,' she said gently. 'But since the changes I can often understand what other people are thinking.'

42

Corydon felt brave. 'What changes?' he asked abruptly.

He heard her hesitate. 'Do you really want to know because of me, or are you just like the losers who plod past every day, wanting a good scream to make them feel cosier at night?'

He didn't understand her. 'I just wondered,' he said, humbly.

Perhaps his shyness moved her. 'All right,' she said. And she began to tell him.

Medusa had been a fiercely independent girl herself, liking books and music better than parties. Perhaps it was because she had no brothers or sisters, and no father either; at least, she had never seen him. She and her mother lived in Kolonos, and her mother did weaving and spinning to eke out their tiny income. Her mother had once been chosen to work on the great mantle of Athene that was given to the goddess every year at her festival, said Medusa proudly. But she herself had hated sewing, preferring to run wild on the mountains with the other girls. She had always loved Artemis more than Athene, loved the wind in her face, the sun on her hair. 'And,' she said, 'Athene was always my enemy. It got so my mother seemed almost like my enemy too.' There had been angry fights every day when her mother had tried to make her stay in and weave, and she had escaped to the hillside. She had learned to fight, too, from the other wild girls, to fight with her fists, with a bow and arrows, with a sword.

One winter day, she had come home long after dark, to find her mother sitting in the front room with a strange woman, a tall woman with a face so hard and stern and handsome that it looked as if it were made of marble. She had run in, giggling, breathless, having been chased, teasingly, through Kolonos by her friends, and seen this woman sitting by the fireside, still, heavy. 'I knew she was my doom,' said Medusa.

She was in fact the chief priestess of Athene, and her mother had dedicated her – 'Sold me,' said Medusa, 'for thirty good silver drachmas' – to the temple for ever. To serve a goddess she loathed, with skills she didn't possess.

The priestesses of Athene were clever, though – 'cunning', Medusa called it. They noticed that weaving and spinning went awry as Medusa's awkward hands were set to them. They noticed that bread-making went badly too, and so did honey-making and olive pressing. At last, one of them thought of gardening. 'At least I was outdoors again,' said Medusa, 'and I could feel the fresh wind of my own maiden goddess warm in my face.' She took over the herb patch, and under her care it flourished. She began to read the many books in the temple's possession, and to learn more and more about the properties of herbs, their power to cure and to change. People from the town heard of her skill, and began to come to the temple to consult her. 'My child is sick, my mother is sick, my dog is sick,' she mimicked. Turning serious, she added, 'I saw a lot of human unhappiness that way. Our bodies – well, no one could think the gods made anything so ramshackle!' and she gave her strange high laugh.

What she didn't know was that she too was changing, that she was getting prettier. She noticed that her hair, which was now very long, was a good colour – corn-gold, bright in the sun like the leaves of some plants. But no one really told her that she was slim and tall and delicate as a flower, that her skin made men want to touch it. Sometimes she would look at her reflection in the well she used for watering the plants and wonder at the face it showed her. 'The priestess caught me once, and gave me a beating for vanity,' she said, laughing again. 'It hurt, of course. But I was fairly happy, though I would not have called it that.'

They had let her make the hymn to the Goddess that last year, and she still remembered it. 'I didn't really like her, so I made her dress in black, as we did, and I said her blacks crackled, and dragged, and that she had a hood made of the bones of men dead in battle. I don't think she liked it. I made other songs for my own lady, the lady of the hills and the beasts, warmer songs. But I never sing those now. I'm not a maiden any more, so she and I have no business together – although, before long . . .'

She paused for so long that Corydon was maddened by suspense. Finally he said, timidly, 'Go on, please. It's as good as a song.'

He sensed that she was pleased, but then she laughed again. 'The next bit is no song for your ears,' she said. But she told him, though he did not altogether understand.

She had met the one who had undone her in the procession to present the Goddess with her robe. She had seen him straight away, as she walked slowly out of the temple into the glare of the sun; there he was. He was tall, dark, with skin that was smooth and dusky, like the black basalt of the temple floor. His teeth were white and he smiled at her. It was like a crack of lightning across the sky. And she, who was supposed to walk with bent head, smiled back. The next night, she had been out gathering herbs by scent as storm clouds blotted out the moon, and she had seen him – smelled him, almost – hiding in the shadows. He took her hand. They talked. And then he kissed her bang smash on the mouth, just like that, no gentleness in it, and that, she found, was what she wanted, his wildness. And they went on. And it hurt her and there was blood on the ground and blood on her dress and she bit him, to show him how it felt, and he laughed. And then the gathering storm broke, and to get away from the rain they ran into the temple and they did it again. And as her blood fell on the floor of the temple, before the altar, it began. The change began. He drew back from her as her hair began to writhe. She felt it quicken into terrible, wriggling life, put up her hand, and a snake bit her. With a last laugh, he slid away, and by his calm she knew she had been taken by a god.

Suddenly she knew that she was undone, finished, over, as she felt her body too begin to quicken with a life that was different, burning, aching. She was not a girl any longer. Now she was a weapon in a struggle between the gods, a struggle that no one would ever bother to explain to her. She knew that she had been filled with power, but the power was not hers to spend.

'I just crouched there in the sanctuary,' she said at last. 'The next morning one of the priestesses came to refill the altar lamps. She wasn't an enemy of mine, though I didn't particularly like her. I stood up, and she *saw* me. And as she looked at me, I looked at her. And I saw her arms turn grey, and her face go impossibly still, the stillness of stone. And there she stood, stone. Her face was frozen into a look of such horror, such hatred. It was my mirror. I had done this to her, though I had not willed it.'

She had known at once that she could not stay with the priestesses. She tried to hide, so that she wouldn't be responsible for more deaths, but they kept coming at her, looking, petrifying, till she was almost hemmed in by what had been friends, companions, now grey and dessicated, dead. Finally, the chief priestess and another drove her out with whips, holding their arms over their faces to protect themselves. Out in the village, people fled from her, but not fast enough; one glance and they dried into greyness. At last she had run out onto the hills, knowing she no longer belonged there either, the grass itself dying

47

under her feet and the animals mad with fear at her coming. She stole a blanket to wrap herself in, and lay for three days under an oak tree, waiting to die. But instead of death, life had come. She had known herself to be with child, her body beginning to be sore, aching, tired. She had known what it meant. Somehow the child she was to have would be part of the gods' war.

And it was there, under the oak tree, that the pirates had found her, sleeping after a week of wakefulness, and they had taken and imprisoned her. 'That was seven months ago, and my time will be soon, little shepherd. Do you know about birthing? Do you help your ewes, in winter? This will be a winter birth too.'

He didn't know what she meant. It was summer now. But he thought perhaps it was always winter for her.

Then a thought struck him. *She* had been driven out, as he had been. 'You were outcast,' he said softly. 'I, too. I was a pharmakos. But something saved me. Something has saved you too. Perhaps the Olympian gods are not the only powers in the universe.'

'Perhaps,' she said softly. 'I do not know what I shall teach my child about that.'

Corydon had been so absorbed in their talk that he had not noticed the passing of time. To his surprise, he noticed it was late afternoon. In the distance, he began to hear a kind of crying, as if someone were running, sobbing for breath, and then crying out. The captain, who had been asleep, sozzled with wine, in the shade of a tree, came suddenly to life. 'That's Belshazzar's voice!' he exclaimed. A moment later, Belshazzar himself came in sight, and what a sight he was. His clothes were stiff with clay and dust, his eyes wide with fright and a kind of lust. 'The Staff!' he cried. 'The Staff! Get it ready! Give it to me! Give it me, give it!'

The captain snatched the Staff up. 'Are you mad as well as dirty?' he snarled. 'It's mine, and anyway—'

But Belshazzar *was* mad, mad with the need for the Staff, the only security and safety in a world of bronze-winged terrors. He could almost feel their breath on his neck. He knew his shipmates were doomed, and he also knew, in the bottom of his shrivelled soul, that he was about to seal their doom. All he wanted was the Staff. With the comforting pulse of its red glow between his hands, he knew he could sit, safe, crouched in the camp, and wait till They came. Then he would stun them, reduce them to the level of the freaks in the other cages. That would be safety. And vengeance.

But the captain had no intention of giving up the Staff. He could see that Belshazzar was mad; he might even let the monsters loose in his present state of madness. And the monsters would hunt them both down. He made his choice; dropping the Staff on the ground behind him, he drew his sword and his dagger and flung himself on the unarmed Belshazzar. But Belshazzar was a quick and cunning fighter. With one swift movement, he seized the captain's wrist before he could raise the dagger, and his hard grip made the captain drop the weapon. Both men dived for it, but the captain managed to plunge his sword into Belshazzar's shoulder. Belshazzar gave a scream, and the two milled in the dust.

Corydon couldn't see what was happening. Medusa was asking him urgently, 'What's going on?' She could see nothing because of the mirrors around her. He didn't reply; he shushed her, his thief-instinct warning him that he must not draw attention to himself. Because he had noticed one thing: the Staff had rolled as it fell, coming to rest only inches from his cage.

He knew he had to treat it as he would a runaway lamb or goat; as a kleptis he had often snatched up the swift-moving. The Staff was just out of reach, though, he tried grabbing it through the bars. His kleptis instincts thought for him; he tore off the hem of his tunic, made a noose, slipped it over the head of the Staff, and pulled tight. The Staff came gently up to his hand, as if it were a lamb who knew his shepherd.

Ignoring the grunts of the two fighting men, Corydon turned the ruby towards the lock on his cage door, and was not surprised when it opened easily. He leaped down and, without any further thought, flung a scarlet beam of light at the lock on Medusa's cage.

A second later he wondered if this had been the most

stupid act of his life. Even the most blundering kleptis in the village might have hesitated . . . After all, she was a monster, and he would never really be able to look at her.

And yet before he had thought this, he *had* looked at her. It was like those times when someone tells you not to look at the sun, and before you can stop, you've done it and hurt your eyes.

He shut his eyes tightly, but before he did, everything about her had imprinted itself on his mind, like an instant painting. Her hair was made of snakes greener than grass; her skin was purple, the faint purple of the evening sea; and her eyes were a dark purple, the bruised colour of plums, and yet they were alive, alive in a way that ordinary people can never be, perhaps. She was also hugely pregnant. Her belly was as full as a grain sack at harvest time, a big yeasty loaf of a belly. He was almost more shocked by her pregnant vastness than he was by her more obviously monstrous features.

He was expecting to petrify, but he didn't. Gradually, he realised that it wasn't going to happen, and he opened his eyes to hers.

She was smiling. 'Gods! That's a relief!' she said. 'Now, let's not question it. Let's release the others and get out before they—' But even as she spoke, the captain and Belshazzar had seen them. In fact, the captain had seen her all too well. As Belshazzar watched, his foe slowly froze into grey stillness. Belshazzar gave a cry of rage. He had seen the Staff in Corydon's hand. Seizing the captain's sword, he lunged forward.

Corydon and Medusa did not wait for more. They ran, with Corydon still clutching the Staff. Belshazzar, blinded by sweat, had not seen Medusa full face. His blindness saved him from the captain's fate, but it proved his undoing, too, for as he ran after the fleeing boy and monster, he tripped on a tree root and fell full length. As luck – his luck – would have it – or as the gods decreed – he fell on the captain's sword, and his lifeblood spilled out. Corydon and Medusa did not know he was dead, for when they saw him trip, they ran on, and it was some minutes before they realised that he was no longer following them.

When they did, they looked at each other, and smiled and smiled. There was no need to say anything. They went on, deeper into the island's hills.

έψιλον

FIVE

Sleepily, Corydon looked at the monster beside him. He did not ask himself why or how, but they were friends now. It was chilly in the hills, but you couldn't curl up to Medusa for warmth because it infuriated the snakes in her hair. Medusa said she was never cold now; it was probably because of the baby, which seemed to glow with warmth like a little fire.

He was almost asleep when he suddenly sat bolt upright. He'd heard the soft sound of a shepherd's pipe. Joy filled his heart. There must be another shepherd boy up here. He began to climb up the hill, trying to follow the music to its source, but try as he might, it seemed to recede whenever he came near to it. He hunted for a while, then suddenly found himself alone on the cold morning hillside. Panic overtook him, and he raced back down to Medusa, who was still sleeping.

As he did so, he heard another sound altogether, a long ululating cry, furious, like beaten bronze, but like a bird screaming for prey, too. Memories stirred again, memories of his rescuers long ago; they had sounded like that. He thought of the Staff and its amazing powers. Perhaps his rescuer needed rescuing – anyway, he might just see. Waking Medusa and grabbing the Staff, he ran in the direction of the sound. Medusa followed, keeping up easily with her long legs, despite her huge bulk. He heard the strange cry again, lonely and gallant. He didn't know why, but he felt his heart would burst if he couldn't help her, couldn't see her soon. Suddenly, the trees he was running through opened out into a small plain of furze. A pitched battle was going on. His heart sang; he recognised them at once. Bronze wings, bronze claws, the faces of birds and women at once; it was them, the ones who had saved him when he had been the pharmakos. They were being attacked by the pirate band.

In fact, what Corydon and Medusa were seeing was the end of a long chase, with Sthenno and Euryale in amused, almost half-hearted pursuit. Now they had finally decided to catch up, out of sheer boredom. There was no possible way for Corydon and Medusa to know all this, but Medusa at least could see that it was the pirates who needed rescuing and not – 'Gorgo!' she breathed. Even she was impressed. Then she remembered to hide her face in her robe, in case she petrified anyone. But as she did so, she realised that Corydon was running as hard as he could towards the fight. She shouted, 'Stop! Corydon!' expecting to see his head sliced off. He was brandishing the Staff, and as she watched from beneath a fold of clothing, he aimed its red jewel not at the bronze-winged gorgons, but at the pirates fighting them. The first pirate went down like a ninepin, and Corydon swung the Staff hastily at the other pirates. They looked at him, and at the hot and glowing red tip of the Staff. Their mouths dropped open. Then they turned and ran.

Quicker than an arrow, one of the bronze-winged creatures made off after them, but before she could catch them, the other gave a cry, so high and sweet it was like a bird: 'Euryale!' she cried. 'Euryale! Look! It's him! It's the mormoluke!'

The pursuing gorgon stopped dead in the air. She turned back at once, and landed directly in front of Corydon.

They looked at each other. Behind her, the other bronze gorgon crept slowly forward, holding out a fiercely clawed hand.

Suddenly, Corydon flung himself into their arms. He felt them start in surprise, then the long brazen wings closed around him, just as they had once before, one day long ago, when his own village and his own mother had cast him out to die. They were whistling and crooning to him in a way that he remembered dimly, and with a

55

shock like a fistful of cold water flung on his hot back, he realised that the songs he had thought were his own were partly learned from them. Even their voices sounded oddly like his pipes, like the syrinx that all shepherds use.

All three cried. The gorgons shed tears of liquid metal.

A chilly cough startled him back to the present.

Corydon smiled at them through his tears. 'Here is another friend,' he said, awkwardly, remembering his manners. 'This is Medusa.'

Medusa smiled. 'Charmed, I'm sure,' she said.

'Welcome,' offered Sthenno, sounding nervous. 'I think you are a sister. We are all gorgons.'

Medusa smiled again. 'Frights,' she agreed.

Of course, her face had no petrifying effect on the two immortals. Yet Corydon noticed at once that there was something wary and forbidding in her expression. He decided to say no more just now. He didn't like talk much, at any time. 'This will be worth a song,' he said happily. The three listened to him, and each thought her own thoughts.

Medusa spoke first.

'Corydon,' she said, 'we are forgetting something. What of the others?'

'The others – oh, gods!' said Corydon, jumping guiltily. He had been so preoccupied with himself and Medusa and the gorgons that he hadn't thought of them once. The poor shaggy Minotaur, all the other lonely creatures . . .

'We must hurry,' he said with new fierceness and determination. What if they were too late?

But with the immortal sisters to fly him to the pirates' camp, it was the work of a moment to reach it. Sthenno and Euryale looked around with surprise, and with distaste.

'You were here?' said Sthenno. 'It smells.'

'I'd go mad,' said Euryale, and she looked as if she might, too.

'You'd get hungry,' said Sthenno sardonically.

Corydon turned at once to the cages.

None of the monsters asked to be released. But in the eyes of each, Corydon could see a glimpse of a dream of freedom, a dream of solitude, a dream of silence, impossible and thrilling peaks of loneliness. Never being looked at again.

All of his warm heart responded. Within moments, he had freed them all. None of them stopped to thank him, but he understood; they were thirsty to be alone. The snake-girl, however, did give him a soft pat with her tail as she slithered into the dark purpling shade of a chestnut tree.

But as they flew or drifted or ambled off into the gathering darkness of evening, only the Minotaur spoke.

In his shy, dark voice he asked, simply, 'Where is she?'

'Medusa?' Corydon was surprised, and a little annoyed. Inside himself he felt Medusa was his. He hadn't known that she had other friends. 'Afar off,' he said, grandly, and seeing the beast-man's shoulders slump, he relented. 'Actually, I am returning to her now. Would you care to follow? But we fly fast.'

'Oh, we needn't,' said Euryale sociably. To her own astonishment, she was enjoying the day. 'Need we, Sthenno?'

Sthenno wasn't enjoying herself as much, but she liked the warm, furry, confused monster before them. There was something comforting about him. And now that she knew the mormoluke was safe, everything felt better. She had worried about him for years. She was the only one who knew what he really was and what he would do, why he was so important. She hated to let him out of her sight. But it was nearly time for one of her prayers, and she wanted to get back to the cave. 'I'll go on ahead,' she said, 'and you follow. That way, I can show Medusa the way.'

Sthenno sped off, through her beloved night sky, racing the stars home. She found the vastly pregnant Medusa and guided her, but the mortal gorgon didn't seem especially grateful to be there. She sat in front of a small fire, her face harder and darker than stone. Sthenno spoke quickly, not pausing to choose her words.

'The others are coming by land. The mormoluke brings

you the Minotaur.' She did not miss Medusa's start of surprise, or the faint blossoming of pleasure in her face. Sthenno didn't miss things; she just didn't always find them very interesting. 'I must go now,' she added.

'Stay and talk,' said Medusa, awkwardly.

'I can't,' said Sthenno, moving from foot to foot. 'It's time. I must make my prayers and plot the new stars. That way, I can understand more about how to help the mormoluke.'

'The mormoluke?'

'The boy.'

'He has a name, you know. His name is Corydon.'

Sthenno smiled absently, then hurried off into the cave. Medusa stared into the flames. Inside her, she felt her unborn child stirring, reflecting its mother's anger. As she thought of the boy and the bronze-winged sisters, the snakes on her head stood up in the firelight and began a dance of rage.

ζήτα

SIX

So, without asking, Corydon and Medusa moved in with Sthenno and Euryale. The Minotaur drifted away to make his own home.

Corydon and Sthenno examined the Staff together. Euryale wasn't interested in the Staff; its intricacies bored her. And Medusa shuddered whenever she looked at it, remembering pain and beatings. But Sthenno knew it was important. Its complex inscriptions were obviously full of meaning, yet they were impossible to decipher. The letters – if you could call them letters – were curling barbarian forms. Some of them almost looked like pictures, but they didn't tell a story.

Corydon couldn't see how they would ever work out what any of it meant.

Did it even matter?

'Yes, it does.' Sthenno was certain. 'Not only now, but

somehow in the farther future.' She sounded grand and aloof.

'But how can we read it?' Corydon wondered aloud.

'The symbols look familiar. I know I've seen something like them . . . It was hundreds of years ago, maybe even longer . . .'

Corydon felt awed. She was so old.

Sthenno darted towards one of the many shelves in the cave. It was littered with fragments of parchment in many languages. She shuffled them, stopping to read a few . . .

Minutes went by.

'Have you found it yet?' Corydon tried not to sound impatient.

'Not exactly, not yet . . .' Parchments flew about like feathers as she rummaged. Then her claw emerged from a pile of unusually dusty and crumbling pieces of writing. She was holding something triumphantly aloft.

To Corydon's surprise, it wasn't a parchment. It was a small clay disc, about the size of Corydon's hand.

Sthenno was right. The figures on it were exactly like those on the Staff. There was the head with the crested helmet. But how did that help? Now they had two indecipherable bits of writing instead of one.

But Sthenno was consulting another parchment. Then she bent and, to Corydon's surprise, laid the Staff delicately on the ground. She rolled the disc along the length of the Staff very carefully, as if she were trying to print its letters on the carved wood. When she reached the end, she stopped and waited. Nothing happened. Then she studied the parchment again, and rolled the disc back once in the opposite direction.

This time the magic worked.

The letters on the Staff began to glow, as if lit from within. They also hummed, loudly, almost angrily, as if a hive of bees were hidden inside. Then, in a golden swarm, they flew over to the wall of Sthenno's cave, where – with much angry buzzing, and some jostling – they rearranged themselves into new forms. The mysterious shapes were replaced by shapes Corydon could read – or was it that he now understood what had seemed strange?

The letters formed words, words that Corydon didn't know.

They said: *Mommou Thoth Nanoumbre Kharikha Kenryo Paarmiath, to whom belongs the holy name of Kronos.*

'Kronos!' breathed Sthenno. 'The king of the Blessed Isles! Of course! Hades' Staff – death is Time's subject, and Kronus is Time . . .'

'But, Sthenno,' said Corydon, as reasonably as he could, 'none of this makes sense. What Blessed Isles?'

Sthenno was impatient, as always. She scuttled around, picking up scrolls and thudding them down in front of him, as if she was searching for a way to make him understand. At last she drew a little map in the thick dust on the floor of the cave.

'Look, here,' she said. 'See, this is Styx, and here, the bridge . . . But nearer, nearer, you will see an island, and it is the Isle of the Blest. And there he sleeps, Kronos. He sleeps. If he wakes, what will happen? But it will anger Zeus. And he is the king of the gods. The ruler of the darkness of this world.'

'What can I do to wake him?' asked Corydon.

'You must say the words on the Staff. The words on the wall.'

'What will happen?'

'I do not know. Sometimes what we do echoes far beyond us. This will shake the Olympians.' She smiled. 'I remember him. Kronos is Time. He is Memory. And' – she smiled again, a battle smile – 'Zeus wants us to forget. His power rests on our ignorance. Any knowledge – even if it seems useless – is a menace to him. Even knowing your own true name.'

Corydon had no idea what use any of this would be, but he could see that Sthenno thought it would help, somehow.

Corydon could see that Sthenno thought it was important, but as he had no idea what use any of this would be, he rarely thought about it after that day. The Staff lay in a corner of Sthenno's cave, another piece of writing that simply gathered dust. Its importance was sheathed in disuse.

Life in the gorgons' cave soon settled into a contented routine, for Corydon at least.

He had a home now.

He loved the big cool eating-cave, with its stone table. He had his own tiny sleeping shelf in a corner of the living-cave, cosy and snug, with a bed he made of bracken. Sthenno never seemed to sleep, and Euryale slept seldom, but they had their own separate caves for their activities. Euryale's was aflame with drawings in ochre and crimson and brown.

Corydon also liked exploring the huge pit where Belshazzar had been imprisoned. Armed with a pine torch, he had found fluted towerets of rock in bright gold, red and rich cream, like milk. Some of the rock formations were taller than trees, others tiny and delicate, smaller than the fingers of a baby mouse. The shapes they formed were suggestive, and Corydon wondered if they were messages from the gods; sometimes he thought he saw the figures of a mother and a baby, of three men on strange monstrous beasts with long legs and necks, and once, he had walked into a circle of tall rocks that reminded him of the pirates' cages.

He had also found the underground river that flowed through the very back of the cave. Euryale had a fishing platform there, and sometimes speared the blind white cave-fish.

Corydon also spent time with the gorgons. He had

become involved in Sthenno's prayers and stargazing, and he began and ended every day with her.

With Euryale, he hunted. After breakfast, he would go to find her and accompany her on her long hunts, or draw a picture of an animal quarry beside hers in her cave. She helped him, too, to round up his own sheep, and caring for them – making cheese from their milk and smoking it over a slow fire – kept him very busy when she was after quarry too big for him.

He tried to teach her the art of kleptis, but she wasn't very interested. He himself still lifted a few beasts, from time to time, enjoying the secrecy.

The ewes came to birth, and he had a fine crop of bleating lambs.

He also spent long hours lying in the gorse, watching the blue sky or looking at the flights of birds.

Above all he felt wrapped in the care of the two gorgons, safer than he had ever been in his life.

At first, he tried to show all his new pastimes to Medusa. He told her about Sthenno's star charts.

She wasn't interested.

Then he showed her a painting he'd done of a deer.

She yawned, and said something that cut him down. 'Oh, well. You can't be good at everything, I suppose.'

He even tried, shyly, to tell her about the art of the kleptis. The slow stalking. The grab. The koumos-pit.

She yawned.

He told her about hunting, about the animals he'd stalked, cut up, eaten. 'What fun!' she said, in a voice of horrible brightness. He knew she didn't mean it. He knew she was saying just the opposite.

Why didn't she like him any more?

It reminded him of the way the village thieves had turned on him after he had been denounced as the pharmakos. One day they were his friends; the next day none of them would look him in the eye. He had tried to ask them what he'd done, but they turned away.

But Corydon was still simple, and he decided he'd ask Medusa what the matter was. On the day when he meant to do it, he noticed that she was in a foul mood. She was making herself breakfast; she clattered the pots to and fro angrily, chipping one in a way that would make Sthenno worried if she saw it. He said as much, and she answered shortly that she didn't much care about Sthenno's worries.

Corydon pressed on, blindly. 'What's wrong?' he asked.

'Nothing.' *Clatter, bang, thump.*

'Don't you want to come and say prayers with me and Sthenno?'

'Prayers! Are you mad?'

'I forgot,' he said, colouring. 'But . . . Sthenno says some gods are good . . .'

'Does she? How nice. Dear Sthenno.'

'Don't you like her?'

'I think she's wonderful, as long as you're fascinated by bits of old parchment and the movements of the stars. I mean' – *clatter, bang, rattle* – 'what could possibly be more thrilling than hearing Sthenno explain her theory about the movements of the Red Planet? Unless it's hearing her deciphering one of her intriguing little scrolls.'

'Well, I think it's interesting,' said Corydon, humbly. He couldn't help noticing that she was burning the barley pottage she was making. He couldn't think of a way to warn her without provoking her further, though. As it was, she spat at him like a furious cat.

'You would!'

Corydon suddenly felt a flame of anger licking at him too. 'You don't seem to like me these days,' he said, loud and furious.

Clatter. There was the pot lid again.

'Why don't you like me any more, Medusa?'

Medusa turned. *Smash!* The pot, full of breakfast pottage, fell into fragments on the stone floor of the cave. The scorched pottage was splattered everywhere, its sharp burnt smell filling the cave.

And her face was a mask of fury.

'Look,' she hissed, low and dangerous, the snakes on her head standing up and hissing too, 'you've got two mothers now. Sthenno and Euryale. That's as many as any boy needs. Right? You don't need me to mother you.

And I've got my own baby to worry about. All right? So why don't you and your goaty leg go and limp around somewhere where I don't have to see you – you stupid little freak.'

Corydon felt he'd been stabbed to the heart. Blind with tears, he ran from the cave. He didn't turn his head. If he had, he would have seen Medusa put her hands over her face in horror. He would have seen her crying. But he ran up the hill, past the thick furze bushes, to hold in his arms the cosy warmth of his favourite ewe, just as he had when he was young.

Was he a freak?

Suddenly, smelling the stink of warm wool, he had to know. He had to ask. He decided to ask Sthenno. He was in such a hurry that he almost fell into her cave from the hillside.

'Sthenno,' he said. 'Sthenno. Am I a freak?'

Sthenno might have answered at once, but she was just opening her mouth when Euryale burst in, holding seven ducks tied together with rope. 'Look!' she said, beaming. 'Delicious!' She began to eat, with much loud crunching of bones and lip licking.

Sthenno eyed her, exasperated.

Sthenno had been studying the mormoluke prophecy when Corydon blundered in. Another being might have wondered how much to tell him, but it came naturally to her to tell the plain truth, unvarnished by politeness.

'You are the mormoluke,' she said. 'That is why your villagers left you for us. They think the prophecy says the mormoluke will be swallowed by monsters and the people cleansed. But they are misreading it.'

Marvellous. His whole life had been wrecked because someone couldn't read.

'What does it really say?' he asked, feeling that unusual anger licking him again.

He could barely hear Sthenno's reply above the sound of Euryale tearing her third duck apart. 'That the mormoluke will become one with the monsters and that together they shall make the whole land clean.'

Corydon was silent, turning this over. At last he said, 'Maybe I'm stupid . . . but what exactly does that mean?'

Sthenno shrugged. 'You will find out. It will unfold. And the stars give me clues.'

Euryale guffawed, her mouth still full of duck. 'Clues?' she said, but it came out sounding like 'kooos?'. 'What clues?'

Sthenno began to explain, with many learned references to stars and planets that were trine and square and aspects and ascendants. Corydon was not finding the conversation as helpful as he had hoped. Maybe I need to ask more questions, he decided.

'What is a mormoluke?' he finally asked. 'I mean – I know I'm supposed to be a daimon. . . .'

'Well, a mormoluke is a mormo-daimon.'

Corydon suddenly felt an enormous giggle bubbling inside him. He had to put his hand over his mouth to stop himself from laughing. He felt sure that if he asked 'What is a mormo-daimon?' Sthenno would say, 'a mormoluke, of course'. In this fashion they could have the same conversation again and again for months. Stifling his giggles with difficulty, he gave it a try: 'What *is* a mormo-daimon?'

Surprised, she turned. 'Your leg. Look at it. It is the mark of your father.'

Corydon looked down at his left leg. He was so used to it that he didn't look at it very often, but now he noticed the hard, dark hoof, and the soft pale brown fur that ran to his waist. He had never thought of it as having a meaning. It was just his leg.

Euryale spoke, so urgently that for a moment she actually stopped eating. 'He doesn't know anything, Sthenno. You must tell him.'

Thus prompted, Sthenno did seem to grasp that he knew nothing at all of what he was. But she also knew that she was not the right person to inform him.

'And if you want to know more, and about your begetting, then my advice is this . . .'

Sthenno scurried suddenly out of the cave. She came back just as abruptly, brandishing a huge bundle of parchment fragments.

'I know it's here somewhere,' she said, rummaging frenziedly.

Euryale began to look around for a snack. She eyed Sthenno's discarded parchments hungrily, as Sthenno flung them over her shoulder. But Sthenno didn't notice, for she had found the parchment she was seeking. In a dreamy voice, almost chanting, she read it aloud.

'*Go out of the cave and follow the stream right to its source in the Cave of the Nymphs. Sit for three days by the cave entrance under the olive tree on that hillside. You must not eat, nor drink, nor move. At midday on the third day, play your pipe. Only in that way can your questions be answered.*'

Corydon thought it over. If he went then he'd be really hungry, but at least he'd find out what a mormoluke really was, what *he* was, and why he'd been exiled. He nodded to Sthenno, waved to Euryale, and picked up the Staff – he wasn't sure why, but he felt he might need it. Picking it up was a reflex, like grabbing a cloak in winter. Then he ran silently from the cave.

He followed the winding course of the stream, slipping sometimes on the wet rocks. Emerging from the shade of the trees, he felt the heavy weight of sun full in his face.

Corydon saw ahead of him a sheer granite cliff face. Before it was the bubbling spring that fed the stream and behind the spring was a large cave entrance. There was an expanse of lush green meadow in front of the cave, as the moisture made the grass grow thick and soft. Hanging in the cave mouth were offerings: small pipes

72

and flutes left by shepherds, milk pails, some women's girdles, wreaths of flowers.

Plainly, this was the place that Sthenno meant. He sat down, and leaned his back against the hot hard rock of the cliff face, where an olive sapling jutted, and waited.

He soon grew stiff and hot in the sun, but he waited.

His belly rumbled fiercely, and he wished he'd had some of Euryale's duck, but he waited.

His mouth was dry as dust, but he waited.

Night came. He gritted his teeth, and waited.

And it went on, and on, and it was so boring he wanted to scream.

Only his monster-strength sustained him, the secret power to endure and survive what no mortal his age could bear.

Then, at dawn on the second day, something began to happen.

But it was too soon. Sthenno had said three days.

Still, he heard it. Thin hunting horns blowing. The belling of hounds. The cries of hunters, high and clear and savage.

And then he saw them, the company of the Moon, Artemis and her nymphs, running free on the hillside, chasing down the deer in their bare feet. They wore rough deerskin tunics. Their hair was loose and tangled and wild; it stood out from their heads almost as if it were alive, and he was suddenly reminded of Medusa.

73

They all carried long, bright spears, or bows. Their dogs ran about them, their muzzles stained with the blood of their kills.

Suddenly, his awe melted into apprehension. He found them much more frightening than Medusa, and his first impulse was to retreat into the cave. But he remembered that Sthenno had said he could not move, and he sat as still as the rabbit when the hawk is in the sky.

They were intent on their prey, and they did not stop to notice one small and shivering boy. He let out his breath, then gave a small whoop; after all, he had seen an immortal goddess. The waiting seemed less tedious, and oddly he felt less uncomfortable, too. In fact, lulled in the arms of earth, he drifted into sleep.

Sthenno had been thinking about her conversation with Corydon. Her thought processes were always swift and darting, like a bird's, but like a bird she would prod at one thing, then flutter off after another. So it was days before she seized on his initial question. Why had he suddenly asked if he was a freak? She put the question to Euryale, who was as ever looking about, dissatisfied, for more meat.

'Euryale, why did the mormo ask me if he was a freak?'

'Well, he was in a freak-show,' Euryale replied. 'And when we saved him, his village had just made him a pharmakos, a scapegoat. Most people would wonder about that.' She went on searching for lost bits of bone.

'Yes, but it seemed that it was only now that he realised. What made him realise? Is it the gods at work?'

'Not exactly,' came a drawling voice from the doorway. 'It wasn't the gods. It was me.'

Sthenno swung round. Medusa looked worse to her every day. Though she didn't mind the snaky hair, she found the almost incredibly swollen belly disconcerting. 'What did you do?' she asked.

Medusa was in fact hideously ashamed of herself. She knew she had made Corydon miserable. She hadn't even seen him for two days, and yet she couldn't say so to this mad, skinny hag. She smiled sociably.

'I called him a freak,' she said, simply. 'It's time he began to find out what he is.'

Sthenno was shocked, despite herself. 'Why say that to him? It's horrible!' she said, her bronze feathers beginning to stand out around her in indignation.

'Well, life is horrible!' shouted Medusa defiantly. 'People who've suffered like he has don't want to hear that the birdies go *tweet-tweet*, they want to know about dust and ash and death and how the gods are cheats.'

Euryale had found a missing duck's wing, and was sitting in a corner, gnawing it. 'You do, we know,' she said. 'But he's only a child. Maybe he still likes the birdies.'

Medusa laughed her high, strange laugh. If Sthenno and Euryale had not been immortals, it would have made their blood run cold. She leaned forward, her terrible lavender face close to Euryale's bronze face. The snakes on her head stood on end and began to hiss softly.

'Well, *you* would *eat* the birdies, wouldn't you? If they sat still for long enough. I wonder you haven't eaten us all. Eating is all you do. You think you can fill that hole inside you with food? You can't. You'll never fill it, you great fat sow.'

There was a long silence.

Euryale got up. Choked on her duck. Blundered from the cave.

'And you, you skinny old witch. What are you plotting in that little room of yours? The overthrow of the gods? You imbecile! They have powers beyond your wildest dreams, and all you have is a few mangy scrolls and a couple of badly copied charts. Do you think any real astronomer would be interested in your ravings? I've known men who spent their lives studying the heavens and who actually discovered things; I bet you don't even know how eclipses happen, do you? You're quite worthless, you mad freak.'

Sthenno was not like the others. She did not break. She shrank, looking half her usual size. But because Sthenno was always afraid that she was useless and wrong, it hurt her less to be told she was. It was not a surprise.

'Maybe,' she said, her voice only a little unsteady. 'But at least I told Corydon the truth. He's gone out to the

Cave of the Nymphs to meet his father. I told him how to do the summoning.'

Medusa gasped. 'But it's dangerous,' she said, all her anger melted. 'What if Artemis sees him? I know her; I was once her votary. She will never forgive him if he enters the cave. She might even . . .' She broke off, unable to find words for her fears.

Sthenno shrugged. 'You said it yourself. He doesn't want to hear birdsong. He needs to meet his father.'

Medusa whirled and ran for the cave entrance. Before Sthenno could speak again, she ran off into the gathering storm. She might have shouted, 'Sorry!' as she ran, but the wind was blowing hard, and Sthenno didn't hear it.

ήτα

SEVEN

Belasmir was nervous, but excited and pleased. He had been granted an audience with King Polydectes. Now he would have the chance to tell his terrible story, and the world would know the fate of his friends. Twitching his garments into order, he followed the attendant into the throne room.

The throne room at Seriphos overlooked the sea. The throne was an impressive but clumsy mass of emeralds and gold leaf, but Polydectes looked much too small for it, like a child in a grown-up's chair – a spoilt child who had thrown a tantrum until he was allowed to sit where the adults did. He had a weak chin and a small beard. His hobby was tulip breeding, and he found affairs of state boring.

'Well?' he asked, testily. 'Are you the man? The one

who's been to the Island of the Hyperboreans and survived?'

Belasmir was taken aback. 'Er – no,' he said, cautiously. 'I'm the one who's been—'

'Oh, well then, I don't want to see you,' said the king pettishly.

Belasmir bowed. 'As your majesty pleases,' he said, equally sulky.

The chamberlain intervened. 'Majesty,' he said, soothingly, 'this is the man who comes from the Island of Monsters.'

'Of course!' The king clapped his hands.

Belasmir felt bolder. He told his story, finishing, resoundingly: 'And majesty, these unnatural creatures have killed and probably eaten all my shipmates, all my fine friends, as honest and decent a crew as any man ever sailed with. I put it to you, king. Shouldn't the seas be made safe for the likes of us?'

The king's eyes were bright with eager excitement. 'Monsters! What a terrible business! They are becoming such a threat to our shipping. Every time we try to go more than a few miles from our own doors – monsters, monsters everywhere! Just look at any map and you'll see 'em. Always lurking in the corners.' He stopped. 'What should we do about it, though? That's the question. For I don't need to tell you that something has to be done.'

'Your majesty,' said the chamberlain. 'I recall that you

yourself had a dazzling notion for how to deal with these creatures only a few days ago. You told your stepson to go to Hades and live with Kerberos. You spoke in ire, but I believe you really *meant* that a posse of heroes was needed to cleanse the dark corners of our world.'

Belasmir could see that the chamberlain was the one who'd had the idea, but that he wanted the king to believe that it was his own plan. He wondered who the stepson was. Poor bloke.

The king clapped his hands. 'Yes! I remember! It was a marvellous plan, wasn't it, Archimedes? Why don't we get started on it at once? Send for Perseus.'

Archimedes left the room. Belasmir waited, curiously. When Archimedes returned, he was preceded by a man who looked like every picture of a hero Belasmir had ever seen.

His skin was smooth with olive oil and bronzed by the sun, his golden hair hung down to his powerful shoulders in ringlets so precise they looked as if they had been sculpted, the folds of his blue cloak were draped like the robe of a holy statue. Every exposed part of him bulged with well-trained muscle. Only the brilliant blue eyes were as flat and empty as glass beads. He did not carry a sword, but he was wearing a bright bronze breast-plate and greaves on his legs, as if expecting battle. His voice, when he spoke, was – resonant, Belasmir thought, impressed. Well, loud, then.

'Hail, father,' said the hero, from halfway down the room. The king flinched a little. Archimedes recoiled too.

'Dear son,' said the king. 'Meet Belasmir, who has come seeking a boon. He has escaped from an island filled with terrible, immortal monsters, monsters who have devoured his crew, including a monster so powerful it can turn men to stone. I thought at once that you were the man for the job. Go with my blessing to this island, and rid it of its terrible inhabitants. And bring me their heads as trophies for my throne room. Then people will say that Seriphos is the greatest kingdom in Hellas.'

Belasmir, watching, saw that Perseus was not as pleased by this news as might be expected of a great hero. Indeed, for a flash of a second, he actually went white. But then he rearranged his features, so quickly and expertly that Belasmir wondered if he'd imagined that first response. He met the king's eye squarely, and smiled a willing battle smile.

'Father,' he said, 'you know how hungry I am for the glory of Seriphos and for my own glory too. But this is a formidable task. Exactly how many monsters were there?'

Belasmir had always had trouble with adding up. He began counting awkwardly on his stubby fingers, not helped by the fact that he had lost a thumb in a fight several years before. 'Six – eleven – er, twenty-one,' he declared confidently. 'Maybe more,' he added, suddenly uncertain again.

'There!' Perseus seemed pleased by this answer. 'Too many for one hero, however great, determined and brave that one hero is. My concern, of course,' he added, looking around at the courtiers, 'is that if we don't manage to exterminate these horrors, they may come here to seek vengeance. We must prevent that at all costs with an adequate attack force.

'So,' he continued, striding up and down the room, 'let us send messengers to all the kingdoms. Let us send to Krete, to Kos, to Khios and Ionia, to Sestos and Setebos and Athens and Ithaka. Let us assemble the heroes for a last great quest. And I, Perseus, shall lead them, lead them against these night terrors. Together we shall triumph.'

'Agreed,' said the king, who had begun to look as if Perseus's voice was giving him rather a headache. 'Where's your mother, Perseus?'

'She's at home,' the hero said, a little sharply. 'Where a woman should be.'

Belasmir wondered suddenly about entrusting his story to a king who apparently couldn't locate his own wife.

'Pity,' said the king, wistfully. 'I always like to see her.' He paused. 'Well, there it is,' he said vaguely. 'Do as the prince suggests. And get this man' – he pointed at Belasmir – 'some fresh clothes.' Belasmir, who had been hoping for sacks of gold, was dismayed that all he was getting was a new suit. 'Majesty . . .' he began. But the king had already left the room, and Perseus was looking at him with his cold and empty eyes.

'You,' said the hero.

Belasmir suddenly felt almost as menaced as he had by the bronze beasts. The back of his neck prickled.

'You,' said the hero, 'you must be our guide, and show us where to find this island.'

'But – but . . .' stammered the pirate. He had no wish to go back to the Isle of Monsters, and especially not with the prince.

Perseus sighed gently. 'I see you are reluctant,' he said. 'Well, after all, not everyone can be a hero. Still, to be on the safe side, we'd better keep you in prison until it's time to depart. We can't have you slipping away. Guard!'

As Belasmir was dragged away, his last sight was of Perseus. He was smiling softly, and fingering the gold hilt of his dagger. Belasmir knew he could obey his new master, or die.

Corydon woke when a dazzle of lightning shone straight into his eyes. Almost at once, there was a clap of thunder so loud it sounded as if the mountain behind him was coming down. There was no rain yet; a cold wind blew hard, and laid the grass flat. On the wind came a sound, the same music Corydon had heard once before: a shepherd's shrill pipes playing.

Corydon remembered. Hastily, he snatched up his pipe and began to play it softly, trying to join in the wild and stormy tune he could hear all around him. There was another crack of lightning, another fierce roar of thunder. Corydon played with all his might; he tried to put the storm into his playing. The storm was getting nearer; he smelled the coolness of rain.

Crash! A bolt of lightning shot into the ground in front of him. All around, the grass burst into flame. At that moment a figure appeared inside the ring of fire the bolt had created. The clouds burst open, and rain poured down, extinguishing the flames. As the thin smoke cleared, Corydon could see the figure more clearly. He could see the curling horns on the shaggy head, the furred legs, the shining cloven hoofs. The remaining smoke blew away, and he saw the face, and it was like no face he had ever seen: mischievous and smiling, but with a great well of sadness and solemnity behind the laughter.

'I have long wished to know you,' said the god.

Corydon gulped. He felt awe, but also a blind terror that made him long to run away. He braced himself.

'Are you my father?' he asked bluntly.

The god smiled. 'Yes,' he said simply. 'You are my son.'

Corydon didn't know what to say. He couldn't hug this powerful being; neither could he just stand there.

Tentatively, he put out his hand. The god took it in his own creased one. Awkwardly, they pressed each other's hands, smiling.

'May I call you Father?' asked the boy, at last.

'Yes,' said the great god. 'It is one of my names. There are many others.'

'I know only one,' said the boy, shy again, tracing a circle in the dust with his toe to cover his shyness. 'And that is Pan.'

The god laughed. 'But that is indeed everything,' he said, cheerfully, slyly. 'Do you love your pipe? Often I have heard you play it, at noontide, when you thought only your sheep were listening. I like the songs you make up.'

'I have heard you, too,' said Corydon.

They were both silent for a moment. The storm had begun to dissipate. Both were wet to the skin. Neither noticed.

'I have come to ask you what I am,' said the boy at last, drawing a deep breath.

'You are the mormoluke,' said Pan. But he did not say it with finality, like Sthenno. He said it as if it were a huge joke between them, as if he already knew that Corydon thought it was a useless answer. They both laughed.

'What is the mormoluke?' Corydon grinned.

'It is a prophecy. Ancient. So old that no one knows

how old. Older than the rocks behind us, far older than the Olympians who now rule all other gods. It tells of a wondrous daimon that will come to the monsters and become one with them. And that together they shall make the whole land clean. He is called the mormoluke, which means the daimon of fear, and his token is that he comes from me. For I am Fear, or Panic. It is one of my names. They will know him by my sign.'

'My leg! Is it really me? But what must I do? I'm only a shepherd boy. And why does the land need cleaning?'

Pan motioned to the cave. 'Come in,' he said, in his low rumbling voice. 'Do not fear, but do not stand under open sky and speak of this.' Corydon followed him.

Inside the cave it was much darker, and the clean smell of rain was enriched by a smell of damp earth.

'Listen and remember,' said the god. 'The knowledge I give you now is stolen from heaven. My little kleptis, my thief; I too steal from those who do me harm. The Olympians have not always ruled the world. Before they came, there were more ancient powers, also immortal. But the Olympians conquered because they made men think that there was only one way to be beautiful, only one way to be clever, only one way to be a real person – their way. Everything else they called monstrous, and they hunted it. They pushed it away from themselves and from the world, into dark places and the corners of dreams. But those powers have lives, boy, and hearts, and loves. And rights. They have been cornered, but they have not been beaten. And it is you who will lead them to victory. Lead *us*. For I am one of them myself.'

Corydon was silent. He was horrified. Make war on the Olympians? Impossible. In fact, he couldn't remember when he'd heard a worse idea. But he didn't want to offend Pan, either. He felt as cornered as he had when the pirates had hunted him. Anyway, even if he could make war on the Olympians, what could he possibly do against their powers? He was bound to lose.

Bound. He wriggled in the tight bonds of the prophecy. At last he said, seeking escape, 'Is it certain I will do this? I am only a thief and a scapegoat.'

The god knew his thoughts. He gave another great laugh, a grin, and clapped Corydon on the shoulder. 'Surely you aren't reluctant?' he said, smiling. 'Why on earth?'

'Well, on earth they have all the power. That does make me a little unwilling,' said Corydon, grinning back, only giving his reply a part of his mind. He was frantically trying to think of a way to avoid the whole thing. He would go back to the cave, tell Sthenno he'd met his father and that he'd explained that Corydon was not the mormoluke, that it was all a mistake, thanks very much, must be off now . . .

'You can do that,' his father said. 'But if you do, they will all die. All your friends. The gorgons. Medusa and her child. The monsters you released. Everyone. Perhaps I myself.'

Corydon realised with a shock that his father hadn't spoken aloud. His father's thoughts had simply materialised inside his head, without need for speech. He had read his father's mind. And his father had read his.

'How?'

Pan smiled. This time the smile was a little wintry. The rain slashed down.

'The heroes are gathering,' he said. 'Soon they will be here. They are Zeus's army. They will stop at nothing to rid the world of monsters.'

Corydon gasped. He didn't know clearly what heroes were, but if his father, an immortal, couldn't hope to win, how could he do it as a mere boy? The pirates . . . And then he stopped. Desperately, he caught at a last, flickering hope.

'The Staff!' he cried.

'Yes. You are finding the beginning of your way. But you still have a long journey ahead. I willed the Staff to come into your hands and it was I who helped you to reach it. But you must learn its uses, and you must learn them alone. There is only one being on the island who can tell you what you need to know, and she has vanished into the inmost fastnesses of the crags.'

'Is it Lady Nagaina?' asked the boy.

Pan smiled. 'No, though that one can be of use too. No, I

mean the Sphinx herself. She knows only some of the Staff's powers. The rest, the greatest secrets of all, you must discover. And it will not be easy.' His smile was almost mocking.

The god began to fade into the mists of evening, into the rain. Corydon suddenly felt terribly alone. He cried out, with all the passion of his lonely life, 'Father!' A gentle hand ran through his hair, touched his deformed leg in blessing, cupped his face. Great arms caught him in a hug. Then his father was gone. Corydon was about to burst into tears, when he heard someone else's sobs ahead of him in the mist, and Medusa burst out of it, running, panting, calling. Crying as if her heart would break.

Θήτα

Eight

Corydon was taken by surprise. 'Whatever's wrong?' he asked, puzzled. Medusa looked at him fiercely for about half a minute. Then, to his great surprise, she suddenly caught him in her arms and pressed him against her, or against the great bulge of her belly. Her hands grasped his head, as if they were trying to push into her chest. He could hardly hear, but she seemed to be saying, brokenly, 'worried about you – why – my fault – so angry – been hateful . . .'

He knew an apology when he heard one. All the things she'd said had been hurting him inside, like a poison that will kill you days after you drink it. But her hug was the antidote.

He hugged her back, as hard as he could for the bulge. Inside it, he felt something stirring: a hard struggling body pressed briefly against his palm. He looked up at her face, smiling at her, expecting to see her smile back. Instead, her face was contracted, and it was as if she didn't see him. Her eyes suddenly narrowed. He saw sweat break out on her forehead. Under his hand, he felt her belly tighten, become as rigid as rock. Then it relaxed, and so did her face.

'That was a nasty one,' she said, smiling now in a kind of relief. 'I've been having them for a few days, Corydon, and they never amount to anything.' But even as she said it, another pain seized her. This time she bent almost double with its force, and only straightened slowly. The ground was wet with the storm-rain, and so were her clothes, but Corydon suddenly saw, with astonishment, that water was pouring out of her. Was it – well, what was it? There was a sharp salty smell with it. She too had seen it; she was looking down at herself in horror.

'Corydon,' she whispered, 'the baby.'

'What about it?'

'It's coming, Corydon. My waters have broken.' Another spasm crossed her face, and she bent forward again, with a heavy moan she couldn't quite repress. Looking at her dress, Corydon saw that it was stained with blood as well as the odd-smelling water. He began to think, his ideas spinning desperately. She might need help. But who could help her? Who?

'I don't need any help,' she said, reading his thoughts.

'It's all quite natural, but it hurts a lot. It always does. So they tell me.'

'But I must get help.'

She clutched his hand, hard. 'Don't go. Stay with me.' And, with difficulty, she added, 'Please.'

So began a long and weary time. She was in pain quite often, more often, it seemed, as day deferred to twilight and twilight to night. There was sometimes blood. Sometimes she groaned aloud when the pain was worst. He knew when a contraction was coming because the snakes on her head would begin to react, waking suddenly and rearing up to hiss long and painfully. Many times he held her hand when the pain was at its height, and she clutched him so hard that his hand was bruised and swollen. Yet at other times she dozed while he played his pipes, or told her little stories that were always interrupted by the waves of returning pain. He told her all about his great father Pan, too, and the meaning of mormoluke, but he wasn't always sure she understood. He didn't want to tell her that the Olympians were sending an army of heroes. He didn't want to frighten her. What was already happening seemed more than enough to scare her.

He was afraid himself. He had no idea what to do to help her, and he felt sure she needed help. Many times he begged her to let him go and fetch Sthenno, Euryale, Lady Nagaina, the Sphinx, his father, anyone. Many times he invited her warmly to come with him back to the gorgons' cave. But she was immovable. He and she had found a shelf of rock lined with moss and bracken in the Cave of the Nymphs, and she had settled on it as if it were a velvet couch of dreams.

'This is right,' she said. 'This is where I have to be.'

Then came a time when the pains were coming so often that there were no dozing respites. Soon Medusa was gasping for breath, hunched on all fours like an animal gone wild. Her snaky hair was all on end, every serpent stiff and furious and agonised. Her lips were drawn back from her sharp teeth. She drew back her robe, but there was no sign of the baby's head. As dawn began to break, she was torn by a pain so terrible that she threw back her head and screamed.

'All right,' said Corydon. 'That's enough. I'm going to get help, and I'm going now. I'll be quick. Hold on, and I'll come back.' He did not wait for her to agree, or protest. He ran down the mountainside in the grey first light, slipping on rocks and hurtling over the small spiky shrubs. His bare feet crushed herbs, releasing a pungent scent, but he hardly noticed. He ran and ran and ran, and at last he saw the cave, saw Sthenno sitting in the entrance, studying her star charts as if there was all of eternity to spare. The sight maddened him. Breathless, he called her hoarsely.

'Sthenno, come – baby – Medusa – now,' he gasped. He panted again. 'At the cave. Come. Quick.'

Sthenno turned and gave a long, high cry. From the sky, Euryale suddenly appeared above them. Snatching up Corydon, Sthenno too sprang into the air. They did not have far to fly. Sthenno plunged towards the ground just outside the cave entrance, and both gorgons burst into the darkness where Medusa lay writhing as wildly as the snakes in her hair. Euryale noticed the sharp scent of blood.

Medusa was almost spent; though Corydon had been quick, it had been eternities for her. She lay on her back, gasping.

Sthenno twitched aside the stained robes. And saw the cord dangling from the gorgon's body, blue-grey. She knew what it meant. Hastily she turned Medusa on to all fours.

'It's the cord. The baby needs to come out.' Euryale sounded worried.

Sthenno suddenly noticed Medusa's clothing, and Corydon's, and her own. 'No wonder nothing is coming out of her. Look at her. Headstrong idiot. The Cave of the Nymphs, and she hasn't even hung up her girdle for the goddess.'

'I hate her,' spat Medusa. 'I hate her. I'm not hers any longer. I'm not, I won't . . .' She rolled to and fro in agony.

Corydon gasped. He wished he had thought of this earlier. He remembered the village women's girdles hanging outside the doors when a birth was in progress; no woman could give birth unless she offered her girdle. The birth goddess alone could loosen the baby from its mother's body. When births had been especially hard, everyone nearby had loosened every knot, and undone their hair.

Hastily, he undid his own belt.

'Don't be silly,' said Euryale gently to the frantic Medusa. 'You want your baby to be safe. I know you do. Let me help you.' Systematically, she began unknotting Medusa's clothing, undoing the coils of two snakes that had twined together, loosening her robe. Sthenno unknotted her belt. And, before Medusa could protest, Euryale had unknotted her girdle and had hung it on the wall. She bowed in its direction.

At first nothing seemed to change. Then as Sthenno and Euryale began softly chanting *Lucina, Lucina, Lucina,* Corydon heard a familiar sound, the sound he had heard before in this very place, the belling of the hounds of Artemis.

Like a beam of moonlight, the goddess herself entered the cave.

She went straight to the writhing gorgon on the bed. Medusa's face was a terrible mask of agony. The goddess was calm and still, like water under moonlight. She took Medusa's lilac hand in her white ones. Then she put one of her hands tenderly on the gorgon's huge belly. She put her other hand inside her and softly drew out a baby, breech first, slick with red and purple blood. She laid the baby on its mother's belly.

Then she looked into Medusa's eyes, and smiled.

Medusa smiled back. 'Parthenos,' she whispered, using the version of the goddess's name that was secret to young girls. It was a kind of apology.

The goddess kissed her brow. 'Forgiven,' she said. 'But you can never go back.'

'I know,' Medusa whispered.

Corydon watched the goddess leave – everyone else was looking at the baby – so only he saw Artemis dash her hand over her eyes, as if to hide her tears.

The baby was golden-brown, with a dark green tinge. He looked as if he had been made of shining stone. As Corydon watched, he wriggled with surprising strength, and seemed almost to be trying to crawl up towards his mother's breasts.

Medusa laughed softly, the happiest sound Corydon had ever heard her make. She took him in her arms and began to feed him, his head looking blacker against her purple skin. Sthenno made a soft cooing noise like a pigeon in a warm nest. Euryale looked up from a quick snack of duck's head, and made an approving noise too.

Corydon found that his belly was aching with a kind of loss he didn't understand. For some reason, he wondered if Medusa would ever hug him again as she had earlier, as she was holding the baby. He also realised that he himself was frantically hungry; he had gone almost four days without anything to eat. He had no wish to share Euryale's meal, though, and he turned his attention back to the new mother and the newer baby.

As the baby spread his hand out on his mother's skin, Corydon gasped. The baby's hand was strangely shaped. He had six fingers. The extra finger came in the gap between the thumb and first finger. Corydon went quietly around to the baby's right, and looked at his right hand. Yes, it was exactly the same.

Corydon felt a moment of horror. The baby was a witch-child, what the villagers called hagseed. Perhaps he might enspell them somehow. They said there was power beyond words in the twelfth finger.

He frowned. That was how his mother had thought about him, how the villagers had seen him when they had left him to die. As the baby tugged and guzzled, Corydon's feelings changed. Yes, he was a monster. Yes, he was a *gorgo*, a frightener. And that made him one of them.

He looked around the cave again. Sthenno had made a fire, and was warming some duck for them all to eat. Euryale, picking at a few shreds of bone, was crooning to the baby, who, with his belly full of milk, was going to sleep. And Medusa was smiling at him in the golden yellow light of the fire, smiling at Corydon, and smiling, and smiling, not her nasty smile, but a truly friendly smile, full of softness and love. The snakes too had lain down and gone to sleep.

Corydon gulped. He wondered what she would feel herself about the baby's hands.

'Have – have you seen his fingers?' he asked.

'No,' she replied. 'I only looked at his face. What's so special about them?'

Corydon struggled for tactful words. 'I think your baby has twelve fingers,' he said, blunt as ever. He couldn't think how to put it otherwise.

Medusa looked down. 'Yes, he does. Oh, well, that will be useful.' She said, suddenly, 'Corydon, it only means he's like us. I don't love you any less because of your leg. I love you more, in a way. It makes you special. And your father has them too. That's how you know each other.'

'Was his father . . .'

'No, but he's very like his father. He'll be a wild one, just like his father is. And like me. And I think we'll need him if we have to fight the Olympians.'

So she *had* been listening when he had thought her deaf with pain. She stretched out an arm to him; the other held the baby comfortingly. She hugged him hard and quickly.

'Would you like to hold him?'

Corydon took the small naked body in his hands. It

99

wriggled, and then, feeling itself unsafe, jerked hard backward, throwing out arms like a little starfish. Then he gave a shrill soft cry, like a gull, thought Corydon.

'Support his neck and head,' said Euryale softly. 'Then he'll feel safe.'

'How do you know so much about babies?' asked Medusa wonderingly.

'Well, I know about animals. The Great Goddess whom we called is the mistress of animals, mistress of hunters. And I am a hunter,' said Euryale.

'Yes, I see,' said Medusa. Suddenly tears filled her eyes again. 'You saved me,' she said, stretching out her hands to Euryale and Corydon, and including Sthenno with a wave of her arm. 'You saved him. I won't forget. Not ever.'

Corydon smiled. The baby gave a soft sneeze, then suddenly Corydon found his hand and sleeve drenched in baby pee. 'You'd better take him,' he said hastily, handing the baby back to Medusa. As he wiped his arm, he noticed that the baby was settling to sleep again. Already he felt he wanted to watch him, protect him.

'Dinner!' said Sthenno, handing round pieces of warm duck and hunks of barley bread.

Corydon was amazed. He had never known the gorgons cook food before. His mouth began to water violently. He caught the food from Sthenno and tossed it down even faster than Euryale had. Looking up, licking his fingers, he saw Sthenno and Euryale watching him with their mouths open. All of them began to laugh. Corydon blushed, then he began to laugh too. The cave rang with the laughter of monsters.

'I taught them to cook,' said Medusa. 'I couldn't face another raw duck.' And they all laughed again.

Over the next few days, Medusa and the new baby stayed in the Cave of the Nymphs and the other monsters came to visit them. Corydon didn't know how they knew where to come, or why, but they came.

First to call was the Minotaur, who had brought some honey and honeycomb that he said he had raised from his own bees. He was living at the far end of the island, and the honey was richly scented with orange and thyme blossoms. Medusa enjoyed it on Sthenno's barley bread. The Minotaur was too shy to stay long, but he held the baby in his furry arms, and the baby went to sleep clutching the fur on his chest. Lady Nagaina came, with a few herbs from her mountain fastness. The herbs helped Medusa sleep and helped her heal. The snake-girl popped her head in quickly and then withdrew. Even the Nemean Lion ambled by, though he was wordless. Only the Harpy and the Sphinx never came. The baby had celebrated its first week of life with a special honey cake Sthenno had made; it was rather hard and burnt, but she was trying. He hated to leave this idyll, but Corydon knew he had to search for the Sphinx. He had to prepare.

Before he left, though, he had another talk with Medusa.

She was singing softly to the baby: 'Great green chunks of greasy grimy gopher's guts.' The baby gurgled joyously.

'I've got to go,' he said, abruptly.

'To look for the Sphinx?' she asked.

'Yes,' said Corydon hesitantly.

'I have three things to say,' she said, suddenly looking more awake. 'First, don't let her get you into a riddle contest. Secondly, try not to look straight into her eyes. And thirdly, TAKE SOME FOOD WITH YOU THIS TIME!'

Corydon grinned. 'But Sthenno said I had to fast. . . .'

'Sthenno would!' she snorted.

'I did get hungry,' he admitted. Then he grinned again. 'Euryale was going to pack me a lunch, but when I saw it I realised I couldn't even lift it.'

'What was it?'

'Two dead deer and half a wild boar.'

Medusa laughed, that new, pretty, soft laugh. It was still birdlike, but now it was like garden birds in spring.

'Don't worry, I sliced some bits off.' He showed her a leaf-wrapped bundle. 'And Sthenno gave me something too.'

'Be careful,' she said, suddenly. 'We can't spare you. There is trouble coming. I feel it.' She cast a glance of appeal at him. But he had already decided not to tell her more than he must.

'I know,' he said. 'That's why I'm going.' He looked at

the baby. 'When are you going to name him?' he asked, teasing a little, to cover the awkwardness of leave-taking.

'When I know his name,' she said. 'Nothing so far fits him.'

'I'll ask the Sphinx,' he said, and set out on his journey. He looked back once, and saw the baby's small black head in the curve of Medusa's arm. He wanted to protect them both from the storm that he knew was coming, a storm that could sweep them away like driftwood lost in a big wave. He squared his shoulders and began to climb, his feet sure of their way over the hard, slippery stones.

γιώτα

NINE

Perseus surveyed the line of heroes. They were not exactly top-class. In fact, there were only two or three who had any experience of heroic quests. They were not, in short, the embodiment of the will of Zeus . . . Not what he had hoped for . . . But the great thing was that the line was long. So much the better. More bodies to put between him and the monsters. But it wouldn't be enough to keep his shivering skin intact.

He knew exactly what to do. He went to consult his *real* father.

Like Corydon, Perseus had to struggle to the top of a very high mountain to see his father. As always, his father's servants tried to keep him out, insisting that his father had a dreadfully busy morning, that Perseus should have arranged a suitable time. But his father heard the sound of his voice, and came bustling out of his enormous office, rubbing his hands. 'Son!' he cried bonhomously, embracing Perseus. Perseus smelled his perfumed hair, felt the stiffness of his rich silk robe, dyed with saffron. His father showed him into his own inner sanctum; Perseus noticed that it had been redecorated since his last visit six months before. Now it was all grey stone and hard iron tables, with an odd-shaped tank of turtles swimming lazily to and fro.

From the enormous oak desk, there was a splendid panoramic view of his father's trading concerns, which were, in fact, the whole earth and everything in it. Perseus could see men farming cattle, for his father; farming sheep, for his father; harvesting grain, for his father; pressing grapes, for his father; mining gold, for his father. Girls preened in mirrors and arranged flowers in their hair, for his father. Women looked worriedly at their faces in mirrors, for his father.

Only a few poets, singers and storytellers ignored his father, and not all of them did. Anyway, they hardly counted.

Perseus's *real* father was Zeus, king of the gods of Olympos. He said this to himself a hundred, a thousand times a day. It was true. It was a comfort when his stepfather slighted him.

This sounds as if Perseus was lucky. But there were limits to his luck.

'Pheidippides!' his father Zeus exclaimed, embracing him again. 'It's been far too long.'

'Um – it's – um – Perseus, Father.'

'Of course! Perseus! My goodness but time flies! The last time I saw you you were only a boy. A mere lad.'

'Father – um – you saw me only six months ago.'

'Yes, I remember now. Anthesterion festival, was it?'

It wasn't, but Perseus sensed that it would be unwise to correct his father again. Zeus was looking faintly cross and put-upon.

The older man ran his hands awkwardly down his immaculate golden robe. 'What can I do for you?' he asked, keeping up the jollity, but plainly meaning, 'Come to the point. My next meeting is important.'

Perseus plunged hastily into the story of the monster isle, Belasmir, his stepfather's request, and his own difficulty in recruiting heroes. His father listened, occasionally glancing into the huge mirror which reflected the world beyond his desk. As Perseus's narrative began to dawdle, Zeus cut him off.

'You're going about this all wrong, son. You can't get people to endure danger by telling them it's danger. You've got to *sell* it to them. Get everyone talking about it. Make them *want* to go. And remember one thing, Hercules. Everyone has only one question in mind when something like a quest comes up, and it's this: what's in it for *moi*?'

And it was then that Perseus had seen his folly. Of course! Men did not sail in search of glory alone; they

107

sailed in search of plunder – treasure, gold, riches that would make their lands famous.

This wasn't a moral crusade. It was a chance to make a profit.

'Father,' he said. 'Thank you. But how can I—'

'Rhetoric, Pheidias, my boy. Rhetoric. That's the name of the game, especially nowadays. Brilliant new invention. I had a hand in it, of course.' Zeus was already on his feet and walking towards the door, breezy, busy, businesslike. 'Get yourself a few good rhetors, and you have all a man needs.' Now his hand was on his office door.

Perseus tried not to resent the way his father had just got his name wrong again. He took the hint and followed his father out of the room.

'We must get together soon!' Zeus shouted after him, already absorbed by his next visitor, a tall thin man with red skin. Perseus heard him tell the stranger, 'Fine specimen, isn't he? That's my son, Philoctetes.'

His father's secretary pattered after him. Like all his father's secretaries, she was beautiful, with flowing hair and heavy, sensuous perfume.

'Perseus!' *They* always remembered his name, thought Perseus bitterly. 'He wanted you to have this.' She handed him a heavy scroll with bright gilded pillars.

Perseus turned it over.

It was *The Heroes' Handbook*, a listing of every active hero in the Hellene lands.

As soon as he reached the palace, Perseus sent for the pirate Belasmir. The ruffian was dragged in, and Perseus greeted him warmly.

'Ah, Belasmir. Just a small matter. My great and immortal father has given me this list of heroes to help with recruitment. I know I can trust you,' said Perseus with forced warmth, 'because you are already keeping many secrets. So I shall ask you to make notes as I read.'

Perseus opened the precious scroll. The first page was headed 'Heroes: Alpha-Grade'.

'Odysseus: Wants watching. Too sharp by more than half. Full of cunning. Apt to dodge the gods' command. Brilliant at rhetoric. Good man with troops. Too fond of his wife and family. Destined to win the Trojan War.'

Perseus shook his head. What was the Trojan War? Baffled, he read on.

'Jason. Greedy little squirt, but very ambitious. Could be a loyal son if given the right treatment. Will win the Golden Fleece.'

Perseus shook his head. What was the Golden Fleece? And wasn't it all a myth anyway?

'Akhilleus. Very difficult to manage. (NB,' said a marginal note, *'get his mother to stop spoiling him). Half-divine. Greatest hero ever. Must choose between glory and a long life.'*

'Well, I don't want him,' thought Perseus. '*I* want to be the greatest hero on this expedition.' He read on: *'Pirithoos: Mainly known as Theseus's best friend'; 'Oidipous: No use to anyone'* and dictated a shortlist to Belasmir, who was sent off to the palace scribe. The scribe wrote personally to all the heroes on the list.

Being Perseus, the list he had dictated invited only the best, the alpha-list – though not Akhilleus, of course. Most did not even bother to say a formal no, and Perseus began to pout, like a little boy who found his friends didn't want to come to his birthday party. Odysseus had written a polite letter regretting that his domestic obligations kept him busy. Theseus had sent him a blunt warning that he was biting off more than he could chew. Jason had written to ask what kind of treasure waited on the island.

Faced with these failures, Perseus thought hard about his father's wisdom. Then he hired a fine rhetor to write a special parchment, which read as follows:

A WHOLE NEW DIMENSION
to being a HERO!

Are you as rich as you'd like to be?
Do you DESERVE MORE IN LIFE?
Do you want to master twenty-five different monsters
AND have days of fun?

Then come on a thrilling adventure cruise with our experienced team of heroes, and discover how much more there is to enjoy with the GOLDEN HOARD MONSTER QUEST!

What is the GOLDEN HOARD?
The GOLDEN HOARD is the TREASURE that vicious monsters
have built up over centuries by ROBBING you, the HEROES.
There's everything you can imagine: gold cups to toast your friends,
gold crowns to wear, and right at the centre of it, a ruby as big as a
ROC'S EGG.

And that's just the beginning!
Some of the treasure is MAGICAL; how would YOUR kingdom
benefit from the power to become invisible, the power to transport
yourself instantly to a distant place, the power to make money grow
on trees?

Hundreds of weapons at your command!
Never-before-seen monsters!
Be the envy of your friends!

Perseus contacted every town crier in Hellas, so that all
day and all night, the sleep of the citizens was disturbed
by men paid to yell, 'Sign up TODAY for the Great
Adventure!' He had so many parchments copied out that
people began finding that their fried fish was wrapped in
leftover Golden Hoard parchments, that they could use
them to line baking stones, that they were good for stopping draughts if you wadded them up. In taverns and on
street corners, rhetors uttered the ringing phrases of
Perseus's call to arms.

Soon, every symposium ended with a story about monsters. The word 'monster' was on everyone's lips. People stopped to listen as philosophers debated the morality of the quest, and disputed whether monsters were malformations of true nature, or signs sent by the gods to show their wrath. In taverns, drinkers sang the 'Monster Song', when they could remember the words; it had a jiggety tune which stuck in the mind.

Within a month, everyone in Hellas knew about the quest.

Of course, the trouble with Perseus's plan was that only the really stupid heroes believed Perseus's rhetors and rhetoric. Some of the brighter heroes even tried to warn the others about Perseus's unreliability. Odysseus, for example, wrote quietly to several friends, advising them that the whole journey was likely to prove disappointing. Despite his wise advice, many of the younger, hungrier heroes, ardent for some desperate glory, were convinced by the advertisment. They flooded into Seriphos, overburdening the inns and camping in the palace gardens.

Perseus looked them over: dim, untrained, essentially monster-fodder. He needed to bring in some class.

So Perseus blanketed the world with another parchment written by the rhetor. This one repeated the story about the Golden Hoard, but added the following:

Once, our great kingdoms in Hellas had these powers.
Our way of life is threatened by the monsters'
theft of these marvellous treasures.
Strike a blow for freedom!
Come with us, and take back what is YOURS!

After Perseus had dumped thousands of these in every town, wives, mothers and daughters began asking husbands, fathers and sons, whether they were going to take back the stolen hoard. Men who refused were sometimes given white feathers; even Odysseus got one, sent anonymously in the post. It didn't make him want to join, but it did make him furious. (Actually, Perseus had sent that one himself.)

Perseus tried other ways of persuading people to join his argosy. He sent out details of special offers:

Luxury Hand-Carved Figurines
Limited edition

When you join the Heroes' Quest™, you receive six individually crafted clay statues of monsters and heroes.

Perseus called the edition 'limited', but in fact so many thousands of the figures were put into circulation that archaeologists would be digging them up for centuries, and labelling them 'votive statues' in dozens of museums. They were greatly desired by children, who built up vast sets of them and used them to play elaborate board games. As Perseus hoped, the children pestered every male relative to join up, so as to get more figures.

Yet still the great heroes failed to sign up. Perseus saw that his only hope with them was to approach them directly, and after much haggling, in which he had to promise half the Golden Hoard that he'd already promised to the men now choking Seriphos, he managed to get Theseus's best friend Pirithoos to join. Of course, it wasn't like having Theseus himself, but it added – well – substance. And Pirithoos brought ten ships, full of eager pirates. Once Pirithoos was on board, so to speak, men began to come in from around the world: from Egypt, from Nubia, from Mesopotamia and the land beyond the two rivers. Perseus tried to keep count; in fact he kept obsessive count, because he wanted as many men as possible standing between him and the monsters. He estimated that the army had reached the ten thousand mark by the first day of spring.

It was through the white feather campaign that Kharmides and his brother Lysias signed up with Perseus's argosy. They were eating breakfast one day, and Kharmides was enjoying the rich new spring honey on his fresh cheese, when a slave rushed in with a roll of papyrus for each of them. Inside both was a white feather.

At once, Kharmides knew who had sent them. It was Amphitryte, their stepsister.

Things had been miserable at home since the death of his father, Kharmides thought. His stepmother and stepsister had never liked him, or he them. His stepmother was obsessed with cleaning, washing the garden paths every day, sweeping the floors every time anyone walked on them. She had always been exceptionally tidy, but it had grown worse since his father had fallen down suddenly in the agora one day, after a dispute with a merchant who had made him pay too much for inferior olive oil.

He still had nightmares about his father's face, crumpled and purple, in the dust.

His stepmother said they had little money now, and it would be hard to get together a dowry for his stepsister. And Amphitryte was a bright, ambitious girl. She too had loved their father, with a jealous love that left no room for him or for Lysias.

Lysias had coped by hurling himself into the wineshop and drinking all day.

Kharmides had coped by trying to keep the run-down family farm going as best he could, though it was hard work, and though his stepmother made him feel like a criminal every time he stepped on a patch of clean floor.

Lately Amphitryte had been slipping out of the house every evening to attend the meetings about the war, meetings held in the women's rooms, the gunaikeons, in the nearby houses.

He didn't know what happened at those meetings, but she had come home more and more excited, almost hysterical, after each one. She had talked and talked about the war against the monsters, about the quest for the lost gold, about the family's desperate plight and her own need for a dowry. She had recited martial poems about clashing swords and the defence of the realm. She had sung songs about never letting the old shield-wall fall. She had begun a collection of figurines of monsters and heroes.

Kharmides knew he couldn't possibly go – not that he wanted to – because there was all the spring cultivation still to do, and weak lambs to get through the spring, and the cows about to calve. He said all this, shortly. He tried to be patient, because he could see that somehow all this was a consolation to her, had helped heal her heart a little after the death of their father.

Now she was trying to shame him with a white feather. Trying to shame him into volunteering for something that looked very like fraud. And like certain death.

But his mother had probably turned in her grave to hear her sons called cowards.

And now Lysias was speaking.

'Come on, Kharmides,' he said. 'No man or woman dares call us cowards. Let's go and join up. It may make our fortunes.'

'Have you been possessed by smiling Dionysos?' asked Kharmides grimly. 'Because this is madness. Even if there were ten thousand monsters on this alleged island, there couldn't possibly be enough treasure for the hundreds going there. It's fool's gold. And you're a fool if you go after it.'

'Maybe,' said Lysias, and for a second Kharmides glimpsed the desperate sadness under his brother's dissolute manner. 'But, Kharmides, I think this is my last chance to make something of myself. To be someone. To be someone else. I can't stand being – just Lysias. I want to be Lysias the Great, or Lysias the Hero.'

Kharmides took his brother by his bony shoulders. 'No, Lysias. Your chance to be someone is to stay here, help with the farm, keep what our father made.'

Lysias sighed. 'I want more,' he said. 'Not Hesiod's works and days, but Homer's epic. This life suits you, but it's killing me.'

And Kharmides knew it was true. His brother was falling apart before his eyes.

So, with an aching heart, he went with Lysias to the recruiting office, knowing that on their return they would have lost and not gained their fortune. At least they got a new set of figurines for Amphitryte. And they got away from the terrible atmosphere around the dinner table.

But as they took ship for Seriphos, singing the new paean written for the quest of the Golden Hoard, with a hundred others roaring out the chorus, Kharmides knew he was making the worst mistake of his life.

κάπα

T E N

Corydon trudged up the mountainside. His legs felt as if they were made of marble; he could hardly persuade himself to keep going. He decided to rest under the shade of an olive grove that shone, silver and grey. The cool shade was welcome; it was good to get the lancing sun off the back of his neck. He slumped down under the trees, on a flat rock, and began opening the pack of food the gorgons had insisted he bring: a few olives, a piece of wild boar meat, deliciously roasted with herbs, a hunk of barley bread, spread with honey, and a piece of the sheep's cheese he'd made himself.

He drank water from his leather flask, and listened to the familiar, dry hum of cicadas and the tinkle of sheep and goat bells. His own sheep were safe enough with Sthenno, though of course they feared her touch. He wondered whether these sheep had a shepherd.

It was his shepherd eyes that caught sight of danger –
what looked like a vulture, a lammergeier, vaning idly on
the hot currents of air steaming off the rock. He could just
make out the shape against the burning sun. As the great
creature hovered, Corydon noticed that there was something wrong about it, different – was it really a vulture?
As he was thinking this, it swept lower and lower, and he
saw that it was not a vulture at all, but a great woman-
headed bird-creature. It landed beyond him, further up
the mountain, behind scrub and rocks and trees; he could
no longer see it but he knew it was the being he sought.
He jumped to his feet, snatching up his lunch satchel
and his water skin, and began scrambling up the steep
mountainside as fast as he could go, his feet bruising
the scented thyme bushes. He ran uphill with burning
lungs. Just as he thought he could go no further, he was
at the top.

And he was confronted by a place unlike anything he
had ever seen in his life.

Born and bred on the island, Corydon had only ever
known a landscape of rocky slopes, gorges, dust, small
scrubby plants with strong scents. Now he saw that the
Sphinx had found, or made, something very different.

It was a flat expanse of emerald green grass covered in
tiny white flowers, which buzzed with bees and flittered
with butterflies. A double line of tall bushes traversed the
space, marking a kind of pathway; all were smothered in

enormous, white flowers; unlike the tiny flowers of the island, these were huge and drooping and voluptuous and deliciously scented. Between them flowed a stream, wide and cool. It led to a white building in the distance.

The building too was unlike the simple village houses; it was surrounded by what Corydon thought at first were white trees, but then realised were tall columns of white marble. The gold crests of the pillars that he had taken for autumn leaves were precious metal, applied delicately in leaf-shapes. He had thought the heavy red round shapes atop the leaves were fruit; now he saw that they were brilliant gems.

He began to walk towards the strange building, hardly knowing what he did. The heavy scent of the flowers, so rich, so sensuous, made him stagger.

He reached the white building in this dazed state, and walked up the steps. In the entranceway was a bowl of water, made of brilliant blue stone shot with gold. Corydon wasn't sure what to do, but after a moment's thought he splashed his hands, feet and face with it to cleanse himself.

'You do well,' came a cool, lucid voice from the depths of the building, a voice that sounded like the water looked.

Corydon saw her emerge directly ahead of him.

The tawny lion's body, with four immense clawed lion-paws; heavy wings that he had thought were brown, but that in the light of the flares in her home shone blue, like the water bowl; the immense woman's head, beautiful, heavy-lidded, golden-eyed, topped by a headdress bright with jewels and gold. It was her.

He remembered Medusa's warning, and tried not to look into her eyes.

'You need not fear me,' came her voice. 'I will not do you harm. And yet . . . you come to me seeking to know yourself, do you not? And that is the most dangerous thing a boy or a man may do.'

'My father said you could explain the prophecy. About me and the war against the Olympians. And how I may use the Staff to defeat them.'

'All in good time,' she said. 'Let us begin with you. What you are, who you are. Can you answer me:

> The camel's humps
> Shifted with clouds.
> Such solitude beheads!
> My arms stretch
> Beyond mountain peaks,
> Flame in the desert.'

Corydon had no idea what she was talking about. The hot sun poured down on his back. She waited. Then she spoke again:

'All night long I think of life's labyrinth –
Impossible to visit the tenants of Hades.
The authoritarian attempt to palm a horse off as deer
Was laughable. As was the thrust at
The charmed life of the dragon.
Contemptible!
It's in the dark that eyes probe earth and heaven,
In dream that the tormented seek present, past.
Enough! The mountain moon fills the window.
The lonely fall through, the garden rang with cricket
    song.'

Again, Corydon found nothing to say. His mouth was
dry and his palms were wet. He thought of the
Olympians, serene above all that made mortal life a dark
passage.

She spoke for a third time:

'Lady, three white leopards sat under a juniper-tree
In the cool of the day, having fed to satiety
On my legs my heart my liver and that which had been
    contained
In the hollow round of my skull. And God said
Shall these bones live? Shall these
Bones live?'

Now Corydon began to understand.

These were not exactly riddles. They were a kind of conversation. It was like when he and Medusa made up songs. He could see this one was about death, so he had a sudden flaring idea. What if he sang his own song of death in reply instead of trying to guess the answer? So he sang:

> 'They told me of your death, and brought me tears:
> For I recalled the many times we sent
> The sun to bed. But, though the time will come
> When you are ancient dust, in distant years,
> Your nightingales will live; and Death, intent
> To pillage all things, cannot make them dumb.'

And at last she smiled. 'Yes,' she said. 'Yes. You know. These are not riddles. Or not for you. These are poems. Because already you know that the world is not single. There are no answers, only conversation. *World is crazier and more of it than we think. Incorrigibly plural.* You are a maker. Whenever you are lost, this is how you will find yourself.'

'That doesn't help me very much,' he blurted out. He had no idea what she meant. What was incorrigible? Of course everyone knew that the Sphinx spoke in riddles . . . but really!

'Because you knew it anyway.'

How could he know what he didn't understand?

'No. What I would like to know is how to protect the

others and defeat the Olympians!' he shouted. 'What I am is only interesting if it helps me do that!'

She spoke again:

> *'You are not responsible*
> *Either for the world or for the end of the world*
> *The burden is taken from your shoulders*
> *You are like birds and children*
> *Play.'*

'You can't take my burdens from me!' Corydon shouted again. 'I wish you could, but you can't.'

'Nevertheless, it is because you are a child that you have found what you know. Let that child play.'

Corydon waited. Finally he said, in a voice of exaggerated patience, 'How – do – I – use – the – Staff?'

'Things are not that simple,' she said.

'Why? Why can't you make them that simple?'

'Because the Staff is not a spade or a shepherd's crook. It does not have a single use that I can teach you. You need to learn instead what it is. Only then will you know how you must use it.'

'I used it before,' said Corydon, sulkily. 'Was that wrong? After all, I did rescue you with it.'

'I do not deny it. But what you did was risky. And it has a price, which you have yet to pay, because you do not yet know what it is.'

125

'How can I learn?'

'Think of what you have already done with it to begin to understand its nature.'

Corydon thought. He had no idea what she meant.

'You yourself said that you released me.'

'Is it a releaser?'

'It is an opener. It is the gateway.'

'The gateway? To what? Or where?' Corydon's head was spinning. How could a Staff be a gateway?

'It is the gateway to the realm of many subjects, where he who has a thousand thousand courtiers rules.'

The underworld!

At last Corydon understood something. But he was still fundamentally fogged.

'Why will that help?' he asked, finally, aware that he could only learn by asking exactly the right questions.

'Did it not help against the pirates?'

'Yes, but you said that was risky. And I don't want to go to the realm of he who has many subjects, at least not much. Or not permanently.'

And yet, as he spoke, a great and startling desire suddenly fired him, to see that lost land, frozen and icy under the baking rocks of the island.

'Only there can you receive the help you need. And the Staff draws on the power of he whom you must all meet one day, and the power of those that serve him. You can harness that power, but at a price.'

'What is this price you keep talking about?'

'What it always is,' she said, and for the first time her voice was not cool or even, but infinitely tired.

He was just about to ask her what she meant, when he suddenly decided that he couldn't bear to know, not yet, not now. 'What must I do?' he asked instead.

'You must do what you can. That is all any man can say. Go. Walk twenty paces down the path, the opposite way from the way you came. Tap with the Staff three times on the ground in front of you. It is the gateway.'

For the first time, he dared to look at her face fully, and was surprised to see large tears in her eyes. She looked tired, her face no longer like crisp-cut marble, but like worn stone, blurred with age.

'Go!' Her eyes began to blaze yellow.

Corydon turned. 'Thank you!' he said, and sped away.

He walked twenty paces, just as the Sphinx had told him. Grasping the Staff carefully, he looked around for somewhere that looked likely to respond to it. A doorway. A window. A rock, even.

There was nothing.

But perhaps the whole earth was a gateway.

He tapped three times, as the Sphinx had told him to do.

He waited.

Nothing happened.

Then he tapped again, more slowly. Three . . . patient . . . taps. . . .

Nothing.

It wasn't working.

Angrily, he hefted the Staff and punched at the parched, cracked earth. *Boom. Thud. Boom.*

Now something began to happen, but not what he had hoped for. The ground remained obdurate. But he heard a shrill voice. 'Go away!' it said. 'Be quiet. Stop banging on the door.'

Corydon banged the Staff harder on the ground.

'Go, boy.' The voice sounded nearer and it was chill with unspoken power. 'Go.'

'I can't go!' Corydon shouted. 'I've got to get to the underworld.'

'Your time is not yet come,' said the voice simply.

'No, I don't mean dying. I mean to the underworld. This is the way.'

'Yes. But you cannot enter now. The door will only open when you strike it under the unlight of a moon at full dark. And the moon is many days from full dark now.'

Corydon gasped. It was true. He had noticed the moon had begun to wane. But it was only just past the last quarter.

'But – I can't wait that long!' he shouted, fury bubbling inside him as hot as lava.

'You cannot help but wait that long,' said the voice. 'The door is not even visible now. Go, and come back in unlight.' There was a thin, witch-cackle.

'But . . .' shouted Corydon. He knew, though, that it was no use. The way was closed.

Corydon was left staring blankly at the bare ground. Angrily, he banged it three times more with the Staff.

Nothing happened.

He wanted to scream at the sky.

He had to do something. But what?

He couldn't just go back to the others and say that he had the key to the door to the underworld but the door-keeper wouldn't let him use it.

Desperately he raised the Staff again and then stopped, struck by a sudden thought.

The words on the Staff! Was now the time to use them?

Why not? Kronos was a power. Perhaps *he* could open the door. Was that what was supposed to happen?

He said the strange, remembered words. They were heavy in his mouth, like pebbles. Like lead weights they fell. And he fell with them, plunging into a sleep so thick and deep that no one could have woken him.

But in his mind he was still standing, in a place he had never seen before, a great forest of broken stone. There were columns lying like fallen trees, stones shaped like fallen flowers, leaves and shards and snowdrifts of stone that had once sung aloft but now lay mute on the ground. He took a few cautious steps forward, feeling the sharp flint-edges under his feet. A heavy, lowering dark sky, purple as a ripe plum, hung over the scene, but there was not a breath of wind, only the hot oppressive air before a storm.

He walked along what might once have been a wide road, paved with stones, but something had lifted and twisted them, pushing them up, pulling them down, as if a giant had been here playing. It wasn't long before he noticed something very strange. Usually when there was broken stone, there were also plants: ivy, thyme, the humble low plants that liked to clamber.

Here there was nothing. Only miles and miles of dust and broken stone. No animals, either; no sound of birds, no sheep, no insects.

It was a dead land. Was this the land of the dead? Corydon began to be afraid.

He walked on and on. Only his monster-strength sustained him on the long, weary way.

Ahead of him he could see a stony heap that looked different. At first he thought someone had simply piled up stones to make a kind of mound. But as he came closer he could see that it was a building, but a strange one, shaped like a huge mountain, but too regular to be a mountain. At first he could see no way in, but as he approached he noticed a tiny door at the base of the peak. Corydon felt that this was where he was meant to go. It took him some minutes to climb the crumbling stone mountain, but he reached the door at last.

It was shut.

Corydon drew in his breath, and said again the words on the Staff.

They hung in the air before him, then melted into a single beam of silver light too bright to look at. The beam shot towards the door and plunged in.

The door burst into pieces. Flint stung Corydon's cheeks.

The silver beam had vanished, as if it had never been.

Ahead lay a long, narrow corridor into the heart of the stone hill.

Corydon drew another breath, trying to quell his fear. He walked in. There was a low, harsh rumble of thunder.

Then there was a sharp crack, and behind him a wall of stone seemed to fall from the ceiling.

His way out was blocked, and now he was trapped in pitch darkness.

Trying not to panic, Corydon felt his way along the walls. The stone was slick, like the stone in the gorgons' cave, and he found that comforting. He took step after careful step. Suddenly he reached a wall.

He could go no further. Now what?

He sat down to think.

His simple good sense helped him, as always. He decided to retrace his steps, feeling his way along the wall, in case he had missed a crucial doorway or cranny. And he was rewarded almost at once. His fingers groped their way into empty darkness. There was a narrow gap in the wall.

Corydon took the turning. He had to squeeze himself along sideways in the narrow passageway.

Were his eyes deceiving him? Was there a faint glimmering of light ahead?

He moved cautiously towards it. As it grew stronger, he saws that it was a pale golden light.

Soon he could see the walls of the passageway, stiff with mysterious carvings and letters in more languages than he could count. The passage grew wider, though he still had to turn his shoulders at every step.

At last he squirmed out.

The breath left his lungs.

He was in a huge, round room of vaulted stone. The walls were pierced by holes like honeycomb, so that the whole room was like a vast beehive filled with golden light.

Corydon saw that every tiny crevice contained a scroll. He wished Sthenno could be here with him. She would have darted over to that crevice there, where a bundle of papyri bulged out thickly, almost spilling onto the golden floor; she would have started reading at once. She would have been excited because some scrolls were smaller than Corydon's thumb, while others were bigger than his legs. The room smelled like beeswax, but it also smelled of old parchment, like Sthenno's cave.

Now what should he do? Which scroll was he meant to read?

As he drifted towards the centre of the room, he noticed a low door in the far wall. He decided to peer through.

It led to another round room, just like the one he was in, another hive of scrolls.

This room, too, had a door, leading to another circle. This new room had two doors. Corydon chose the right-hand door. It led to another room.

And another choice.

And another.

Now Corydon was beginning to feel lost.

The airless rooms, thick with dust and the smell of beeswax, gave no clues about direction. They were all perfectly circular and all identical. His shepherd's senses depended on the stars, on the free air in his face. Here there were none of those things he used to find his way. Here he was utterly alone.

More rooms, and more, and more. By now it was beyond Corydon even to retrace his steps.

He wandered on, tormented by thirst and by the cold prickles of a fear that he had never known in the wild places of the land, a fear that made him sweat and shiver. Looking at all the scrolls was somehow sad; who had made them, written them? Were their creators now drifting on the cold winds of Hades?

He longed to read them, if only to seek the guidance for which he had been sent, but the few he picked up were in utterly unknown languages, and Corydon had only been able to read slowly and haltingly even in the language of the Hellenes.

Finally, he sat down in a room exactly like all the others.

He knew there was only one thing left to try.

So, aloud, he spoke again the words that had been engraved on the Staff.

And the magic worked at once.

Where there had been nothing, there was, suddenly, an old man, the oldest man Corydon had ever seen, sitting at a low table. The table was covered in fragments of scrolls, papyri, pieces of parchment.

The old man's swirling black robes were thick with dust and spider webs. His dusty cloak was lined with brown fur, holed by the activity of centuries of moths. His hair was long and his beard dangled wispily below his waist. His eyebrows were shaggy nests for mice. On his head he wore a dented black fur cap, with a dangling tassel which he kept tossing out of the way. He smelled strongly of old clothes, musty and unclean. On his desk was a sign that had once been shining gold, but was now so dim and tarnished that it could hardly be read. Corydon thought he could make out the letter K.

The old man was very carefully and gently joining two small pieces together, marrying the broken letters into wholes.

134

Corydon crept forward and waited for the old man to notice him.

Minutes went by.

Finally, desperately, Corydon coughed.

The old man looked up at once. Corydon saw his face for the first time, a deep nest of soft folds and wrinkles. He was frowning.

'Shhh!' he hissed, and went back to his slow and careful mending.

Corydon went on standing. Finally, he coughed again.

'What do you want?' asked the old man, not looking up from his task.

'I think I need help,' said Corydon rather despairingly.

'Can't find the codex you want, I suppose.'

What was a codex? Corydon began trying to explain his request. 'Well, partly. You see—'

'Don't tell me. I know. You never learned to use a catalogue, though admittedly our finding list is incomplete – new accessions, you know . . .' Muttering, the old man began shuffling slowly over to another corner of the room. 'You young people are all the same – no sense, no manners – still . . .' Still muttering, his claw-like hands pawed through a pile of small pieces of papyrus, and as he sifted, the old man murmured, 'Staff, Staff, Staff of Hades, pomegranate, haima, death, no, not that one – no – not that one, too old for you, not very suitable – Ovid – no, not that one, Claudian, overrated – no, no, not Pope – never did care for couplets – Lancelyn Green, not bad but a bit reticent – Hughes – dear me – now, here it is! This one, this one! HERE!'

The final cry was almost a scream of triumph. The old man turned, and in his hand he held out a small piece of papyrus, a torn fragment. On it was written:

$$\beta \text{ Top } \Pi \text{ infra } \Lambda \text{ supra } \Theta$$

Corydon stared at it.

The old man hurried back to his desk and picked up his mending work. He began delicately pasting together some broken letters.

Finally, Corydon asked, 'Er – what should I do with this?'

The old man looked up, with a quick spidery tilt of the head. 'What do you mean, you stupid boy? Do? It's a shelfmark, of course. A shelfmark.'

'What?'

'A shelfmark. A key to finding the scroll you want.'

'But – how do I use it?'

'The first letter tells you which room it's in. The second letter tells you which floor it's on. The third letter tells you which shelf it's on. The fourth letter tells you where it is on the shelf.'

Corydon was beginning to feel a mixture of fury and despair. He felt trapped.

'Please,' he said. 'Please. Show me. You know why I'm here. Please.'

The old man's face softened miraculously.

'It's a long time since anyone said "please",' he admitted, grumbling. 'And I know of your quest, of course I do. I know everything. I contain it all. See? All stories. Yours too. And the Olympians. But they don't say "please" to me any more. And you did. Follow. Yes, follow me. Quickly. Too much to do.'

He shuffled off into the next room, Corydon panting behind him, stammering thankfully, trying to keep away from the dusty, torn folds of robe that swirled in front of him. They crossed several rooms, and to Corydon's surprise the old man seemed to know every step of the way to the right book; his footsteps never faltered. Finally, he dived towards one tiny hollow and pulled out a scroll so small it disappeared in his hand. It was dull green.

'Here,' he said. 'This is what you need. But remember this, and remember it well. You do not need this now. It is one piece of the puzzle. Later, you must make another journey. Then you will see what all this means.

'By the way,' he added, turning to go, 'did you see the very fine engraving on the wall over there? Owes not a little to Dürer. I believe it's a depiction of Giambologna's statue of Apenino – but it might be useful, yes, indeed . . . Remember. Memory is mine. My gift. Farewell, Corydon Panfoot. We will meet again.'

Corydon tried to thank him, but before the words were half out, the old man had shuffled away into the dimness of the library.

He was bewildered. Who were Dürer and Giambologna? More magic words? He looked at the picture. It showed an old man, made of rock, looking a little like Kronos himself. He was a giant, though, hundreds of feet higher than the surrounding trees. From the foot of the giant, from his ankle-bone, gushed a fountain.

Very nice. Not much use, though.

Carefully, Corydon took the scroll over to the table in the middle of the room, and unrolled it.

There was unfamiliar-looking writing on it and he had a moment of blank panic, but then, at once, the magic of the scroll began to work. In the bare margins, a picture grew, a picture of a boy. To his astonishment, Corydon saw that it was himself, Pan-leg and all. The boy was digging a hole, then the picture somehow changed. Now the boy was burying – no, planting something, planting it deep in the earth. Where was it? The picture seemed to widen, and Corydon saw to his surprise that the landscape was snowy, frozen.

Then he saw what was in the hole.

It was the ruby of the Staff.

As he watched, eager to see what good this would do, the vision began to fade. 'No!' he cried, frustrated.

The walls of the library began to crumble and dissolve.

The scrolls all around the walls burst into red flame. Shadowy figures ran to and fro, hurling flaming torches, fanning the fires. Corydon couldn't run – his feet seemed mired in the ground – but all around him the library was consumed in an avalanche of fire. He watched, terrified, uncomprehending – was this really happening?

Seconds later, the fire burned itself out.

And then Corydon stood, untouched, alone, in a ring of black ash.

Then that too faded into the sweet-scented dark of a night on the Isle of Monsters. Corydon lay on the cold hillside.

He was awake, and it was getting lighter every moment.

How long had his journey taken? He didn't know. Hours?

Something about the air felt wrong. Colder than it should have been.

He got up, slowly, stiffly. His bones ached. He felt as if he'd been lying, cramped and chilled, without the slightest movement, for—

What was that?

It was a silver fritillary. And there was a crocus.

With horror, Corydon realised that it was no longer summer.

It was spring. Early spring.

As the thought hit him, he picked up the staff and began to pelt, frantic, down the hillside, surefooted as a goat, trying to outrun the terrible knowledge that he had somehow lost months – months! – in the library. Who knew what had happened, while he lay frozen in time?

Were any of the others even alive?

λάμδα

ELEVEN

The Cave of the Nymphs had come to seem rather small, with three gorgons and a baby monster living in it.

Sthenno spoke. Her voice was cold and bleak. 'They are coming,' she said.

Medusa hoped she didn't look as weary as she felt. Sthenno had announced terrible dangers so often. She had told Medusa of the killer bees – or was it ants? – something too tiny to be seen – that were about to invade the island from Africa; she had panted out her dread of the imminent plague of rats infested with a vile disease; she had prattled of a city wiped clean by the eruption of a volcano. The silliest prophecy of all was when she announced that men would learn to throw thunderbolts that could destroy whole countries.

'What is it this time?' Medusa asked.

Sthenno flinched at her tone, but brandished a parchment.

'I've made a note of it all,' she said. 'They are coming. The children of Ares, the children of Zeus. The sky burns red along the horizon from the red planet of blood and war. They are coming, they are coming, and we are for the dark.' Her voice rose in a sharp cry, almost a scream.

Medusa did feel some slight alarm. While Sthenno's other prophecies had been highly specific, this one was troublingly vague, as if she really had glimpsed something from beyond the world. And there was the fact that Corydon wasn't back yet. She knew that he was trying to find a way to use the Staff, and for the first time she wondered seriously why it had been so urgent to do so.

Euryale laughed. 'Why need we fear, sisters?' she asked. 'After all, we are immortals. What can any do to harm us?'

'Well,' said Medusa, 'my son and I are not immortals. Corydon is not immortal. Lady Nagaina and the Minotaur are not immortals. The Sphinx cannot die, but she can be killed. So too yourself.'

'I do not know how I can be killed,' said Euryale stoutly. 'And if I do not know, does anyone?'

Sthenno spoke again. 'The gods themselves descend upon us. Can you not feel their weight, piled above our heads, like a storm about to break?'

142

The baby gave a sudden cry, as if he had understood her.

'I shall name him now,' said Medusa. 'I name him Gorgoliskos, little gorgon. Gorgoliskos, soon I will show you to your father, in the hope that he may help us.'

'Who is his father?' Sthenno asked, gently.

'He is himself a god,' said Medusa, her head high. 'I do not know whether he will acknowledge his son. But I do know that he will remember.'

'You will tell him he has a son?'

'I am not sure how,' Medusa admitted. 'I have never seen or spoken to him in his true form. But I think we should leave this place, go back to your cave. Ideas may come to us there. Corydon will return.' She hoped she sounded more certain than she felt.

Kharmides was glad to reach Seriphos. Lysias had been seasick the whole way, throwing up violently every hour of every day and finally lying white-faced among the other groaning victims of the ocean's swell. There were a few, like Kharmides himself, who did not suffer; there was one man, an Egyptian, who enjoyed the voyage so much that he was trying to tell the other questers that the sea wouldn't make them as sick as eating crocodile steaks. 'It's the fishy flavour they have,' he said, chuckling. 'Like fish that's spoiled in the sun. No one can eat it without chucking it right back up again.'

Kharmides gazed in amazement at Seriphos harbour, where a huge argosy of ships was being assembled for the expedition to the Monsters' Isle. Unlike the old crate in which they sailed, the new ships were triremes, sleek as adders and as deadly in battle, armed with archers and spearmen as well as swordsmen. Three decks of rowers meant they looked like hedgehogs stuck with quills. They had bright, empty blue eyes painted on the front, and huge, billowing square sails. They were beaked with bronze, each one with a fierce hard metal spike on its prow, ready to smash into an enemy fleet.

Seriphos was by now a garrison town; armed heroes were everywhere. And since they were all idle, there were daily brawls and lootings and drunken orgies. This was not a disciplined army. It was the dregs of Hellas; anyone who had ever failed at anything was here, hoping for miraculous success. Also here was anyone who couldn't run a whelk stall in Piraeus and make a go of it, including all those who didn't know what a whelk was and wouldn't have been able to count three of them if they'd been placed in a row. There were crazy dreamers of every kind, and there were greedy sharks who grew fat selling them unbreakable picnic kits, and cheap armour so brittle it broke as soon as you put it on.

The new shipload of hopeless cases was not welcome.

Nonetheless, Kharmides liked having solid ground under his feet. He helped the drooping Lysias to a lodging

144

that was more like a kennel, and went out in search of supper. All over Seriphos, campfires glowed like emerging stars in the dusk. On his way to an inn where he might buy dinner, he ran into another of the hopeful heroes, and hailed him.

'Have you heard?' the fellow asked eagerly. 'Perseus himself is to address us all tomorrow, and we sail for the Isle of Monsters on that very day.'

'You know,' Kharmides said dryly, 'I can't help wondering . . .'

'Whether he'll be at all impressive,' supplied the other soldier with a grin.

'Or whether he'll be a gigantic bag of wind, as I suspect,' said Kharmides, even more dryly. They smiled at each other.

Kharmides returned to Lysias, but his brother did not react to the news about Perseus as he had. Lysias was beside himself with excitement and pleasure.

'You mean, we're going to see our leader tomorrow?' he asked breathlessly.

'Well, we're going to see Perseus, anyway,' said Kharmides doubtfully. 'Get some sleep. We want to be up early so we don't miss a good spot. I want to hear what Our Beloved Leader has to say. I do, really.'

The next day, both had their wish.

Kharmides stood among the throng of sweating warriors and would-be heroes. The atmosphere was tense with excitement; everyone was waiting for Perseus. At the front of the crowd was a large platform hung with flags and banners. The banners showed Perseus's new symbol, the head of a monster. The flags were golden, to represent the treasure; they showed the silhouette of a muscular hero with sword raised, standing over a cowering dragonlike creature. Some people among the crowd had brought banners of their own, saying 'Perseus Is Great' and 'Our Beloved Leader'.

'He probably paid them to bring those banners,' said Kharmides. Lysias looked pained.

Just then trumpets began to sound. 'He's coming!' said Lysias excitedly, craning his neck to see. Perseus ran up the steps to the rostrum and turned to face the crowd, his fist raised in the air The onlookers broke into cheers. He smiled, showing his very white teeth. Kharmides had to admit that he was an impressive specimen, muscular and tanned, with blond curling hair. But from the first words he spoke, Kharmides felt chilled – and worried, too.

'Heroes of Hellas!' he cried. 'You have come here today to set free your lands and your families from the dread menace of the monsters!' Everyone cheered.

'And let's not forget,' Perseus added, 'that these creatures have also taken the wealth that is rightfully yours. Let us take it back – together! Let us band together into one irresistible force! The will of the gods is with us, we cannot fail!

'You have chosen me as your leader!' More cheers. Perseus pretended to look modest. 'And I shall lead you into terrible danger. But we fight for freedom, for our rights, for the gods who made us men! Who will come with me?'

A great roar answered him.

Kharmides saw that Lysias was carried away, that everyone else was at least half-convinced. He suddenly felt very lonely. Hemmed in by the vast crowd of would-be heroes, every one of them panting with desire to be off, only he could see that the man before them hadn't an idea in his head.

Why was he alone immune to this man's spell? For it was a kind of spell, he realised, his vision suddenly clearing. A silver flame flickered over Perseus's brows; yes, the Olympians really *were* with him, were acting through him, he saw. Why? They were using Perseus, and he was using the ragtag army, that was clear. Ideas, speculations began rolling through his mind; had the man done the gods some favour?

The point was, did the gods really intend him for heroic glory? Or were they using him to punish each other? If so, they could be about to use all these idiots for some dreadful purpose. They would brush aside the lives of these men as easily as a good housewife might destroy a nest of black beetles, or a farmer burn a pile of weeds.

And which gods? The silver flame and the eloquence

147

of Perseus looked like Athene's work. Which meant that Zeus was behind the hero. Kharmides suddenly felt sick and worried, but he looked around him at the ecstasy from which he was excluded, and knew he was trapped. He would have to see it through now, if only to protect Lysias from the anger of the Olympians, anger he felt sure was brewing and building.

'On to the Monsters' Isle!' The men began flooding on to the ships that stood ready at the quayside. They were so eager to be off that some pushed others off the narrow gangways and into the water in their hurry to get on board. Kharmides was not so eager, but even if he had wanted to get away, the crowd bore him irresistibly forward. All he could do was to uncork his wine flask and pour out a last libation to the powers of earth, for already he knew that on the Monsters' Isle they might be the only hope.

μι

TWELVE

On the island there were many ways to notice the passing of time. The long hot summer waned into the mists and rains of autumn, and then the biting winds and thick frosts of winter. The days grew shorter, then began to stretch out again. Lambs were born on every hillside. Spring flowers painted every grassy pasture, and village girls wove the blossoms into bright garlands. Gorgoliskos began to smile, then to laugh, then to crawl. It was full spring.

Where was Corydon? Where? None of the gorgons ever saw dawn light without asking themselves what had become of him. Sthenno sought reassurance in the stars, Euryale in food and in her pictures, Medusa in her baby and in her heart. Perhaps it was silly of them, but each felt certain he would come back, except in the deepest hours of darkness, when each felt certain that he was lost to them.

149

And he did come back. One cold spring morning, he pelted into the cave as though wolves were after him. He flung himself on Medusa, kissed her, swung Sthenno around, her flapping wings brushing his head. He looked for Euryale, was reassured when he heard her scratching out a new drawing.

Then he sat down to tell them the dreadful news: that he felt certain an army of heroes was coming to exterminate the monsters, and he still did not know how to use the staff to defeat them. He thought they might cry or rage at him. But all three of them were oddly kind.

'You have a piece of the puzzle,' Sthenno said encouragingly. 'That is what Kronos said, and he does not lie, though he can twist the truth. You will see the whole when the dark door opens.'

'You must go on hunting,' urged Euryale. 'You are on the scent. You will find prey.'

'You are getting closer to yourself,' said Medusa, 'and that is the key. Sthenno's scrolls know this and so do I.'

He tried to content himself. But their love and faith made his failure harder to bear.

For now there was nothing to do but wait. Wait for the dark of the moon. Wait for whatever warfare the Olympians unleashed. Corydon roamed the gorgons' cave desperately, Staff in hand, occasionally tapping on likely-looking rocks; there might be another door somewhere . . . He also tried planting the ruby on snow-clad slopes, even in a snowy bale of soft new wool.

But he achieved nothing beyond exhaustion, which at least brought sleep.

Medusa woke to the sound of Gorgoliskos's crying. Sleepily, she rolled on one elbow, tucking his small head against her. He found her breast and his crying ceased as he began to feed hungrily. Medusa put her own head down, drowsy. It was the grey hour just before dawn. Medusa felt grey with tiredness herself, but she felt warm and comfortable too.

Gorgoliskos, satisfied, dozed in her arms. Sthenno paced restlessly. Medusa felt herself infected by both the baby's sleepiness and Sthenno's restlessness. A bit of sea air would help with both.

'I'm going for a walk by the shore,' she said. 'Can you watch him?'

'Of course,' said Sthenno. 'Be careful.' Medusa laid the now-sleeping baby on the bed and pulled a dark deer-skin cloak around herself.

As she slipped out of the cave, she acknowledged that one of the reasons she haunted the shore was that she never quite lost the crazy, irrational hope that someday Gorgoliskos's father might somehow come there.

She wasn't even sure why she thought this might happen. But hope lived in the parts of herself that were all feeling and no reason. As she trod the stony little path down to the bay, the pink and gold clouds that lit the sky were banners of optimism.

When she came over the crest of the rise above the cove, she knew why she had felt this way. Usually the cove was an empty stretch of sand and shingle, its placid waters slowly sliding the grey slates to and fro.

Today, it wasn't empty.

On the beach were men. Hundreds – no, thousands of them, sitting around watchfires. Their ships lay at anchor, rocking on the open sea; their ships' boats were drawn up neatly on the beach. By their sides Medusa could see the glint of bronze swords and spears.

Not pirates, or shipwreck victims. This was an army. And not just any army; this was the army of Hellenic heroes. She saw the glittering arms, the combed, oiled hair, the swords, the shields, the banners and flags. She saw the green-and-white feather crests on the helmets.

Instinctively she dropped down behind a rock on the edge of the path.

As she watched, astounded, she recognised one of the men. It was Belasmir, the pirate. She heard him saying nervously, 'Lord, Lord, they may be nearby, may be behind any shrub—'

The tall man cut him off, asking, 'Are the scouts back yet?'

'Not yet, Lord,' said a third man. He looked worried.

So did the tall, fair-haired man, who appeared to be the leader. Medusa could see that he was really afraid as well as worried. He kept glancing around. Now she noticed him doing it, she also noticed that everyone was jumpy; they kept looking anxiously inland.

As she crouched there, she suddenly heard a long, terrible, piercing, ululating cry.

The army heard it too. With a great clatter of metal, almost every man sprang to his feet. Some of them drew their weapons or brandished them. The tall blond man was shouting at them, running about as though maddened by hornet stings, trying to get them to form a battle line.

With a sick feeling in her belly, Medusa knew that Euryale had found either prey, or the missing scouts.

And unless she thought of something quickly, the whole army would soon be after Euryale.

Medusa suddenly saw it all.

The army was here to hunt for the missing creatures of the pirate show. She crouched lower; she had to get away to warn them. And Gorgoliskos, so tiny and so vulnerable . . . She had to get back to him. Now.

But she must not be seen. Drawing her dark cloak well down, she tried to stand up in absolute silence, bracing her feet so she did not dislodge even a pebble. Every muscle in her body ached to run, to race as fast as she could, but she forced herself to move slowly and silently, putting each lavender-soled foot down as carefully as if she walked on the skin of her friends.

She had moved five paces away. Ten. Now she must risk a sound or two.

She began to run. She ran desperately, her breath tearing her throat. Her feet flew along the stony path, crushing spice bushes and releasing clouds of heavy harsh scent. As she drew near to the cave, she began to cry out: 'Sthenno! Sthenno! They're here! The heroes! Euryale – needs – help! Where's Corydon?'

With a bound Sthenno sprang out, Gorgoliskos in her arms. Medusa took the child, and picked up her sling, strapping the baby to her chest. Then the gorgon took wing, Sthenno carrying Medusa, her instincts guiding her until they began to hear the clashing ring of bronze that told them where Euryale was, and that she was fighting for her very life. As Medusa saw Euryale, she also saw the army of heroes flooding towards her like a great human tide. Euryale was striking out all around her, using claws and feet-spurs, even her bronze wings. Heroes fell at her feet, but there were always more.

With a loud cry, Corydon burst into the thick of the battle. He had the Staff in one hand, and he swung it wildly. Men fell like leaves, but not even the might of the Staff wielded by a small boy could stem the tide. As the other gorgons watched, horrified, a sword slashed open Corydon's arm above the elbow.

'Medusa!' hissed Sthenno. 'Unhood yourself! Look at them! It's the only chance!'

And Medusa knew that Sthenno was right.

Sthenno dropped through the air, landed in front of Euryale and Corydon.

In one swift movement Medusa flung back her dark hood.

The snakes on her head, roused by the sudden cold air, stood up on end and hissed. Her eyes flashed green light. Her mouth opened and she bared her teeth, fierce and pointed.

The men in front of her looked her full in the face. They didn't even have time to scream before their terrified open mouths hardened into grey rock.

A few others tried to fight, and were petrified. The rest simply turned tail and ran for it.

Medusa was left standing by Euryale and Corydon, surrounded by hero-statues. The Staff pulsed redly.

Euryale was bleeding; her golden blood flowed out over the grass. A hero had struck her hard in the arm. Sthenno tore off Medusa's cloak and began to staunch the bleeding. 'This is deep,' she said. 'We need the herbs in the cave.'

'I'm fine,' said Euryale through clenched teeth. 'See to Corydon.'

Corydon soon found his sword-cut bandaged, but his heart was still thundering. He'd been dismayed by how weak the Staff seemed against an army.

'Anyway, it's all over now,' said Euryale reassuringly. 'Medusa scared them away.'

'But they will be back,' said Sthenno. She said it with a black dread in her voice and in her heart that she had not felt for many long centuries.

Perseus sat on the little strip of beach, still erect and straight as became a hero. All around him were men bleeding, men crouching in terror, paralysed by fear. Some had even jumped into the water and swum back to the ships. But a few – and Perseus was very glad to hear their voices – were talking of their moments of glory in that battle. A singer had already begun to put the deeds of one, a young man called Lysias, into song fit for a hero:

'With his sweeping bronze sword, the god-born son of
   Poseidon
Pierced the brazen skin, just as a hot knife
Cuts into a soft cheese when a housewife is preparing
   supper,
Or like a cottager puts his axe to a great tree and fells it.'

The singer strummed his lyre, waiting for the Muse to tell him more.

'Lysias the housewife!' giggled one young hero, Demetrios. He had been frightened, and now wanted to

156

think that everyone else had been afraid. Lysias's heroism had shown him a self he didn't like.

'Shut up!' Kharmides was feeling confused himself. He had been amazed, but also horrified, by his brother's courage. Lysias had cut through the thick of the battle as if he was himself a god, shouting to others to follow him. But Lysias wasn't a god; he was a mortal man. And Kharmides knew that when he had landed the damaging blow on the dreadful, birdlike monster that towered over them all, it had been a parry that had slid under the monster's guard. 'He isn't the son of Poseidon, anyway,' he muttered crossly.

'Yes, Demetrios, silence!' said Perseus firmly, coming over to the group and clapping Lysias on the shoulder. Lysias looked up, beaming. This was what he had always dreamed of: to be a hero among heroes. And to have Perseus notice him . . .

Kharmides sighed.

'Lysias is an inspiration to us all,' Perseus pronounced. 'He has shown that even the most terrible monster can be slain by a hero of good faith.'

Kharmides smiled wryly. 'My brother's deed is praiseworthy,' he said, 'but aren't you forgetting that it was *not* the most terrible monster that he managed to wound? The most terrible monster is the one that appeared at the end. And she has made her own memorial; the place where she appeared is now permanently surrounded by a guard of honour made of stone.'

His sarcasm annoyed Perseus. 'Look, I know that,' he said, almost snapping at Kharmides. 'We do need to make a plan. And I will make one.'

'Make one quickly,' suggested Kharmides. 'She may be back at any moment.'

'Do not fear,' said Perseus, looking around hastily. 'Even if she does return, we can defeat her. We will triumph! How not? For we are the heroes of Hellas, and our bodies, our minds, have been prepared for this battle for many months.'

'Our bodies will make nice garden sculptures, too,' said Kharmides, 'unless we find a way to kill her.'

'I think we can find a way,' said Perseus.

'I have a plan,' said Lysias. Everyone turned towards him. Gratified, he went on. 'Well,' he said, 'I was looking her way at first – she was wearing a cloak, and when she did no one was petrified. What if we threw a blanket over her?'

'Brilliant,' said Kharmides dryly. 'Go right up to her with a nice bit of fabric, and say, "Would you mind putting this on for a minute?" I know you've got a lot of idiots assembled here, Perseus, but even they seem unlikely to try that – *no*, Lysias, it shouldn't be you. If it's anyone, it should be him.' He jerked his thumb at Perseus.

'I would gladly do it,' said Perseus with dignity, 'but I do see your point, Kharmides. And you must not do it,

Lysias,' he added. 'We cannot afford to lose our greatest fighter, can we?' Lysias glowed. 'We must think of a better plan. I will consult my great and heavenly father. He has been behind us from the beginning. He will surely help us now.'

Perseus took a black ram and some firewood and moved cautiously out of the camp, looking nervously all around and scuttling between bushes. There was a flat stone on the rim of the bay which he thought would make a fine altar. He tethered the ram to a scrubby bush, and then bent the animal over the stone, holding its head back to expose the throat. Its golden, unwinking eyes met his; he read consent in its stillness and silence. A good omen. He drew out an obsidian knife and, in one swift movement, cut the ram's throat. Its brilliant red blood spurted on to the altar, and the heavy smell filled the air.

Carefully, Perseus made a fire. Even more carefully, he skinned and dismembered the ram; he took the organs, the fat and the bones, and draped them in the skin, placing these pieces neatly on the fire. The rest, the good meat, he roasted on a sharp stick. As the scent rose upward, his belly growled. It never occurred to him to invite anyone to share the meat. When it was done, he devoured it, his teeth ripping off chunks of delicious flesh.

As he had expected, the scent of the sacrifice brought results.

In the smoke from the fire, a wavering image of his great father began to be visible. He too was eating, a vast lunch, with those who shared his empire, by the look of it.

'You need help, my son?'

Perseus noticed that his father was avoiding using his name. He plainly had no idea what it was.

'We had an – accident – at our first battle.'

'Yes, I know.' His father looked mildly amused. He took a bite of the ram-bone, and juices dribbled down his chin. 'She's a tricky customer, isn't she?' He chuckled. Took another bite. Spat a fragment of bone, politely, into a dish in front of him.

'It's all thanks to Athene that she turned out this way,' he added, with his mouth still half full. 'Wonder why she did it?' He took several more bites of his lunch, chewed thoughtfully, then focused on Perseus. 'Now it's a problem,' he said. 'It needs a hero's solution.'

'There can be no heroes without you, O great one,' said Perseus.

If his father sensed the flattery, he was nevertheless pleased by it. 'Oh, well,' he smiled. 'Yes, true enough, they're mostly mine. My sons, my good boys.'

'And you helped them,' said Perseus. He tried to look appealingly at his father, but found it hard to humble himself enough.

'And I shall help you too,' boomed his father, now carried away by one of his generous moods. He wiped some fat from his heavy chin. 'I shall give you many gifts. Make you great. The winged sandals of Hermes. The magic shield of your sister, Athene. Hermes! Athene!'

The gods he called for appeared. Thin, black-clad Hermes looked very sullen. Markedly reluctant, he handed his winged sandals to his father. Then he stuck out his tongue at Perseus, and ran off laughing.

Athene was more serious, and her eyes glowed with happiness. Her grey gown was spotless, immaculately ironed, set in clean folds over her ample, solid bosom. She took the brightly-polished shield from her arm and handed it to Zeus with the greatest respect.

'Great father,' she said. 'Great Perseus. Take this and gladden my heart by using it to destroy that wicked woman, that defiler of my temple, that harlot, that stupid, sex-mad, love-crazed—'

'Er – thank you, Athene,' said Zeus firmly, before she could say any more. Athene fell silent, reluctantly. She even stayed for a few minutes, hoping to be allowed to say even more about Medusa's evil ways. But Zeus kept looking firmly away, and eventually she left.

Perseus was beginning a long speech of gratitude, one which began, 'Great father of the lightning stroke,' an opening he rather liked, when his father stopped him, too, with a gesture. Perseus, disappointed, rearranged his face in lines of happy gratitude.

Cramming some more roast ram into his mouth, Zeus said, 'Wait. There's more. I've got another gift for you, a wonderful surprise; no hero ever had such a gift before. I won't say a word now. But I will tell you one thing; you'll be more than a match for your twittering gorgons with all my gifts to help you. Now, you understand, don't you? Use the sandals for attack, and don't look directly at her – use the shield as a mirror. See? And use your last gift as your most powerful weapon. They can do nothing against you when you have it. Or should I say him?'

His father chuckled again, and then rolled himself in the smoke of the fire as if it were a warm cloak.

He was gone. Perseus was left alone, holding the bright shield and the sandals. He smiled delightedly at his own heroic reflection in the shield's mirror-surface. He knew in every fibre of himself that the gorgons' days were numbered.

VL

THIRTEEN

In the cave, Corydon watched as Gorgoliskos tried to stand up. He pushed with his small hand, its many fingers outstretched, then fell back, defeated. He gave a small wail, his face crumpling. Medusa picked him up and cradled him gently, then laid him on his back. He gurgled up at her, then smiled widely, almost toothless. Corydon smiled too; he couldn't escape the dark knot of anxiety inside him, but seeing the baby playing eased him.

'You are very nice and tiny and pretty,' said Sthenno, awkwardly, from behind Medusa. She didn't really feel sure what to say to a baby, but she found him fascinating, as if he were a new constellation whose meaning she had to fathom. Gorgoliskos was interested in Sthenno, too. He stretched out his hand and curled it round her hard bronze claw; he smiled again. Sthenno tried to make a cooing noise. It sounded rusty, thought Corydon, but it sounded real too. She meant it.

Euryale looked up from her meal of calf's head; the heroes had brought a large number of animals with them, and she was enjoying the change from the isle's wild game. She smiled, and then said, 'Someone has to be practical. These people' – she gestured at the bay – 'are here, and they are not going away.'

'All we can do is wait.' Corydon spoke almost curtly. He felt hideously angry, and somehow ashamed. Why couldn't he help everyone *now*?

'Why are you so certain that your way will get rid of them?' Euryale demanded crossly. Truth to tell, she had not been pleased at having to be rescued by the others. Euryale saw herself as invincible. Now she had been wounded, and by a mortal. Deep inside, in a part of herself she didn't dare look at, Euryale was afraid, for the first time in her thousands of years on earth. 'But they could still overwhelm us by sheer weight of numbers. There must be at least ten thousand of them.'

'Surely not that many?' Medusa replied, tickling Gorgoliskos's tummy. He laughed, a strangely deep-toned laugh, like a growl. The sound was so sweet that it made Medusa relax. She almost felt she couldn't be bothered to worry about the heroes. She caught Gorgoliskos's hand and kissed it.

'Listen, Medusa. Stop lollygagging with your son and

listen. They will come back and you can't fight them alone.'

Suddenly an idea hit Corydon.

'What about the others?' he found himself saying. 'The other monsters, I mean. Couldn't we *all* join forces?'

There was a silence. None of them felt very enthusiastic about joining. Monsters didn't join. They kept to themselves.

'It's an idea, I suppose,' Euryale admitted. She was still unwilling to admit how much her own encounter with the heroes had shaken her confidence. Perhaps they did need help. 'We could fly out by night to the lairs of the others . . .' Her voice tailed off, but Sthenno took up the idea.

'We should at least warn them in any case,' she said firmly.

Corydon was thinking aloud. 'What about the Sphinx, and Lady Nagaina? The Harpy – though she's probably not much of a fighter. And the snake-girl. And the Minotaur, though I don't know if he would come . . .'

'The Staff will save us,' said Sthenno, with sudden confidence. 'It will save us all.'

'But we may be dead by the time Corydon is able to learn to use it,' said Euryale, irritated by Sthenno's confidence, 'unless we can defend ourselves.'

'We will make a plan,' said Sthenno, still confident, 'when the others arrive.'

'Arrive?' Euryale laughed, and gestured towards the beach. 'Don't you think it would be saner to meet somewhere else? Rather than assembling right on top of an army determined to destroy us? On top of Hades knows how many men? Why don't we just walk down the shingle and introduce ourselves?'

Now Sthenno looked annoyed. In any case, she did not want to leave her charts and parchments, especially not now when she might need them at any moment. But she could see that Euryale was right. 'Where shall we meet, then?' she asked.

'When shall we three meet again?' Medusa asked, her smal joke concealing worry. She had already picked up Gorgoliskos and had slung him to her chest.

Corydon spoke, hesitantly. 'I think the most defensible place is Lady Nagaina's fortress. Medusa, you and I will go there now with Gorgoliskos. And Sthenno, Euryale – you must go to all the others and invite them to join us there.'

'All right,' said Medusa. 'But you must cover the Staff. Its light could catch their eyes. And they have Belasmir with them' – Corydon shivered – 'and he might recognise it.'

She peered out of the cave. It was almost dark, but the waning moon had not yet risen. Perfect.

And then they heard it.

A slow, solid thud.

And then another.

As if someone had dropped a giant rock, picked it up, and dropped it again.

Thud.

Thud.

It was getting louder. Now it was like a tree falling nearby.

Thud. Thud. Thud. And faster. Like a whole forest of trees.

The water in Euryale's cup began shaking with every thud. Gorgons and boy looked at each other, then sprang for the cave entrance. They looked out, and—

O, great gods! What was it?

It was thirty, no, fifty feet high, gleaming dully in the faint twilight, as if it were made of brass. It was man-shaped. It held a huge spear, and carried a shield emblazoned with two crossed lightning bolts. At its side was a sword. It was like a Greek soldier, a hoplite, but its size was like five hundred hoplites massed together. And it was moving, walking in the sea as if it were a child and the sea a mere puddle. But there was no gaiety in its terrible, slow, solid movements.

It turned its head from side to side, as if it were searching for something. As it did so, Corydon caught a glimpse of its eyes through the eyeholes of its helmet. They were molten, like lava erupting from an active volcano, and like lava they shone red.

'*Run!*' Corydon could only whisper; his mouth was dust-dry with fear. But Euryale heard him. She did not argue, but she paused.

'*Go on!*' Medusa urged behind him, in a soft hissing whisper. '*Get the others! Warn them!*'

'*Meet at the stronghold!*' Corydon urged. He could still hear the giant's terrible footsteps.

Silently, keeping their wings from clashing, Euryale and Sthenno stole out into the open, crept behind the rocky overhang that formed the cave mouth, and then took off. Corydon and Medusa peeped cautiously out of the cave entrance, preparing to follow on foot.

But Sthenno's feathers had given a soft rattle as she spread her great wings.

The giant's head snapped round.

It let out a monstrous roar, like a charging animal, and lifted its spear. Corydon and Medusa looked at each other, frozen with absolute horror.

Corydon knew he must do something. But what?

He picked up a rock and threw it down and to the right, past the cave entrance.

Aroused by this new sound, the giant turned his head again, with another bull-like roar.

Medusa and Corydon scuttled into the shadows at the cave entrance.

But Gorgoliskos, scared by the loud noise gave a cry of terror, a loud scream.

The giant thudded towards them, running full-tilt, his enormous feet a menace to all life as he crushed plants and even trees in his wake. Medusa stood still for a second, mesmerised by his size and power, then she ran to the back of the cave, Gorgoliskos bouncing in his sling. Corydon tore after her.

In a few thunderous steps, the giant reached the cave entrance. He bent down low. He tried to push his gigantic fist into the cave, but it was so big that he couldn't get it through the entrance. He gave a roar of frustration.

He took a step back, then kicked at the entrance, using his great foot as if it were a battering ram. He seemed impervious to pain. He kicked again. And again. And again. He managed to make an avalanche of tiny stones from the scree above the cave mouth, but the granite rocks held. He tried to poke his spear, then his sword, into the entrance.

The sweat of fear dripped into Corydon's eyes. He and Medusa could just see each other, and Corydon knew that Medusa too had managed to dodge this menace, diving and rolling from side to side to avoid his thrusts.

The giant's great bronze fists were scratched and bent with the pounding. Silently, Medusa pointed this out.

So he wasn't a god or a titan; there might be hope. There might. Medusa held onto that, as firmly as she held Gorgoliskos. Corydon clutched the Staff desperately, as if its wood could give him courage.

But the giant didn't go away. He kept at it, growling with animal frustration.

After what seemed like hours, a small man, seemingly an ant compared with the giant, ran up to his huge leg and tilted back his head, shouting something. Corydon couldn't hear what he said, but he heard the giant's voice boom out, 'Yes, Lord.' Then the giant, at last, walked away into the deepness of night.

The two fugitives waited almost an hour before they dared to venture out.

When they did, all seemed quiet. The stars shone fierce and prickly overhead. The crescent moon had risen, low and golden. It showed the heroes' encampment, and beyond them, immense and shining, the hulk of the giant, standing to attention and watching the camp. Corydon caught a glimpse of his huge red eyes. He shrank back, but his cloak was enough to hide him. The darkness added a layer of protection and they managed to slip past the camp and up the stony track to Lady Nagaina's stronghold.

Medusa hugged Gorgoliskos to her, feeling the piercing fear that only a mother can know. But as she hurried onwards, she also felt certain, somehow, that Corydon would manage to save them. It was only Corydon who felt that every one of his steps might take him – take them all – over a precipice.

*

170

Perseus surveyed the metal giant Talos with pride. He had never felt so happy in his life.

He remembered Talos from his lonely boyhood. Occasionally his true father had claimed Perseus for short visits, but Zeus was easily bored by his many children, and Perseus had mostly been handed over to one of Zeus's many nymphs. The nymphs had also found the small angry boy boring, and had often left him alone, playing dismally on a beach, by a cave.

Once, though, the nymph of the moment had been one of Aphrodite's train, and Perseus had been taken to Kytherea, Aphrodite's island. It was lush and green, and in every part of it Perseus could hear the giggles of girls through the trees, as his father Zeus chased them, caught them ... It had been so embarrassing. He had stalked crossly along the beach, kicking up puffs of sand, and had suddenly noticed the giant, keeping pace with him, knee-deep in ocean.

At first, Perseus had been terrified. He remembered hearing his nursemaid telling another boy that 'Talos will get you if you don't go straight to bed'.

But the giant made no move towards him.

And suddenly Perseus had somehow found the smooth metal body reassuring. Talos wasn't interested in nymphs at all, or in chasing them ... Perseus had thought, guiltily, that the giant looked and acted much more like the king of the world than did his father ...

Talos did not speak, but simply walked along with the lonely boy for an hour or two.

It was Talos's task to guard Aphrodite's isle, and he had no intention of failing in his duty, but perhaps too he had meant to comfort. Perseus remembered wishing that a giant like this could obey *his* commands, guard *him*.

And now his wish had come true. It was like having the best toy ever.

Talos would help them break out of the bay and onto the island hinterland. Thinking of this, Perseus felt released, as if he could suddenly fly. His heart was feather-light as he thought of returning to Seriphos in triumph.

Talos was also a present from his father, Perseus reflected. Zeus must really love me, he thought, to give me such a wonderful toy.

Already Talos had proved his worth. He had immediately discovered the monsters' secret lair, and had tried so hard to destroy it that he had run the risk of injuring himself. He had obeyed instantly when Perseus had ordered him to stop. Now he was the best sentry imaginable, tirelessly watching the land, alert to the slightest sound. He missed nothing.

Everyone was sleeping more soundly, guarded by this great brass giant. When Talos had first arrived, some of the heroes had shrunk back, afraid, but after his great discovery of the monsters' foul lair, they had acknowledged him for what he was. Now only Perseus was restless, trying to map out what to do next.

Suddenly, he remembered his father's other gifts. He almost laughed aloud. He had been so eager to welcome Talos, that he had completely forgotten to try the winged sandals. And yet a moment's thought revealed that if he wished to be the glory of Hellas, he must not leave all the heroic deeds to Talos. He must do some himself to be worthy of an epic or two. Or three. But of course he must not take too many risks. Thinking it over, he pulled on Hermes' winged sandals.

They were rather frisky and hard to manage; the right sandal even tried to take off on its own before he could strap it to his foot, and he had to pounce on it to pin it down. While he was doing that, the left sandal landed on his back and began tickling him with its feathers. Impatiently, Perseus wrestled them both to his feet, but then they grew sulky, and refused to fly. Perseus had to promise that he would play with them later if they would behave, and then they took off so quickly that he barely had time to grab his sword. Soaring straight up into the air, they showed no sign of hovering over the land, as he had hoped. Instead, they seemed to be making for the moon. The air grew cold and thin.

'Stop!' shouted Perseus. Disliking his tone, the sandals grew sullen again. They folded their wings crossly. Perseus dropped through the air like a wounded bird.

When he was inches above an immense grey rock, they listened to his pleas and resumed flight. Perseus shot upwards again. His stomach lurched and he turned green.

After several hours like this, Perseus was both airsick and angry. At last, by bribing them with a promise of new inlaid leather uppers, he managed to persuade the sandals to fly levelly over the land at a height of twenty feet or so, so that he could look for monsters. Almost at once, he was rewarded. Ahead of him, clambering and running over the stony hillside, he saw the figure of a woman, and with an uncontrollable shudder he recognised her by her green snaky hair. Beside her was a boy, limping but surefooted.

To his surprise, he saw that the monster-woman was carrying a sling, the kind of sling that Hellenic mothers used to carry their babies.

At once he realised what must have happened. She must have stolen a baby in the night and she was doubtless taking it to some terrible altar of Hecate to be sacrificed. He imagined the altar thick with dark blood, in some dim grove adorned with the body parts of previous sacrifices. Such a sacrifice would increase the monsters' strength, too, might even give them power to defeat his army.

But Perseus knew that he couldn't tackle this gorgon on his own, not yet, not now. He hadn't brought his shield, and his control of the winged sandals was precarious at best. And who knew what dark magics the limping boy might command? However, his sly brain was working. He followed her, not too closely, as she climbed up a spiral path, through an oak grove, then over a swift stream and upward towards the high snowy peaks of the mountains.

Perseus tried to get the sandals to rise, but they complained that they were tired, that they had been flying all night, that they were not mountain sandals, and that the air was cold. Perseus had an idea. Instead of bargaining with them, he bent down and hit them with the flat of his sword. Sulkily, the sandals began to climb, flying higher as he wished. This allowed him to see that the monsters were heading for a tiny whitewashed village, the red tiles of its roofs visible in the faint light of dawn. By the village, Perseus saw a tall stone, and peering, he could see that it was riddled with tiny holes. A red mark on its side showed that an iron ring had once hung there, but Perseus wondered if the redness might be blood. This, surely, was the altar the monster was trying to reach. He could also see a larger, deeper hole at the apex of the stone, but he was not high enough to see into it. 'Perhaps,' he thought, 'that's where the baby's blood goes.'

But even Perseus could see that dawn was no time for a sacrifice to Hecate. The monster would have to keep the baby somewhere until the witches' hour of midnight, when Hecate would be abroad.

So would it be tonight? Perseus cudgelled his tired brain. The moon was in the last quarter. Sacrifices to Hecate took place at the moon's dark, which would begin in two days' time.

Perseus tried to keep his tired eyes fixed on the snaky figure, though terror of her power made him look away often. He had no wish to meet her eyes and be turned to stone himself. Every time she moved her head, he flinched. It must have been at one such moment that she vanished suddenly from his sight. He flew angrily to and fro, searching for her, but there was no sign of her. Not even a footprint.

There was nothing for it but to go on to the village.

Perseus decided not to fly in and land in the main agora. They might take *him* for a monster if he did that. Instead, he landed just outside the village, and began strolling along the track as if he were a traveller coming from the nearby coast. As was usual in these small places, a woman was outside sweeping up the goats' dung from her front doorstep with a thick birch broom, and she was gossiping with a neighbour who was sitting in the sun doing her spinning, the white wool soft in the early light. The little place was poor, but frantically clean. The men, meanwhile, were all playing dice outside what must be the tavern, with vine-leaves over the lintel. They looked surly. A bunch of sheep-thieves, thought Perseus disdainfully.

When Perseus came clanking along the street in his breastplate and greaves, the peace was broken. The women looked up. One even gave a little scream. The men looked up too, and one of them was obviously about to go and fetch the spears, when Perseus spoke. Clearly, these simple people were not used to visits from great heroes. He would calm and reassure them.

'I come in peace,' he cried, waving his arm. He saw to his relief that they understood him. Then suddenly the whole village poured out into the street and began making much of him. A woman pressed a flower into his hand; a young girl gave him an apple. An elderly woman stroked his shining armour; a young man grinned admiringly. Perseus practically purred.

The villagers decided to take him to see their headman, and he was followed up the street by an excited gang of children; the boys were already imitating his swaggering walk, pretending to be him. Perseus smiled, showing his white teeth. For perhaps the first time in his life, he felt a real desire to help simple people like these. And imagine their gratitude and respect if he did . . .

The headman was quiet, serious, silent, but he welcomed Perseus and offered him coarse red wine in a simple pottery krater, with some rough barley breads to dip in it. Perseus accepted, and sat down.

'Has anyone here,' he asked, 'lost a baby?'

There was a long, hard silence. Then a woman stepped forward.

'My baby, my baby!' she cried. 'Have you seen him, great sir? Oh, have you seen him?'

The other villagers were silent. The woman burst into tears.

'How long ago did you lose him?' Perseus asked as gently as he could. The woman simply went on sobbing.

'I fear your child is in the hands of a fiend,' Perseus declared. 'But fear not, little mother! I and my peerless band of heroes, accompanied by the great metal giant Talos, will rescue the child from the monster who has stolen it.'

The mother looked at him gratefully. 'You are too good, sir, too good. They will not listen, they do not understand. You understand, sir, you know a mother's heart.' To his surprise, Perseus felt touched by this outburst. He patted the woman on the arm.

For a moment the village headman seemed to be about to speak, but then he changed his mind. He shrugged instead, and all the other villagers shrugged, too, and murmured to each other. Perseus noticed that they were still wary of him, but he felt sure that he could win their trust by restoring the stolen baby.

'Well, to arms,' he cried. 'The monsters may attack while I am gathering my men. Ready your spearmen in

178

case. We will return in force.' He turned to leave, already planning exactly what to say to his army.

'Sir . . .' It was a pretty young girl. She looked up at him adoringly. 'Sir, you do know about Sylvia; they did warn you?'

Perseus frowned. 'Is Sylvia the mother? Grief does strange things to women,' he said firmly. The girl smiled hesitantly, then decided not to try again. Instead, she waved.

With that, he marched out of the village; as soon as he was out of sight, he coaxed the reluctant sandals into the air and took off for the beach camp. He remembered that he had promised to play with the sandals, and decided to give his servant the job. He had more important things to think about.

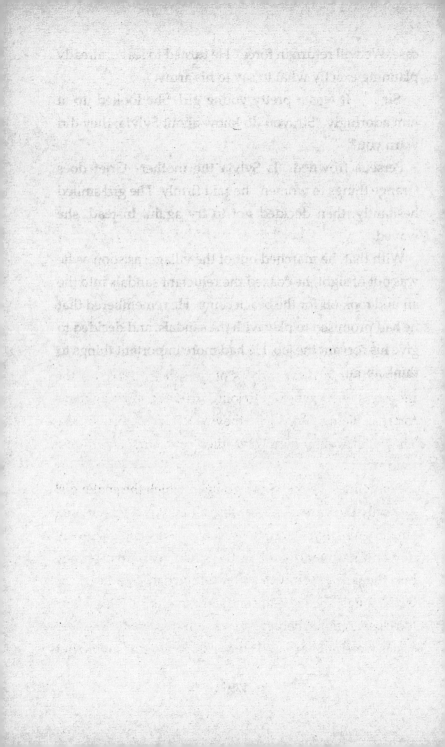

FOURTEEN

By now, every one of the monsters knew what they were facing.

Sthenno and Euryale had spread the news; it had reached the farthest corners of the island. And yet the monsters were reluctant to join forces at Lady Nagaina's fortress. Being monsters, they were used to solitude. They all had their own ways, their own lands, their own food.

Sometimes weeks would go by in which the snake-girl saw only the birds. And she liked that; she liked her own small peninsula, where the sun warmed the rocks every day and she could bake in the sun's heat, then plunge into the jade-green water to hunt for fish. She liked the birds' songs; she liked to eat them even more, if they flew too close. Against heroes she was almost defenceless. Her scales were not hard and shiny, like a dragon's mail, but yielding and silken, so tender that she had always hated to be touched.

She knew, however, that she had to give up her lovely private loneliness. She slunk reluctantly to Lady Nagaina's stronghold, praying that it would not remind her too much of the pirates' show.

The Nemean Lion lived alone, too, in the small sandy desert in the heart of the island. No one came there; it was wild and weird and of no use to the villagers. The lion had a rock, too, one where he could bake in the sunlight and enjoy cooling sleep during the evening. He did not think or reflect on what he was. Sometimes he felt hungry, and then he ate. Otherwise he simply enjoyed the sun and then the coolness and the stars. When he was told of the heroes, his shaggy head drooped to the ground. He liked it in his desert. It was wide and free. Those new people would disturb him, and he knew his peace was over. He set out for the stronghold, but he stopped to nose his rock, and lick it a bit, to say goodbye to it in case he never saw it again. It never occurred to him that other people might think this was funny, or silly.

The Harpy didn't mind society quite as much. She was neither sensitive like the snake-girl nor intrinsically solitary like the lion. She had known sisters; one of her sisters was Iris, the rainbow-winged messenger of the Olympian gods. But the Harpy would miss her daily flights; she loved to coast on the currents of the air, riding the warm winds that rose from the land, soaring, and dipping, and swooping. The only thing that cheered her was the thought of a little mischief. Perhaps she might snatch food away as others were about to eat it? Or pull their bedclothes from them? These minor torments pleased her as she landed, her wings giving off the reek of sulphur.

Of course the Sphinx hated leaving her home. But unlike all the others, she was calm. She understood necessity and force; they were her being. And the Minotaur was just hoping to see Medusa again, though he didn't say so, not even to himself.

Lady Nagaina had built her fortress because she didn't ever want to see anyone, human or monstrous, again after the torment of the pirates' show. She had hated being *seen* by people; people who laughed, people whose voices went through her head and set her temples throbbing, people who screamed when they saw her. People who gazed at her five heads and counted them, awed, eventually shouting *'Pente!'* in triumph. Even after several months in her stronghold, she still had to push the thoughts of these people away from her, resolutely, if she was not to spend the whole day in darkness. Now it seemed that she would be doubly invaded; the monsters were already filling her stronghold with their oddly-shaped bodies and angry voices, but they were there to prevent a further and worse invasion.

The fortress itself was hewn from the mountainside, seeming to cling onto the edge of the cliff like a limpet. Atop the fortress tower was a great dome that looked as if it was made of crystal; no one knew how Lady Nagaina could have come by such a thing. In fact it was made of her own poisonous secretions; she had mixed her gaseous poison with her acid poison, and moulded the substance into the dome. It had hardened quickly in the mountain air. Now it was her bedchamber, her favourite room.

On the first day that the monsters were assembled, the Nemean Lion had roared all night, missing his rock, and complained that it was too hot at night. The snake-girl had refused to eat and had sat unhappily hunched in her chair. The Harpy had flown round the room with loud screeching cries, even flying off with Gorgoliskos once. And Lady Nagaina had lain in bed all day with a separate wet cloth on each of her heads. Corydon began to feel that the situation was hopeless. How would he ever get them to cooperate enough to fight?

Yet fight they must; his monster-sense told him that he and Medusa had been spotted approaching the stronghold – he'd felt sharp eyes in his back as clearly and coldly as one can feel a knife. He had kept turning his head, but hadn't managed to see who it was. It was sure to bring the heroes down on them all. Their only chance was to be ready. Sthenno and Euryale and Medusa all understood, but he couldn't persuade the others to have a proper council of war. It didn't help that Lady Nagaina never seemed to eat, so there was very little food in the stronghold. It didn't help that Gorgoliskos had been crying fretfully all afternoon; it seemed he was cutting a tooth, which meant Medusa was snappish and irritable too.

It seemed silly for a boy to take the lead when there were so many beings that were thousands of years old assembled. But it was obvious that there was only him. However bad things seemed, there was nothing for it but to get on with trying to form a plan.

He called up and down the crumbling spiral stairs.

'Come to the dining room if you want to save yourselves!' He chose the dining room because they could be fairly warm there. It was the only room with a fireplace – designed for cooking, except that there wasn't much to cook.

The monsters began to appear. Medusa came first, and gave Corydon a warm smile. 'Good idea,' she whispered. The snake-girl drifted in, and coiled herself into the smallest possible heap next to Medusa, who had decided that she must learn this waif's name. 'What are you called?' she asked, as kindly as she could. The girl began to tremble, but answered in the faintest possible whisper. 'It is forbidden to use it, but it is Lamia.'

'Who has forbidden it?' asked Euryale, sweeping in

with bronze wings clashing. Euryale was restless. And, of course, hungry.

'Nobody. I myself. It doesn't matter,' said the girl, drooping even more, her voice sinking so low that it could hardly be heard.

'All right,' said Medusa hastily. She exchanged a glance with Corydon.

The Nemean Lion entered obediently, his claws skittering on the stone floor. He gave a soft rumbling growl, and settled in front of the fire.

Sthenno rounded up the other monsters by nagging them.

It took half an hour before all the creatures were at last ready to begin making plans, sitting sulkily, or in some cases furiously, around the table.

Almost at once, the Harpy became restless and managed to tread on the lion's tail. He gasped, singeing the Sphinx's wings. Everyone snarled at everyone else. Medusa banged on the table and shouted for quiet. The noise went on, not words, but moans, complaints and growls.

Medusa, growing desperate, banged again, more loudly. Finally the monsters fell into sullen quiet. They all looked at her, and then at Corydon.

He swallowed, and breathed a quick prayer to all the Muses for inspiration. 'We are met,' he said, 'because an army wishes to destroy us. The heroes are even now coming into the village below us on the hillside. They have the metal giant with them. We cannot fight him with tooth and claw. We will have to think of another way.'

'We also know,' Sthenno interrupted, 'that Corydon, the mormoluke, will save us! He will find out the uses of the Staff.'

Corydon blushed, and made a silencing gesture. Medusa glared at Sthenno for interrupting, but as usual she was impervious to Medusa's stare.

'He cannot do that yet,' said the Minotaur. 'The moon is still a night away from full darkness.'

'As Corydon was saying,' Medusa said, very loudly and clearly, 'the leader of the heroes, Perseus, is assembling his VAST army a FEW miles away. They will certainly attack as soon as they know where we are. We need to make battle plans. We have to hold them off until Corydon can find out how to drive them away for good.' She spoke very slowly, and it irritated the Harpy.

'Don't talk as if we are stupid, Medusa,' she said. 'What battle plans can we make? Why don't we just ATTACK? Most of us are pretty powerful. We'll just do the best we can.' The Harpy flew round the room to applause from a few of the monsters.

The Sphinx sat silently. 'I have seen war,' she said, reflectively, 'and I know its ways. I have seen Agamemnon and Menelaus, Odysseus and Epaminondas, Philip and Alexander.'

187

'Who?' asked Corydon, puzzled. 'Not in a battle. Doesn't it often mean colours?'

'No matter. I have seen them. We need to plan our attack and coordinate it.'

'I do not know what "coordinate" means,' said Lady Nagaina, puzzled.

'It means that we all – work – together,' said Medusa, as patiently as she could, though the snakes on her head gave away her irritation by rearing and hissing.

'All right,' said the lion. 'I will work with you. What shall I do?'

Corydon was so grateful that someone was willing to help that he almost hugged the lion, even though he was pretty sure that the beast had no idea what was going on. The Sphinx said, thoughtfully, 'My friend, you are fearsome indeed, with your fiery breath.' The lion threw his chest out a little; no one had ever praised him before.

'You, with Sthenno, and my flying friend here' – she gestured at the Harpy, who was careening around the ceiling, shrieking with laughter – 'will fall upon the enemy's left when diversion is most needed. The Minotaur may accompany you – if he wishes.' The Minotaur looked down, sullen and reluctant. It was obvious to everyone that he, especially, did not want to fight. 'We must have a signal,' the Sphinx went on. 'Meanwhile,' she said, still calmly and thoughtfully, 'Euryale, Medusa and myself will attack the centre. Our goal will be to kill

Perseus himself. I think his army is a mere rabble. It will disintegrate if he is lost. The snake-girl, Corydon and Lady Nagaina will guard our retreat to the stronghold.'

'I don't want to guard the rear!' said Corydon crossly. 'Surely I should be part of the attack, with the Staff?'

Medusa patted his arm. 'We don't want the Staff to fall into their hands, though, do we? We need to keep it safe. And you with it.'

Corydon could see the force of her logic, but he still felt he was being tidied away, as if he were a baby like Gorgoliskos. He felt it more because a tiny part of him that he wouldn't look at was relieved not to be fighting. Almost at once, Lady Nagaina spoke his fears aloud.

'What about the metal giant?' she said, her voice taut with anxiety. She had been terrified by the mere rumour of him.

'I will try to take care of him as best I may,' said the Sphinx. Her glacial calm reassured them. And they were all secretly relieved that one of their number felt able to manage him.

Medusa found all this hard to visualise. 'Could you draw the battle plan for us?' she asked.

Luckily, Lady Nagaina didn't believe in dusting, so there was plenty of dust for the Sphinx to use. She drew her battle plan in it.

'They will deploy in lines,' she said, marking lines in the dust to indicate the heroes.

189

At once, predictably, the lion asked what deploying was, and the Sphinx explained that it meant telling people where to stand to be ready for the enemy.

'Then the lion, Sthenno and the Harpy will form up on our extreme right, with the Minotaur,' said the Sphinx, making a round mark to show their position.

'But that's the left!' the Harpy complained.

'It's *their* left,' the Sphinx explained, patiently, coolly. Medusa's snakes hissed derisively. 'So it's *our* right.'

'Oh.' Corydon was secretly glad that someone had explained this, though he hadn't had any intention of asking himself.

'So that's all right,' said Sthenno, trying to be helpful. Lady Nagaina shook all five of her heads, confused. The Minotaur dropped his heavy head lower still.

'And we can take them almost on the flank,' continued the Sphinx.

'What flank?' asked the Harpy.

'Well, an army of Hellenes always faces forward so it can join its shields to make a shield-wall. If we can attack from the side – you call it *the flank* when it's a battle – then we have a better chance of getting past their defences.'

Medusa leaned forward, attentive, engrossed. 'So what is this other round shape here?'

'That's us,' the Sphinx explained. 'You and me, and my clawed huntress friend here.' She indicated Euryale. 'We attack the centre.'

'But didn't you just say that it was better to attack the flank?' asked the lion, baffled. Corydon sighed.

The Sphinx used her delicate ivory claw to show the centre attack sweeping forward. Dust flew up. 'You see,' she explained, 'if we attack at two points, he won't be able to reinforce both flank and centre without opening a gap in his lines that we can exploit. A gap that will let us reach Perseus himself.'

Now Corydon noticed a small line in the dust behind Medusa's group. 'What's that?' he asked eagerly.

'That is you, my dear mormoluke, with Lady Nagaina and the snake-girl. You are our rearguard. You keep us safe from attacks from the rear, and can also be used to reinforce us if we are in dire need.'

Everyone looked at the fine lines of the Sphinx's sketch.

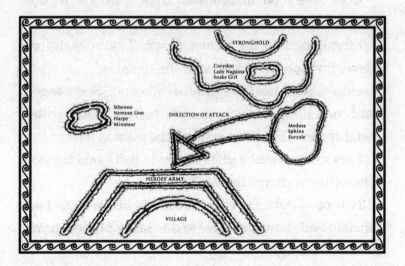

'That's much clearer,' said Euryale, pleased, 'and I think the drawing itself might have power to make it come true.'

'Perhaps yours do,' said the Sphinx courteously. Euryale took this as a signal to go over to a corner and begin scratching a sketch on the wall. She was warming to the idea of hunting Perseus, and drew him as prey, with antlers. The scratching noise made Lady Nagaina feel irritable, and she abruptly left the room to get away from it.

'Men are more dangerous than ever in rutting time, when their antlers are new, in their pride,' said the Sphinx. 'But antlers may catch on one bramble. And that bramble may be their downfall.'

'Can we go?' whispered the snake-girl. 'Or is there more?'

'Does everyone understand what they are to do?' asked Corydon, rather desperately.

'I think so,' said the Nemean Lion. 'I am to wait for a signal. But I do not know what the signal is.'

'How about this?' suggested Sthenno. She banged, hard, on one of Lady Nagaina's pottery plates with a metal spoon. The spoon cracked the plate in half.

'I am to wait until a plate cracks in half,' said the lion. 'Then I am to charge the left?'

'No, no. Look, Euryale will clash her wings. Then Sthenno will show you what to do,' said Corydon, trying hard not to laugh.

'I know what to do,' said the Harpy brightly. 'I'm supposed to be a nuisance.'

'That should be easy,' muttered Sthenno to Corydon. Corydon grinned, his mood a little eased by the jokes. But his heart still felt black with dread when he thought of the day to come.

Medusa could hear Gorgoliskos crying again, and knew he must be hungry. She ran up the twisting stairs and seized Gorgoliskos, holding him tightly on their shared bed, hugging him to her and finding his warmth and coos comforting.

Then it struck her hard, like a slamming door. What on earth was she going to do with him tomorrow? She couldn't take a baby into a battle. She couldn't leave him all day; he would get too hungry. And she couldn't desert the others.

She thought, 'I must leave him here. He will be safe. And I will try to come back to feed him.'

It wasn't a very good idea. But the world seemed devoid of very good ideas just now. Unless you counted Gorgoliskos himself, who often seemed to Medusa the only good idea she'd had in her life. She kissed his soft downy head, and if she had been humbler, she might have prayed to any gods that could hear for his life.

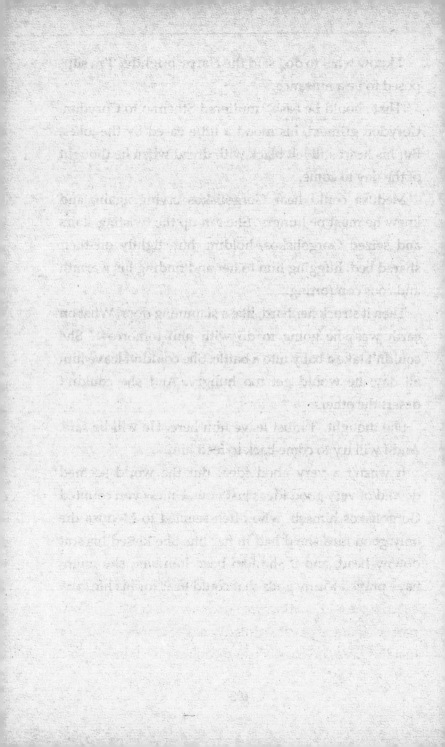

όμικρον

FIFTEEN

The heroes were to assemble in the village square. All the way up the hill there were moans, and complaints, and grumbles, and the whole force seethed with rumour.

Most of the rumours came from Kharmides. He had been unable to hold his tongue.

'Where exactly is this alleged Golden Hoard?' he asked. 'I haven't seen so much as a nugget since I arrived on this god-forsaken island.'

'Don't say that,' Lysias protested. 'It's probably hidden in the mountains, to protect it from us. Why, I bet we're moving towards it now.'

'Well, I suppose we might be,' Kharmides agreed, pleasantly enough, 'but perhaps you can tell me how exactly we are to find the cave where it lies? We've passed about six caves already, not to mention the one that the giant tried to open and couldn't. That one looked a likely bet. Except, of course, that there was a real live monster in it. Somehow, when we found that out, Perseus vanished. Just the moment for a hero, and they all seemed strangely absent. Where was Pirithoos? Where was Jason? I tell you, Lysias, it's what they call a rich man's war and a poor man's fight, and I don't care who knows my opinion.'

Kharmides was an annoyance, but the views he expressed found an echo in many. Most of the heroes had been hoping to scoop up huge mounds of treasure from puny monsters as soon as they landed. Now they were finding that marching in blazing sunlight in full armour up a mountainside from which monsters might emerge at any moment was not much fun. They had all been unnerved by the frightful gorgon with her power to turn men to stone. They were not yet sure that the metal man could defeat her. So they murmured, fearful, doubtful, but they reached the village eventually, and found Perseus waiting for them, with the other commanders.

They were all wearing their parade armour, gold and dazzling in the sun. Their servants, travelling on horseback, had brought it. Perseus the shield of Athene, which flashed, brighter than the sun itself.

Beside them, Talos waited, still as a brass statue, his eyes glinting redder than lava.

The army drew up. Perseus began to speak. He explained his battle plan, got them organised into units, sent this man to the left under Pirithoos, that to the right under Jason, still others to the centre, which he intended to command himself. Pirithoos's party were delighted when Talos was assigned to them. Lysias and Kharmides were there too; Kharmides was relieved not to be under the ever-dislikeable Perseus, but Lysias was heartbroken; did the leader not trust him? He must prove himself worthy, then. His face went hard.

When everyone was in battle order, Perseus spoke.

'You know our purpose, gentlemen. Against us is ranged the foulest brood ever to face mortal men. But we fight in the power of the great sky gods. Is not the presence of the metal giant Talos proof of that? Victory will be ours! Onward, sons of the Hellenes! Set free the land of your fathers!'

'Didn't he do this speech back in Seriphos?' muttered an elderly soldier.

The shield whispered to Perseus, 'Well done, my good lord. How handsome you look, and how wisely you speak. But do hurry, and kill that snaky-haired – creature!' Its soft voice had become a venomous hiss. Perseus jumped. But he remembered what he had meant to say.

'Not only are we assembled here to destroy a horde of monsters, but to rescue a tiny and helpless baby, stolen from his cradle by the hideous gorgon who turns men to stone. We know that she will sacrifice the infant to her dark mistress Hecate in exchange for magical powers unless we can prevent it. His mother weeps even as we stand here, ready for battle. Will you help her? Will you help her and save her baby?'

There was a moment's silence. Perseus led the woman Sylvia forward. At the sight of her tear-stained cheeks, even Kharmides felt a longing to help, and a horror of the monsters. The silence was broken by a mighty roar, so loud that it was audible in the stronghold itself. 'We will triumph!' the heroes roared. 'We will triumph!' With that they turned, and ordered by their commanders, formed up in battle array.

The heroes did not have long to wait.

After a few moments, they saw two great shapes flying, like gigantic black eagles drifting on the winds. One had wide-open metallic wings. The other had wings that looked blue in the bright sunlight. The two great birds swept down towards the centre.

One was the brazen monster they had wounded; the other was some new monster, wearing a tall crown, with a woman's head, a lion's claws . . . The centre almost broke and ran. But Perseus shouted, 'Hold! Remember the baby! Remember the treasure! Remember your manhoods!' Most heeded him, and turned towards the oncoming monsters. The archers fired their arrows into the sky. They bounced off Euryale's wings, and the agile Sphinx managed to dodge. Then an arrow almost struck the metal-winged creature in its exposed underbelly, but the other monster knocked it aside, and dropped like a stooping falcon, claws outstretched. The other glinting-winged monster attacked, too.

And then they saw what every man had been dreading. It was the snaky-haired gorgon, men's last sight. She simply walked towards the front line, in the middle of pitched battle, and it was enough. Coached by Perseus, they tried hard not to look at her, but it was like trying not to look at the setting sun; everywhere, men caught her eye, and stone took their soft flesh and devoured it. The closer she came, the harder it was to avoid her gaze. The only way was to turn around, and then those who did were easy prey for the deadly claws of the Sphinx and the other gorgon, who kept stopping her work to give happy gurgling cries.

Beyond these creatures, they could see some dreadful lizard-woman with no fewer than five swirling, swooping heads, and next to her a smaller, slighter but no less deadly spectacle: a slender green snake-like body with the head and torso of a girl. And beside her was the goat-footed demon many had dreaded in their cradles. Though not giants of fear like the gorgons, they looked rich in hideous magics. There was no escape that way.

But then Perseus's head cleared. Carefully using his shield to prevent himself from catching Medusa's eye, he summoned his great ally. 'Talos!' he shouted. 'Come over here! We need you!'

With great thundering footsteps, Talos landed beside Perseus.

The Harpy had not bothered to follow any battle plan. Now, seeing Talos's leap, she forgot all about signals, and flew up as quick and bright as a tropical parrot, flapping around Talos's head, harassing him, making him blink his fiery eyes. With huge fists, he tried to snatch her from the air, but she was too quick; it was like trying to swat an annoying fly. She kept shrieking in Talos's ear, and spitting gouts of venom over his face. The venom damaged his shiny plating, making the Harpy laugh happily.

With a final roar of annoyance, Talos managed to slam his shield into the Harpy.

She dropped like a stone.

He caught her. She was only stunned. But now she lay in his fist, crumpled and ragged. He examined her carefully.

His eyes began to glow so brightly that many had to shield their eyes from the red radiance.

Then Talos himself began to glow, like a piece of metal that the blacksmith takes from the heart of the forge. The red light radiated outwards from his chest, which was almost white with heat.

It was then that Talos slapped his hand into his chest. The Harpy was flung onto the near-molten metal.

She gave one terrible scream. Corydon shuddered as he heard the death-cry. The smell of burnt feathers filled the air. The Harpy's body slid to the ground, no more than a few blackened feathers and a pile of ashy bones. He ran forward, sobbing, furious. But the snake-girl caught him and drew him back. 'No,' she whispered, looking hard into his eyes. 'No. The Staff. No.'

He found himself obeying her.

But someone else had also been roused to battle-fury by the Harpy's death. With the bellow of a charging bull, the Minotaur rushed into the fray, goring and tossing heroes right and left. In the thick of the battle, the maddened monster came face-to-face with Pirithoos.

The Minotaur gave a savage roar.

Pirithoos swept out his sword, trying to block the great creature's charge, but the Minotaur dodged surprisingly nimbly. 'Evil rogue!' he shouted, startling Pirithoos, who had thought him a speechless animal. 'You and your friends kill and kill and kill. The plain is choking in the bodies of the slain. Your dead as well as ours! Why don't you stop? Go home!'

Pirithoos showed his white teeth in a grin of fury. He threw his spear at the Minotaur, but it missed its target as the great creature dodged. The Minotaur seemed to Pirithoos to have the unstoppable energy of a great storm wave, flung up by Poseidon Earthshaker from the depths of the sea. The bull head swept low, like a wave crest breaking, and caught Pirithoos in its sharp horns. Then the head lifted, tossing him high, and flinging him down, as a sea surge flings jetsam onto the shore. Pirithoos lay still, his blood darkening the ground. The Minotaur stood shaking, staring down at him. Then, with another roar, he hurled himself back into the attack.

The gorgons too were stung to new fury by the Harpy's death, and they attacked Perseus's forces with ferocity, trying to fight their way through to Perseus himself. He had taken up a station behind Talos, however, which made their task seem nearly impossible.

'What's – happened – to the diversion?' gasped Medusa, fighting hard with both sword and glance. 'Euryale, have you clapped your wings?'

'Three times,' said Euryale grimly.

'Try again,' said Medusa desperately, staring angrily at a hero. He rippled into granite. Euryale clashed her wings desperately.

And the lion heard, as did Sthenno, because this time the wind was blowing their way, carrying the sound. They swept forward towards the remnant of Pirithoos's men. When they saw a lion as big as an elephant charging towards them, most of the men scattered to the four winds. They were accustomed to danger, but they were not accustomed to gigantic lions, nor to brazen-winged monsters. Perseus saw them breaking. As the Sphinx had hoped, he at once sent his reserves to plug the gap in the line. This weakened the centre, made the men there more ill-at-ease, despite the presence of Talos.

Belasmir had stationed himself somewhere sensibly far to the rear, but his piratical eye was always alert for treasure. He had only come on this stupid expedition because it was obvious that if he stayed in Seriphos, Perseus would have him killed. Now, he glimpsed the flash of the ruby atop the Staff.

He recognised it at once. Carefully skirting the deadly combat, he crept up behind Corydon, Lady Nagaina and the snake-girl, all of whom were watching the battle so intently he was able to make a surprise attack.

Corydon felt himself felled by a great weight and a hideous stench of unwashed body. He cried out. Belasmir was on top of him, gripping the Staff in both hairy hands, pulling, tugging.

Corydon fought back, kicking Belasmir hard in the shins. Belasmir pummelled him ferociously, almost wresting the Staff away. Corydon bent down and bit the huge hand, drawing blood, and Belasmir gave a scream, but hung onto the Staff. His grip tightened.

'O gods,' sighed Lady Nagaina, bored. 'How tiresome this is!' The snake-girl trembled at her side. 'Cover your mouth,' suggested Lady Nagaina, casually.

'What are you going to do? Remember that you mustn't hurt Corydon . . .'

'Oh, he'll be all right. I'll just get rid of this smelly little man quickly.' Lady Nagaina had always hated the pirates.

Now, she opened one of her five mouths and breathed out a ferocious wave of brilliant green smoke. It poured towards the man and the boy. When it hit them, its deadly power was all too clear. Both began spluttering and choking. The snake-girl watched in horror as Corydon writhed, foam on his lips. Slithering forward, she snatched him away from the green cloud. But Belasmir still lay within it; it almost seemed to follow him as he writhed, choking, drowning in Lady Nagaina's poison.

Soon he lay still. The green cloud wandered into a group of Jason's men, who had been blundering up the hill to the stronghold. They too perished in its livid embrace, almost vomiting up their own lungs.

The snake-girl gave a great shudder of horror.

Lady Nagaina said, 'Well, that was so exhausting. I really must lie down.'

'You can't,' said the snake-girl, frantically.

'Yes, I'll just catch forty winks.' And with that she slithered off to the stronghold. Luckily the heroes didn't notice that she had gone. The snake-girl was left to hold the rear with Corydon, who lay on the grass, gasping like a beached fish. But he still held the Staff.

Meanwhile, the Nemean Lion and Sthenno had smashed through the heroes' reserves, as if they were made of fragile china. The lion was heading for the village, when he turned and saw what was happening in the centre. Nothing was going well. Euryale had been wounded again, and there were still many men between them and Perseus. The hero had been using his shield adroitly, making sure Medusa never got a chance to turn him to stone. And it was only a matter of time before Talos caught one of them in his terrible grasp and subjected her to the same fate as the harpy.

Was it his fault? The Nemean Lion felt dimly that it was. He roared in shame and anger. His flaming breath just reached a wooden village house. The flame licked up the wood like a hungry dog eating a bone, and devoured it. The woman living in the house screamed. The Nemean Lion looked around, puzzled. Then he noticed that some of the village houses were on fire; the glow of the flames almost eclipsed the radiance of Talos. The air was filling with smoke and he felt himself choking.

Lysias suddenly noticed the fire. The monsters! They must have done this! He ran towards the village, brandishing his spear, determined to kill the demon who had done this; he remembered Sylvia, the mother; he must at least save her, for her baby could not live without her . . . She must see her baby again, it would be too cruel if . . . These thoughts tumbled through his mind as he ran.

Then he saw it. It was the huge lion which had smashed their line earlier. It was trotting into the village square. He ran towards it, shouting his new battle cry.

The lion turned, still puzzling over what had happened, and saw a man running towards him, waving a spear.

He didn't look friendly. His face was all twisted. He was yelling. The lion didn't like yelling men. He growled warningly. A small jet of flame shot from his jaws.

The man came on.

'That is how he set this fire,' thought Lysias, watching the beast. When he was a spear's throw away, the lion's growling was so powerful that the small jet of flame had become a fountain of angry golden fire. There was no way to get close enough to inflict any damage with his sword. 'That's fine for me,' thought Lysias, for the spear was his favourite weapon, and he knew that he usually found his mark.

He pivoted on one heel, and threw.

The spear flew through the air and hit the lion full in the chest.

But it bounced off the lion's skin.

Lysias felt surprise rather than fear. Why hadn't it worked? Then suddenly he saw that he was weaponless and that this monster was about to attack.

The spear had bruised the lion, and he didn't like being bruised.

Angrier than ever, he sprang. He caught the man in his powerful jaws and shook him. He had him by the throat. The man was kicking his legs, but soon his kicks grew weaker and weaker. He hung limply in the lion's jaws.

The lion opened his mouth, and the man's body fell to the ground. He didn't move. He didn't speak. His face was purple and there were marks on his throat. His eyes were open and accusing.

Looking into Lysias's eyes, the lion realised that he had killed him.

He didn't like killing things. He could bear it only if he did it so quickly that he himself didn't notice that it had happened.

The lion wept huge fiery tears for what he had done. He saw now that perhaps he could have just run off. Was that what they should have done? All of them?

As the fiery tears flashed into the ground, he thought about why he had done it. He didn't like yelling, and he didn't like being bruised. But he liked killing even less.

'Why did the man come?' he wondered.

Perhaps he had come to rescue the people, thought the lion sadly.

'It was my fault the man died,' he thought. He must tell the others. They could help him understand. And perhaps he might still help them.

He walked through the embers of the burnt houses, his bright tears lighting his way through the grey smoke.

In the centre, full battle was still raging, but Medusa's power had been weakened by the haze of smoke which had settled on the battlefield. She didn't know where the smoke was coming from. But it made it harder for men to see her, and so did the drifts of green gas that came from the stronghold.

The stronghold!

Medusa suddenly remembered Gorgoliskos. He must need food badly. She shouted to Euryale and pointed at the stronghold. Euryale shouted, 'Retreat!' and the two began fighting their way back together. The Sphinx kept fighting; she was tireless.

Perseus saw them go, and immediately his mind began whirring. Where were they going?

Like a fruit falling from a tree, the answer thudded into his mind. The baby! Of course! They were losing, so they were going to sacrifice the baby to increase their dark powers!

He saw the face of the baby's mother in his mind, and he felt strong and brave and heroic. Ordering Talos to watch carefully and to come at his call, he set off. With the winged sandals to help him, he flew fast and high, landing outside the stronghold door while the monsters still toiled up the hill. In the smoke and gas haze, Corydon and the snake-girl didn't see him.

Euryale and Medusa climbed fast towards the stronghold, gathering up Corydon and the snake-girl as they went. Sthenno and the Minotaur saw them retreat and began edging back to the fortress as well.

Panting, Medusa almost fell into the entrance. She tripped over Lady Nagaina's collection of rare sunshades, and almost broke three of them. 'Damn!' she said.

There was something wrong.

She had expected Gorgoliskos to be crying for milk. But the tower was entirely silent.

Medusa ran to the bedchamber.

And saw an empty basket. Gorgoliskos was gone.

SIXTEEN

Medusa looked on the bed, although she knew she'd left him in his basket. She called: 'Lady Nagaina!' Had the stupid creature picked him up, trying to be helpful? The thought sent a jolt of worry through her; Lady Nagaina knew nothing about babies.

Lady Nagaina peered down from the upper bedchamber, one of her sleepy heads showing over the balustrade.

'Where's my baby?' Medusa demanded, her heart so tight with fear that she could barely get the words out.

'Nooooo idea,' the head yawned. 'I've been asleep.'

'Medusa,' called Euryale. Something in the terrible urgency of her voice sent Medusa whirling towards her. Euryale was at the window. She pointed.

And Medusa saw him.

It was Perseus, his golden hair escaping from his helmet, his shield flaming in the fiery light of burning.

He flew high. Under one arm he held a bundle. A bundle wrapped in a shabby old deerskin.

'Gorgoliskos,' Medusa breathed. She was about to spring from the window when she felt Euryale seize her arm. 'Help me!' Medusa cried desperately. 'Fly me to him!'

'Too late,' said Euryale, her own breathing fast and panicky. 'Look.'

Below, Perseus had rejoined Talos and the remnants of his army. He was holding the baby aloft, and everyone was cheering.

'But why?' she almost sobbed. 'Why do they want him?'

'Well,' said Sthenno, entering and putting surprisingly gentle arms around Medusa, 'from what I overheard, they think he's one of them. They think they're saving him.'

'But they'll find out . . .' Medusa couldn't finish the sentence. 'And how will they even feed him?' she wailed. Sthenno and Euryale hugged her, petted her. 'We'll get him back,' they said. 'We'll get him back.'

Corydon knew that it was futile to tell her that it would all be all right. He contented himself with pressing her arm and holding the Staff fiercely aloft. He knew now that everything depended on him. It was the dark of the moon this night.

All the other monsters began to drift in from the battlefield; only the lion was absent. 'We'll get him back,' they all said. But none of them could really understand the ache of Medusa's empty arms.

'We can do it!' The snake-girl sounded brave for the first time. 'Medusa, you should have seen how the Sphinx drove Talos away. She hypnotised him; he looked into her eyes, and even he had to do her will, he just kept walking backwards and then he fell over, and everyone laughed. And when he got up he was dazed, it was as if he didn't work as well; so I just know we can get your baby back for you, really . . .'

The words piled up like thunderclouds in Medusa's head. She barely heard them, but they beat against her terror and loss like rain on a shutter, throbbing until she felt she might go mad. She clutched the table to stop herself from doing anything fierce.

There was a soft hissing noise and a sad Nemean Lion, weeping huge fiery tears, sidled in. He was still grieving for Lysias.

Medusa thought he was crying for Gorgoliskos, and put her hand gratefully on his head. His tears stopped in surprise, and she hugged him tightly, liking his warmth and also his ungainly clumsiness, sensing that he too had lost something fundamental.

'Are you crying over Gorgoliskos?' Sthenno whispered.

'I killed somebody,' whispered the lion.

'We all did that today,' said the Sphinx, her voice mid-winter-cold. 'And we have lost one of our number, the

213

Harpy, and we must take action to make sure we do not lose another. Gorgoliskos is precious to us all. We will do whatever we must.

'Here is my say,' she continued. 'We must send an emissary to Perseus and ask him for the child. Medusa, I do not wish to cause you distress, but you must know that the hour will come when they will discover Gorgoliskos is one of us, and when they do he will be in danger. We must act before then.'

Corydon spoke. 'But they think they are rescuing him. Will they give him up so easily?'

'Perhaps not,' said Euryale. 'But they might be persuaded.'

'How?' Medusa asked, her voice tiny, shrivelled with fear.

'One of us must shame him,' said Euryale, firmly. 'He is their leader, and he longs for glory. If one of us could defeat him in a single hand-to-hand combat, then his honour and glory would crumble into dust in the eyes of his men. They are a rabble; they would disperse. And those who remained could easily be rounded up.'

'But why would he do it?' Corydon asked sensibly. 'He has the metal giant.'

'We must make it a public challenge, before the whole army!' Euryale could imagine the scene. 'That would make it impossible for him to say no without laying bare his own cowardice.'

'Is he a coward, then?' The Minotaur was surprised. 'He fought hard.'

'Yes, he is. I have seen it today,' the Sphinx replied. 'He is here to flee his own cowardice. He will flee from it further, into our arms.'

'Do not forget,' said Sthenno, 'that the Olympians stand behind him. We have no choice; we must win this war, or disappear from the earth. Such is our fate; it's all spun on the distaff of the sky.'

There was a silence. No one knew what to say, or whether to believe Sthenno. Corydon held the ruby of the Staff in one hand; it felt warm, as if it were comforting him.

'Won't they attack us when we come to bring the message?' Medusa was eager to grasp at any straw, but the plan seemed impossibly fragile.

'We must trust in bearing olive boughs. They should respect this sign of truce,' said the Sphinx.

'And who is going to fight him?' asked Lady Nagaina wearily.

There was a silence.

'It must be me,' said all three of the gorgons at once. Irritably, they begged each other's pardon, paused, then each began to make her case.

'I am the strongest,' said Euryale flatly. 'And I am the only one who likes fighting.'

'I am the wisest and the most full of cunning,' said Sthenno. 'And the fastest flier.'

'I am the only one who can turn men to stone,' said Medusa impatiently, 'and besides, it is my child we are fighting for.'

The others accepted her right, and bowed their heads. Corydon added, 'And if I can find out how to use the Staff, you won't have to.' Medusa ignored him, her eyes much too bright.

'You – you will look after him, if – if I should fall,' said Medusa, hesitantly, to Sthenno and Euryale and Corydon. 'You will have a chance – then – to rescue him, to try again. Don't leave him with them, will you? For they will not understand him or love him as he deserves.'

'We promise.'

'Now, we must go at once,' Medusa concluded, desperate to recover her lost baby.

'We will bear the challenge,' said Sthenno and Euryale.

'No,' said Medusa. 'Only one of you must go. It will be no safer with two.'

'Then I will do it,' said Euryale. 'Sthenno's wisdom is more needed than my strength. There is an olive tree on the hillside; I will not forget.' And before anyone could argue, she had soared down to the bottom of the stairwell, unbolted the door, and slid out.

po

SEVENTEEN

It was full dark, the dark of the moon, and Corydon was once more at the heavy black door to the land of many. He had groped and stumbled his way to it by starlight, and now he felt certain that he had found the right place. But he could still see no door or aperture. He pounded on the ground with his Staff.

Nothing. He almost despaired. Then, to his amazement, he heard a voice beside him, a furry and resonant voice.

'The dark moon has not yet risen,' said the Minotaur.

Corydon sprang to his feet. In the faint light he could just see the heavy black curls of hair on the Minotaur's forehead. His horns were heavy too. Corydon noticed that his head was wrong for his body, like a mask, or a helmet built for a grown-up fitted onto a child.

'Why are you here?' Corydon asked.

'I am to accompany you,' said the Minotaur in his soft, rumbling voice. He put out a strong brown hand in appeal.

'Do you know where I am going?'

'I know you go to the realm of the dead,' said the rumbling voice softly, as if whispering a secret. Yet Corydon was amazed to hear him say openly what even the Sphinx had avoided: the word *dead*. It reverberated in the air. 'I have been there once before. That is why she sent me to accompany you and to teach you the way.'

Corydon was glad; the Minotaur's warmth and solidity suddenly seemed comforting, rocklike.

Grimly he settled down to wait another hour.

He sat for long enough to make him feel as frantic as a bound prisoner, but at last something began to happen.

The ground in front of him creaked, groaned, and formed itself into a new shape. It was a doorway made of the darkest, smoothest obsidian. It was perfectly plain, with no carvings; a flat black door to nowhere. Resolutely, he pushed his fears aside and took up the Staff. He struck the door with it as hard as he could.

The door swung open. They stepped in . . . and both fell, down, down, down into the darkness. Corydon stifled a scream in terror as he felt the cold air rushing past, felt himself falling, began to anticipate landing. He tried not to panic, tried to keep a tight hold on the Staff, and on the Minotaur's firm warm hand, but he couldn't hold on.

As he let go, Corydon landed hard, his shoulder hitting the ground, jarring bone. If he had been an ordinary boy, his collarbone would have snapped like a dry twig. As it was, he was bruised and shaken. He sat up and looked around.

They were lying in the middle of a plain of ice and snow that stretched as far as the eye could see in every direction. The light was soft blue-grey, like snowlight on a cloudy winter's day.

As he looked around him, Corydon noticed light white flakes of snow begin to fall. As the snow fell, it froze at once to the bleak ice. There could be no snowballs, no play. Only a desperate scrabble not to fall at every step on the slippery surface.

'Come on,' he said. With a groan, the Minotaur rose. His hard bare feet were able to grip the ice more securely than Corydon's light sandal, or his Pan-foot. Corydon had never found walking so difficult; he was usually surefooted even on a mountainside fringed with frost, but here his foot slid at every step. Together, they began to struggle forwards.

'Why are we going this way?' asked Corydon.

'This is the way to the River Styx,' the Minotaur said. 'It is the only way.'

'Yes, but how do you know?' asked Corydon, his Pan-foot slipping yet again. The cold was beginning to bite through his shepherd's sheepskin cloak.

'I can smell the shades,' the Minotaur said. 'Do you not see them, beside us, see where they are going? So must we go. They cluster around the River Styx.'

At first Corydon had thought that the light floating things travelling along the ground were blown snow, but he now saw that if watched carefully, they took on human shapes, faint ones, like shapes remembered from long ago and drawn badly. With a jolt, he realised that they were the dead, drifting around him, brushing against his warmth in a vain effort to warm themselves.

One of them found a low moaning voice. 'Haima!' said the voice. 'Haima!'

The others began to take it up, their voices rising in a great sucking roar. 'Haima! Haima!' It was a cry full of the pathos of those who cannot speak. It was not even breathed. It was blown, drifted, like the snow of which they seemed part.

As they cried, the shades began to fasten themselves to Corydon, lying across his head, shoulders, arms, across his mouth, across his eyes, blurring his sight.

'Haima!' they cried.

'If they reach your blood,' the Minotaur said thickly, for his mouth too was crusted with the white ice of the dead, 'they will drain you dry. Blood allows them a few seconds more of life, warmth. And they will kill you to have those few seconds. Use the Staff. They may respect it.'

Corydon hastily drew out the Staff, and brandished it. Its redness glowed achingly in that bitter white waste-land. Corydon had never realised before that its stone was red as blood, but the dead saw it as blood; they clustered frantically around it.

'Do not let it fall!' shouted the Minotaur warningly. Corydon caught firmer hold of the Staff and waved it again, in a gesture like brushing away flies. The shades drew back, but thousands of them followed its red light, like bats following a lamp. Holding this radiant red glow aloft, Corydon and the Minotaur picked their way slowly, painfully, across the endless ice, along with the numberless dead.

It never got any lighter or darker; the snow kept falling, but it didn't get deeper because it was so blown by the restless, bitter wind. After a few hours, Corydon felt he had been walking in exactly this way for years. But they could tell that they were getting nearer to the Styx, because the shades thickened the air about them more and more. The ruby light shone on their thin, ragged bodies. Sometimes, Corydon thought he caught glimpses of the people the shades had once been; faces with beaky noses, for example. But for the most part they were all alike, drifting and desperate.

As they went along, the air seemed to change subtly. At first Corydon couldn't quite think what was different. Then he realised that there was a new sound, very faint, but growing clearer as they plodded and slithered forward. It was the sound of a rushing river. As they continued, the noise grew louder and louder, until it filled their ears. The shades, too, heard it and pressed forward frantically.

'Why do they want to get there so badly?' Corydon asked, shouting to be heard above the roar of water and the whine of the wind.

'So they can reach Hades' mansion. That's where they can enter the Hall of Poesis.'

'Why do they want to go there?'

'To choose a new shape and be reborn.'

'They get to choose?'

'What they choose is the outcome of all the choices of their life. So it is just. Those who love power choose to be eagles or kings. Those who love wealth choose to be rich. But some become jackdaws, some misers. They are supposed to learn from this. But some take eternity. They miss their way.'

Corydon almost slipped on a slick black rock. They were struggling across a landscape of heavy boulders, flung as if by giants. Sometimes they had to climb down sheer rock faces to keep moving forward. The shades found it easier; they poured over these cliffs like falling water.

Corydon kept the conversation going, to distract himself from the tiredness, the cold. The Minotaur's voice was the only bright, warm thing in the landscape.

'Why do they want to? Be reborn, I mean?'

'They are bound to life. It takes many, many lives before one may let go of the wheel of life, even though it burns like fire.'

'Why is it like this?' Corydon was getting hoarse from shouting, but he had to know. Above the roar and the screeching, he heard the Minotaur's soft rumbling reply. 'I don't know, but I know it wasn't always like this.'

The roar from the river was now so deafening that they could no longer hear each other, even by shouting. As they drew nearer, it began to hurt their ears. And at last, they saw what was making the sound.

A great torrent of black water roared along the bottom of a gorge that was hundreds of feet deep, with sheer cliffs on either side. Corydon pressed close to the edge of the cliff, and saw that the river was thick with slabs of ice, so many that they crashed into each other, splintering or forming new, larger floes. And this mighty river flowed over an enormous cliff face, forming a waterfall whose roar exploded in Corydon's frozen ears. Ice floes flung themselves over the edge of the waterfall, smashing on the rocks below. Corydon saw souls clinging to some of the ice floes as they were hurled over the edge. They might not be able to die twice, but Corydon could see that they were screaming.

There was no possible way for a mortal to cross. It was indeed a river of death.

'How . . .' he tried to mouth to the Minotaur, but the Minotaur raised his hand and pointed.

Corydon looked, and to his astonishment he saw a thin, rickety bridge spanning the gorge. Many pieces of it were missing, the ropes looked ragged, and some of the dead fluttering across it were falling into the river, but it was the only possible way to cross. As they began to walk towards the narrow bridge, they saw a tall figure standing on it. Frost clung to his eyebrows and to his hair, and yet he was naked except for a rag around his hips. Livid purple and bluish flesh showed that he was parched with cold. His hands were black with frostbite. He looked withered, and his voice was cracked and splintered, like breaking ice. As he harried the souls across, he noticed Corydon and the Minotaur standing by the bridge.

'Why do you come here, living souls? This world is now barren. There is nothing for you here, nothing for you or for anyone.'

'We want to cross!' shouted the Minotaur into the wind. The strange old man looked up at the sound of his voice; he seemed more attentive to sounds than to sights. 'I know you,' he said, his eyes narrowing to try to see better. 'You have been in this realm before.'

'Yes,' admitted the Minotaur.

'I told you it wouldn't work,' said the old man, and he began to cackle, shrilly, heartlessly.

'Yes, you were right,' said the Minotaur.

'What is he talking about?' bawled Corydon.

'I was here before. I tried to enter the Hall of Poesis and be reborn as an ordinary man instead of a monster. I loved a woman who would have nothing to do with me. Queen Pasiphae. She was my mother. She hated me and she ran from me. She shut me in a great underground place. Despair led me here.' He sighed. 'But it didn't work.'

Corydon hardly knew what to say. The Minotaur's misery was more chilling than the wind. Yet the furry monster seemed to draw courage from having told his story.

'It is not for that reason that I have returned, Kharon!' the Minotaur said. 'I am here to escort my friend. He has business with Hades.'

Again, the old man's nearly-senile laugh rang out. 'What business can a shepherd possibly have with the Lord of the Dead? Don't waste my time.' And he began to turn away.

'We will give the proper payment if you let us cross!' yelled the Minotaur hastily, at the retreating figure.

'Do you know,' snarled the cracked old voice, 'what the proper payment is?'

'Isn't it two obols?' said Corydon. He remembered the villagers placing these small coins on the eyes of the dead, for their crossing fare.

'That is only for the dead,' said the gatekeeper. 'For the living, the price is a drop of their blood.'

'One drop?'

'One drop.'

Corydon was puzzled. It sounded simple enough. Yet there was something sly in the terrible old man's smile.

He was handed a bronze bowl to hold the blood.

He took out the knife he used to free sheep from thornbushes, and for whittling. He held it to his arm.

'Stop!' said the Minotaur. But he forgot to shout, and Corydon didn't hear him. The knife bit into Corydon's skin. A bright bubble of deep red blood appeared, and dropped into the bowl. It made a faint ringing noise as it fell, strangely audible above the roar of the river.

As soon as the drop touched the bowl, as if the sound were a summons, thousands of shades poured towards Corydon. They flew, arrow-swift, back over the narrow wooden archway, many falling into the river in their haste. With one voice, they cried, 'Haima!'

In a second Corydon was so thickly covered in them that the Minotaur could no longer see him. Thousands clutched his arm, and a few managed to get their white, starved lips to the cut on his arm. He heard them sucking and saw some of his blood running into their ghostlike bodies. As the blood began to work on them, they began to solidify, to gain weight and dimension. They were no longer white and rag-like. Within a minute, they were recognisable. And the one sucking the hardest began to push the others aside; they gave little moans, but yielded to his fierceness.

Corydon looked down. It was the pirate Belshazzar.

But suddenly the Minotaur acted.

He shoved the nearly-solid Belshazzar aside. But at once more of the dead rushed on to Corydon's arm, like a swarm of dreadful birds. Corydon began to reel as more of his blood was drained by the desperate dead.

The minotaur snatched the knife from Corydon's hand, and used it to cut right across his own wrist. Then he aimed an arc of blood at a place ten yards from where they stood.

With a moan of 'Haima!' the shades fell away from Corydon and drifted towards the new supply of life.

'Run!' cried the Minotaur. His monster-strength helped him bear his wound; Corydon too managed to stay on his feet despite the ringing in his ears. Together, they tore across the bridge, heedless of its rickety condition, leaping the gaps. As they did, more of their blood dropped into the Styx. The shades plummeted after it, forming a new waterfall of tattered white. As each of them plunged into the river, they gave a shriek of horror. The Minotaur's monster-flesh closed over his wound. Ice had already formed on Corydon's smaller scab. Both stopped running.

'What – happens – to – the ones – that fall – in?' Corydon panted.

'They are carried to the waters of Lethe,' said Kharon. Corydon jumped; he had not realised the old man had followed them across. 'There they forget everything, forget all desire, even the Hall of Poesis. But the River Styx burns them with its cold. Yes, it burns. It hurts.'

Corydon looked at Kharon. Bits of ice clung to him. 'You have been down there too,' he said, not making it a question. Kharon nodded. Two tears ran down his cheeks and froze instantly. 'I have forgotten everything,' he said. 'It is better. But I remember the pain a little.'

Corydon felt so sorry for him that – very cautiously – he put out a hand and touched the old man's shrivelled arm. Kharon jumped. The warmth of the boy's touch seemed to burn him. But then his face twitched. Corydon saw, with wonder, that he was really smiling at last. 'Thank you,' he murmured, so softly that Corydon could hardly hear.

They had reached the far side of the bridge. Corydon and the Minotaur stepped off it, into deep snow. Corydon sank into it almost up to his knees.

'Wait!' came the cracked old voice. 'Let me give you a warning. The waters of Lethe – do not touch them, taste them, or your mission will fail. Many seek them. But they promise and do not fulfil. You may lose your memory but you can never lose your pain.'

Corydon called back an awkward 'Thanks!' The

Minotaur gently brushed his brown, soft hand against the old man's frost-rimed cheek.

They set out, beating a heavy way through the snow. The Minotaur went first, pushing his way through the drifts with his strong body. Corydon followed in the track he made.

σίγμα

Eighteen

There was no sound. They'd somehow left all the shrieking shades behind. And the wind had dropped to silence. Now it was so quiet that Corydon spoke once or twice just to make sure he hadn't gone deaf. His feet and hands grew colder and colder and colder. They began to hurt, a dull grinding pain that gradually grew in sharpness, as if his hands were being crushed in a mortar and pestle. His legs, too, ached with weariness. But there was nowhere to stop, no sign of anywhere they might rest. And if they lay down in this snow, they would never rise; Corydon could see that. He managed to talk himself into staying upright for countless more miles, countless painful footsteps. But then his legs began to slow, and he just couldn't make them move faster. He crumpled hopelessly into a drift, and had to struggle out, soaked to the skin. The twentieth or the fiftieth time this happened, he lay still like a felled tree.

Slowly, Corydon closed his stinging eyes. He could go no further, his sturdy shepherd-boy strength long since exhausted by the cold, the terrible aching silence, the white endlessness of the snowy landscape. Only his Pan-strength, his monstrousness, had kept him from dying.

Warm and gentle hands lifted him. The Minotaur picked Corydon up and slung the exhausted boy on his great hairy shoulder.

'I can walk,' whispered Corydon, his pride stung at being carried like a baby.

'I can carry you,' the Minotaur rumbled softly. And after a few more muttered protests, Corydon accepted his kindness. Lulled, rocked by the big creature's warmth, he fell asleep.

When he awoke, everything had changed.

They were now in a landscape of mountains – still snowy, but carved into high peaks, sharp, angry-looking peaks shining with silvery mica, grey and impenetrable.

And directly ahead of them was a castle.

It was by far the largest building Corydon had ever seen.

At first, he had taken it for a part of the mountain, unable to imagine that anything so enormous could be made by hands, or even by divine powers. Like the mountains, it was tall, peaked, frowning, but now that Corydon looked at it more closely he could see that it was a little at odds with the wintry landscape. There was a spareness and elegance about it that refreshed eyes tired with snowy wastes. True, it was grey, but it was silvery grey, with a mysterious soft glow, a kind of starlight glimmer. There was a fragile beauty in the curves of its towers and windows that belied its hard iron gateway. The windows were too high to see into, but Corydon thought he could see flashes of colour, as if brightly-dressed people were moving about household business inside. The windows were round, and quartered; the tiny panes, too, glinted frostily. It was their delicate curves that helped Corydon find courage. They plodded up to the gateway and the Minotaur pulled on a long, tarnished chain that hung by the gate. A single bell chimed, faint and sweet. To Corydon's surprise, the iron gates began to open, slowly, and rustily, as if they had not been touched for a long time. They opened inward, and Corydon and the Minotaur walked into a castle courtyard that was filled with snow. Stone archways rose all around it, like the long stems of stone flowers.

All around were iron suits of hoplite armour – the breastplates, the round shields, the spears and swords, the feathered double-crested helmets. Corydon wondered how they had come there; had the dead brought them?

One of the helmets was raised, as if pushed by an invisible hand.

There was a shout, and the suits of armour began to march towards Corydon and the Minotaur. With spears bristling like the quills of an angry porcupine, they didn't look like the friendly hosts for which Corydon had hoped. They advanced towards the travellers, at a quick-stepping pace, like an army that had forgotten to bring its bodies.

'I don't think they're going to offer us hot baths,' said Corydon dryly.

The Minotaur said, seriously, 'No. They may not be real, though. Try using the Staff.'

Corydon brought it out. As its red light hit the first rank of active armour, the illusion crumbled, and the armour tumbled to the ground, collapsing into shields, swords and other bits and pieces, little heaps of battle debris. The second rank crumpled too. Now all the armour lay around the courtyard, innocent, as if it had never moved.

Corydon noticed something. Where the snow had been scuffed away, the grass underneath was brilliant, emerald green, not dead and yellowing like grass under snow should be. The castle felt alive, in all kinds of ways that were wrong here among the dead.

He was just about to find out how right he was about that.

They moved towards the narrow gateway that separated the courtyard from the rest of the castle.

As they passed under the archway, Corydon saw another courtyard ahead of them, also surrounded by those aspiring stone arches, like trees, like flowers. But this court was different because the ground in it – some-how – was not covered in snow, but bare, hard earth. Frozen, brown-black, but bare.

The relief to the eye was amazing. Corydon darted for-ward. The Minotaur shouted a warning, but it was too late.

As Corydon ran, the ground came to life all around him. A plant burst out of the ground, thick, dense, and already dauntingly huge. With savage speed, it grew, its long, hard red thorns encasing Corydon in a kind of cage. As he watched in horror, it began to put out leaves that twined like worms all around him. Then it burst into flower, and its enormous red blooms were scented with poison. As Corydon inhaled their odour, he felt his brain reeling.

'Help!' he cried feebly.

He heard the Minotaur hacking despairingly at the plant with one of the swords left behind in the courtyard, but he could feel that the great plant was growing far faster than the Minotaur could cut it down. With his last wits, he lifted the Staff and brought it down with des-perate strength on the body of the plant ahead of him. The plant gave a thin wail, and began to wither. In sec-onds, its leaves turned vivid gold, then red, and blew off in a sudden, spiteful gust of wind, and the plant itself sank back, almost sullen, into the black earth. The air around him was clear, and Corydon felt his strength returning.

But he was beginning to be aware of a different kind of tiredness. Always one test after another, one fight after another. Could he never find anything simple any more – rest, warmth? The humble pleasures of a shepherd had never looked so alluring, and he longed for his calm and solitary home. He had never wanted adventure or heroism. And yet here he was in a land of ice and snow.

It was as if the Minotaur knew what he felt. He took Corydon's hand, and said, softly, 'We cannot give up now. We have come too far.'

Corydon shook himself. Medusa, the baby. Sthenno and Euryale. The others. He would help them, and then he could rest.

'I want to help Medusa,' he said, 'but I'm so tired.'

At the mention of Medusa, the Minotaur smiled. 'I too am here on her account,' he admitted. 'She bade me come with you. And I will never abandon you.'

Corydon was surprised, and very pleased. His heart grew warm, and in that warmth he found he could go on. They advanced towards the next archway.

The new courtyard seemed simple snow underfoot, but as they entered, someone else approached from the other side.

It was a man as tall as a cyclops, twenty feet or more, and broad in proportion, carrying a huge branch of olive wreathed in ivy in one hand, and an axe in the other.

He was green-skinned, the deep green of winter trees. His eyes were red and glowing. As he came forward, fire erupted suddenly from four lamps on the four corners of the courtyard. The fire, too, was green. And everywhere the giant stepped, the snow melted away from his feet, leaving huge and spreading patches of greenness.

'Travellers,' the giant boomed. 'Travellers, be welcome to the court of my lady.'

'Who is your lady?' asked Corydon suspiciously. He felt wary of the giant's gleaming axe.

'She is the lady of this kingdom,' said the giant, a little sternness coming into his voice. 'You should give her the respect she deserves. She rules here, in this castle, and one day may rule this whole kingdom.'

'What is her name?' asked the Minotaur in his soft voice.

'We do not say her name,' the giant said. 'That is a secret. But we call her the Lady of Flowers.'

Corydon looked around. Despite the patches of green caused by the giant's feet, the courtyard was bare and desolate. He could not imagine why a lady of flowers would live here.

'You have passed the tests,' the giant continued. 'But one more trial awaits you.'

'Who made the tests?' Corydon asked. 'And why are they there?'

'I made them,' the green man said, simply and a little sadly. 'And my lady made me in order that I could defend her. I was made from a single flower – perhaps you know this – a flower of winter, that pierces the snow.' He smiled.

Corydon felt uneasy. For one thing, the giant looked nothing like a flower. He was more like a tree, with green and mossy bark. Corydon decided his story was true only in the way that Medusa's poetry was true; it meant something, but in a difficult, unreachable way.

The giant had also answered only half of Corydon's question. 'Defend her from what?' he persisted.

'From the king of this realm, of course,' said the giant, as if this were something everyone knew. He gestured around him. 'Do you see any flowers?' he demanded.

Corydon said no. The conversation was odd, surreal. But he felt it was somehow important.

'They were blighted,' the giant said. 'They have been driven under the ground. But one day they will return.' Two tears rolled down his cheeks. The liquid was yellow, like sap, or nectar. 'Come,' he said. 'My lady herself will explain everything to you. Then you will understand. I am not for explaining, but for defending. Come in. Come in and accept our hospitality.' He led the way through the main door.

They were in a long, wide hall, roofed and vaulted. The first thing Corydon and the Minotaur noticed was the enormous fireplace, with a great log fire blazing in it. 'Come and warm yourselves,' said the giant, and both of them obeyed eagerly. As the logs crackled and the ice and snow melted from his clothes and hair and eyelashes, Corydon began to look around him. He noticed at once that the ceiling was made of something that showed the grey sky beyond; it was clear and frosty-looking, like ice. Why did it not melt?

He suddenly felt too tired to find out more.

'Come, eat,' boomed the giant. A table had been laid, with roast goat meat, fresh cheese such as Corydon himself might have made, vine leaves, pottage with honey, good bread, and honey cakes dressed with small golden flowers. Corydon moved forward, his belly giving a great and happy rumble.

The Minotaur took his arm. 'No,' he whispered urgently. Corydon's heart sank. 'But – I'm so hungry,' he pleaded. 'Just a few bites.' The food smelled wonderful and homelike. Somehow it made him remember his mother, making food for him after he had been out playing on the hillside. Her barley bread had smelled just like this.

'No,' said the Minotaur. 'Not now. Or you will have to remain here for ever.'

'Here,' rumbled the Minotaur softly. From his pack he

got out a strip of dried meat. It was dull compared with the lovely banquet set out on the table, but it was food, and Corydon ate it gratefully.

'You will be able to eat here – after you have slept,' the Minotaur said. 'You must refrain only till then.'

And Corydon was almost asleep already. Stumbling with tiredness, he was led to a small chamber where another fire burned brightly. In one corner was a bed, and Corydon pulled off all the blankets, took off his soaking-wet sheepskins and tunic, lay down on the floor as he liked to do, and went to sleep at once.

When Corydon awoke, pale and wintry sunlight filled his room. He yawned and stretched. A woman in black was moving about, laying out fresh clothes for him. His own clothes; they had been washed and dried. She added a new cloak he had never seen before. It was finely woven, with a green and gold border of leaves and flowers, and its colour was dark red, the kind made from the dye of the madder plant.

'Did you make that?' he asked.

She turned around. She had a face he found hard to read. It was a set, hard face, the face of one of his own people, worn into seams and lines by life, inclined to cruelty and prejudice, but under the harsh lines there was a timid kindness, and a tentative peace, as if this woman, like himself, had reached a haven of warmth after a long struggle through the snow. She smiled at him.

'Yes,' she said. 'Now you are wearing the lady's colours and you are her servant. As I am.'

'I am no one's servant,' said Corydon, 'but I thank the lady for her kindness and will be glad to repay her.'

The woman frowned, as if puzzled, but then smiled again. 'Come,' she said. 'Break your fast. Your friend awaits you.'

Corydon put on his clothes and the new cloak; wearing it, he felt fine and free, swinging his arms to watch it rise and fall. He tried to follow the woman along the long corridors at a lordly walk, a hero's walk. He didn't know what was coming next, but he no longer minded. He was delighted to be warmly dressed, and to be walking towards breakfast.

The woman in black led him to a small room. The Minotaur was sitting at a wooden table. 'Eat,' he rumbled, himself chewing. And Corydon smelled the same delicious barley bread that he had so longed for the night before. There was corn bread, too, and a comb dripping with honey, and a bowl full of the petals of a flower coated in more honey. There was goats' milk to drink, also a small, rich, red fruit, bursting with seeds, that Corydon had never tasted before. He ate and ate and ate.

And the woman in the harsh black garments brought more food, and smiled, and hummed in a way he found hauntingly familiar, but he was too busy eating to think it out, find the exact memory. As he was wiping his mouth after the last possible bite, she touched his shoulder, and her touch sent a kind of thrill through him. But her words were blunt and simple.

'The mistress wants to see you,' she said.

Corydon looked at the Minotaur, who nodded calmly, then followed her down a long stone corridor. As he passed one window, he looked out, and saw to his surprise that the castle stood by the sea, a grey and wintry sea that left long streamers of foam on a beach that was dim with fog. The smell of the salt came to him in a rush. He almost stopped, but she beckoned to him and he walked on, through a doorway of light grey stone, past frail carved stone flowers, tiny turrets sculpted of ice, of salt, into the shapes of leaves and fruit, past pictures of flowers scratched on ice mirrors. The style was delicate and very elegant, but somehow he was reminded of Euryale's drawings; these were hunting pictures – someone was trying to use them to catch flowers, to make flowers come true.

As he thought of Euryale, he felt a rush of longing for one of her bronzy, prickling hugs. He thought of Medusa, of the baby, and suddenly the whole slow procession through the land of the dead became unbearable; he wanted to run back to them all, fling himself into a battle, defend them at once from the heroes. He realised, for the first time, that they might all be dead already. His stay with Kronos had lasted months. What if he had been down here for years?

It was as he thought this that he passed through heavy wooden doors, into a great hall. At the end sat the woman who had summoned him, surrounded by what looked like a small lake of spilled paint. The colours were rich and deep and shocking in the pale room.

She looked so small and far away that he thought at first that she was only a child. She was shrouded in her long bright hair, the pale gold of the new moon, but he could see a delicate, pointed face.

In front of her was a heavy olivewood loom, the biggest loom he had ever seen. Woven cloth hung down and swept across the floor in flowing waves of colour that threatened to engulf the chill dullness of the land and bring it surging to life.

The cloth was blue and red and gold and green and scarlet, and as he came closer he could see that it was not one, but many, perhaps hundreds of pictures made of wool.

At first, his eyes couldn't settle, couldn't make sense of what he was seeing.

But as he came closer still, he caught sight of scenes he recognised: Belshazzar's death, himself and Medusa on the mountainside, the Sphinx speaking to him, his father, the heroes landing, the sad charred body of the Harpy, the Minotaur's triumph. His body went cold with shock. Was this magic?

'Is – everything – here?' he asked the tiny, childlike figure.

She did not stop weaving. The loom clacked briskly and she drove the shuttle swiftly on. The thin threads followed eagerly, accumulating into a great weight of colour.

'Yes,' she said. 'Art selects, but I make.'

'Yes, art selects,' Corydon said eagerly. 'When I make a song I have to leave things out or put them in. The song is free because I choose freedom.'

'The song is a cage,' she said in her tiny voice, like rustling petals. 'And so is this whole world. Look, little singer. Look and beware.'

With her finger, she pointed to one image, the largest.

As Corydon looked it seemed to grow, filling the whole frame of the loom. It began with a tree, a tree with leaves green as emeralds. As he watched, the picture seemed to come to life, like a sleeper waking. The tree tossed in the wind. Its boughs began to be weighed down with heavy red fruit, round and rich, which then fell to the ground in thick showers, like drops of blood.

Flowers sprang up around the tree, as if the fruit brought them into being, huge purple flowers with sharp sword-like leaves.

And she herself was there, the weaver, picking them. Corydon saw a man with her. He was tall, dark, and his face had a stillness that somehow reminded Corydon of stone, of Medusa turning living men to stone. The man was talking to the weaver. He had something in his hands, something red and round that dripped crimson madder gore. Corydon felt sick – he thought it was a heart. Then he saw that it was a fruit, a pomegranate, one of the tree-fruits, and as he watched, the man squeezed it so its juice ran down his hand like blood. He held it out to the girl who did the weaving.

Corydon couldn't hear much of what he said, only fragments. It was something about 'love – marry', and it sounded as if she was refusing. Finally she pushed him away with both hands.

The man did not smile, or sigh, or look angry. His face was hard and still. Like ice.

He did, however, draw a heavy iron sword from its sheath, and laid it to the root of the huge tree. The girl gave a cry of horror, but the man swung his sword hard, just once. As Corydon watched, the tree began to sway, to fall, and the girl began to cry, in fright and terror.

Next it was bewildering; there were hundreds, thousands of people building something out of wood, highly polished golden wood. The wood, he now saw, came from the tree, which lay, felled. As the thing being built grew, it became a vast palace. But as it grew, something else began to change.

The sun went in. The grass began to yellow and fade. All the leaves turned orange, then brown, and they fell to the ground too, and were blown away by the freezing winds. Snow began to fall on the new palace. Icicles decorated it.

And now the whole land was snow and ice and winter for miles and miles, for ever.

The man with the hard face turned to the weaver, and asked her something. The weaver turned away, caught up her long purple skirts, and ran over the snow. The man did not follow. He stood gazing after her, his black cloak flapping in the icy wind.

Corydon lost focus. He looked up at the weaving girl. The shuttle rattled in her flying fingers as the bright cloth ran across the floor like a pool of blood.

His eye was drawn to another image she had made. A crag, the one where her castle stood. The weaver was standing there. Some shades were with her, and to his surprise he recognised one. It was the woman in black who had brought him his breakfast and his new cloak. She was a little shadowy, but as he watched she expanded and became more solid, as the shades who had fed on his blood had done. He soon saw why. The shades around the weaving girl were absorbing some energy from the ground. He looked more closely, and found that the land around the weaving girl was dark purple, not with blood, but with reddish-purple flowers, like narcissus, but full, richly coloured. Blood-purple. He could almost smell their heavy scent, the picture was so real. And now he could begin to hear.

The weaving girl said, 'You are all mine, lost mothers, lost daughters, lost children.' And the dead bowed to her.

246

She did not smile, but her face lightened a little. She looked less cold.

The woman who had served Corydon said, 'He will come for you, my daughter.'

'Then we must make defences,' the girl said, her face stern. 'Do you have any suggestions?'

A large man whom Corydon recognised as the green giant said, 'I can help you. I might be able to fight him. Green is hard to kill for ever.'

'We will all bring our knowledge,' said another man, 'and weave our own webs. Make our own strengths into guards against his might.'

'And one day, someone will come who will free us all.' It was the woman in black who spoke. 'But we will find it hard to hold out till then. I have seen it. A weapon is being made which will be our undoing. Unless we can somehow work against it.'

'What is this weapon?' the weaving girl asked, like a child who does not want to be frightened.

One of the shades who had not yet spoken replied. Corydon thought he looked like a small and lost boy, about his own age. 'It is a staff. Its wood comes from the world-tree, which Hades felled to win you. Its stone is the pomegranate which Hades tried to make you eat, to bind you to him for ever. The stone carries all the desire and anger of Hades' heart, the heart of a god. Together, the stone and the shaft are invincible.'

Corydon tightened his grip on the Staff. He felt awed by its sheathed might.

'Perhaps not,' said the weaving girl. 'Both may still remember that once they lived and grew. Perhaps we can wake that memory in them.

'But now our first care must be to save ourselves. I have dreamed a castle, shrouded from his eyes. We can go there, and wait until the hour comes. And the boy, too, will come there.

'One thing first, though,' said the weaver girl. 'I must try. Just once. To help him, to heal the wound he made in this land.'

As the others began trying to dissuade her, that picture faded, as if it were a hillside suddenly engulfed in grey curtains of rain. Corydon found himself looking at a new picture.

The man with the hard stony face was holding the Staff in his hands, turning it this way and that, almost as if he were searching it for something. Suddenly, the weaver girl was standing beside him. Corydon saw him start, then with a cruel smile he held out the Staff. Red fire flooded from its ruby tip.

But the girl was unmoved. Her hair was lit red by the fiery glow, but the Staff seemed to have no power over her. She smiled, and put one hand on the ruby tip. As she touched it, the Staff began to shake and vibrate, almost as if it were trying to shake off the dark hands that held it, as if it were trying to fly to the girl. Then the girl put her other hand on the wooden shaft, and wrenched it from the man's hands. The tall man looked surprised. Then the girl lowered the Staff so that it was pointing at his heart. The man pushed the Staff angrily so that it glanced aside and struck him hard on the thigh. Then the man gave a terrible cry, like a soul wrenched out of its body. He fell writhing to the ground.

The girl's face went white. Clearly, she had not meant to hurt him. In her horror, she dropped the Staff.

But it did not fall. Instead, it began to spiral upwards, as if it meant to pierce the sky. Soon it was far over their heads. It disappeared into the clouds.

And now, Corydon found that new pictures of the Staff crowded in: the Staff bursting out of the ground like a sapling, but much faster; the Staff standing like a sentinel in hot dry golden sand, casting a sharp black shadow. Then a shape he knew: the heavy wings and lion's claws of the Sphinx, and her golden eyes examining every inch of the Staff. She did not touch it. Then a group of men in blue and white robes, approaching the Sphinx, all of them carrying ankhs, crosses with globes of blue lapis above them. And the Sphinx bowing low to the men. And following them. And one of the men picking up the Staff and carrying it, carefully, reverently. And the men saying the names Ra and Osiris.

Then a wide river, wider than anything Corydon had

seen or imagined, and a huge city, and a temple above it, white with statues, and the Staff in the temple. Then suddenly red fire and burning, as of war, and the men in their robes running from soldiers – no, *pirates* – it was them; he recognised Belshazzar, Belasmir, the whole crew, and they snatched up the Staff and hit the Sphinx with it.

And that, Corydon saw, had been the beginning. But it did not tell him anything. It did not tell him how the Staff could protect them all from Zeus's army of heroes and their metal giant. He understood it all, and it was not enough. He wanted to cry with rage and frustration.

'You do know the answer to your question,' said the weaving girl. 'But you have not yet found a way to unlock what you know. I can help you.'

'Please, lady, help me,' said Corydon. 'My friends will die if you don't.' He managed to stop himself from adding, 'For the sake of all the gods, if you can help me, then do it!'

'You love them. They are all your mothers,' said the girl. 'I know what it is to lose a mother. I will help you, and I will tell you what you must do. But I will exact a price, and it is this: you must return here, bringing the Staff, once you have used it to help your friends. Do you promise?'

She looked straight into his eyes.

Corydon tried not to think about making that journey again. Hastily he raised his hand. 'I promise,' he said.

She paused, nodded. 'Here, then, is what you must do.

You must ask the servant who brought you here to tell you my name. When you have my name, you must draw a circle from its letters and you and your friends must stand within it. Be sure there is no break in the writing that encloses you. Then take the Staff, drive it into the ground, and speak my name aloud three times.'

'Wh-what will happen?'

'I cannot tell you that. But this is your only chance.'

'Please, lady, please. Tell me your name.'

'Alas, I can never do that. And there is another reason. But I cannot tell you that either.' She smiled. 'It is difficult, Corydon, for us, for we are alone always, and life itself is a question without an answer for such as we. Do as I suggest, though, and you will save your friends, as you were born to do.'

She turned back to her weaving. Corydon saw that she would not speak again.

He felt on fire with furious impatience. Without even saying goodbye, he rushed to the doorway, searching for the woman in black. He ran through the palace, calling, 'Hey! You! Please! Come!' The vision of Talos glowing with terrible fire was piercingly bright in his mind, and he began to feel all the panic of a lost child. Suddenly, he saw her at the end of a corridor, her black dress dragging on the ground as she carried a flaming torch to the dining chamber. He ran up and plucked at her dress. He was panting, weeping.

251

'Tell me!' he demanded. 'Please tell me. Her name. Tell me.'

Her eyes searched his, seeing his desperation. For a long time she looked at his pleading face and desperate eyes. Then she lifted a fold of her robe and dried his tears with it. The tender gesture surprised him. As she did so, her lips opened, and she whispered. 'Her name is Persephone. Persephone. Now go. Beware. Go.'

Corydon began running. As he ran, he found to his inexpressible relief that the Minotaur was running beside him with long effortless strides.

'We must hurry,' he panted.

'Do you have the answer?' the Minotaur asked.

'Yes!' Corydon flourished the Staff triumphantly. 'Do you know the way out?'

'Yes,' said the Minotaur. 'But we pass the fountain of Lethe. We must be careful.'

Corydon and the Minotaur struggled on through the driving snow. Eyelashes frozen once more, lips cracking in the cold wind, belly roaring with hunger . . . Corydon felt as if he'd been doing this harsh journey all his life.

Suddenly, the Minotaur stopped, and sniffed the icy air.

'I think we turn west now,' he rumbled softly.

Corydon had no idea which way west was; the dim light that served as a sun in the underworld was too diffuse to use for directions. But he turned obediently to follow the Minotaur, even though that meant facing directly into the icy blast of wind blowing the snow into his face.

'It is not far now!' shouted the Minotaur.

'To where?' Corydon shouted. The wind tore his voice away; he could barely hear himself.

'To the way to the upper world!' The Minotaur put his head down and fought his way through a huge snow-drift, his powerful arms heaving the snow back. A frozen lump caught Corydon in the face. He spluttered, but the Minotaur didn't even hear. He seemed to be desperate to move on, and quickly. Well, Corydon wanted to get home too. He put down his head and kept plodding on, his mind wandering with the drifting snowflakes, whirling with the wind. He thought of things he hadn't had time to remember for months; Medusa's poems came to him in flashes, and so did his sheep, their soft warm stink; the taste of charred lamb with the old kleptis gang of village boys; the festival of the flower god and the village streets full of petals redder than drops of blood; the smell of fresh goats' cheese on the day he had been driven from the village. No thought stayed with him for long, but each seemed to swirl into his tired mind, freeze there for a few seconds, then melt into air.

After hours of aching, slow progress, he saw what seemed like a faint black blur on the horizon. It grew larger as they fought their way towards it. To his surprise, Corydon saw that it was a low stone wall, half-buried in snow. Set in the wall was a gate.

Corydon stared at it, puzzled. Through the gate all he could see was snow, endless snow all around. Moreover, the wall was so low that it was possible simply to climb it and bypass the gate altogether. Yet the Minotaur was making directly for the gate.

And there was something odd about the gate itself; it wasn't made of metal or wood, but of – could it be? Bone? Something white, that gleamed like a skull laid bare.

Corydon put his hand on the gate to feel the material. As he did so, something very odd indeed happened. He smelled barley bread – rich, strong, just-out-of-the-oven barley bread. His empty stomach gave a roar.

And there was something else. At the edge of his hearing, a soft voice singing something he almost knew but couldn't name. He took his hand away, hastily, in fright. Then he put it back. The delicious scent and the song returned. Now the Minotaur, growing impatient, pushed the gate open. To Corydon's surprise it opened easily, and both walked through.

Corydon's mouth fell open in amazement.

The snowy world of underearth had vanished. He was surrounded by smooth grass, so smooth it looked as if it had been painted. His feet trod a brick path, warm from the sun. Banks of rich white and red flowers rose on either hand. And straight ahead of him he heard the murmur of a fountain. Somehow the sound reminded him of the song he had heard at the gate. Wondering, a little afraid, he pressed forward, and so did the Minotaur.

'Is this the way out?' Corydon whispered.

'Yes, I think so,' the Minotaur replied. He sounded dreamy, peaceful, as if he had been sleeping in the sun. Corydon frowned. He felt sure something was, indefinably, a little wrong.

He looked back through the gate, to the snowy way they had come . . . where was it? All he could see were gentle, grassy, sunlit hills, sparkling with flowers.

Corydon was puzzled, even a little scared. But the sun was so warm, and the fountain's murmur so pleasant after the howling wind, that he almost didn't care. The scents of the garden were delicious too, and as he got closer to the fountain he became aware that the smells he had noticed came from it, not (as he had supposed) from the flowers. As he stumbled forward, dizzy with the heavy perfume, Corydon felt his eyes beginning to close. 'Must stay awake,' he whispered. The Minotaur grunted, but had already collapsed onto the tiled margin of the fountain, his great heavy head resting on the rim. Corydon felt his legs fall from under him, and he too began to fall, down, down, down . . . into velvety, rich blackness . . .

ᴛᴀᴜ

NINETEEN

'Wake up! Corydon!'

The loveliest voice in the world was calling him.

Corydon sat up in his small wooden bed. A band of clear white morning light crossed the floor of his bedroom, turning its wood to soft gold.

At the end of the bed sat his mother.

She laughed.

'Wake up, sleepy! Your father wants you to help him drive the goats up the valley today! Here's your breakfast – eat it in bed like a lord for once!' She handed him a rich pottage of honey, grain and goats' cheese, but he could still smell barley bread.

'I've made some bread for your lunch, too,' she said, smiling eagerly at him as she noticed him sniffing. He saw how pretty she was; her hair was black, glossy, tied straight back from a friendly, lively face. She was wearing a black dress, its hem gaily embroidered with red and white flowers. Her eyes were dark, and something about them reminded him of something, someone – no, the memory was gone. And besides, what could it be but a memory of her?

What was happening to him? How . . . ?

'Come on, Corydon, eat up,' she said, and he held out his hand automatically for the pottage and began sipping it; it was delicious and warming and runny, as he liked it. The room seemed full of light. Outside, he could hear a bird singing.

'I think I had a bad dream,' he said after a while, slowly, for that was more and more how the world of the dead came to seem – a bad dream of snow and ice. Had there been a monster, too? Pirates? He shook his head, confused. It was all growing less and less clear as he sipped the pottage.

His mother smiled again and put a tender hand on his forehead, stroking back his hair. 'Poor darling,' she said. 'Po po po! A bad dream, my love? Never mind, little one – it's morning now, and your mother is here. And,' she added, laughing, 'your father is waiting!'

Still feeling dazed, not sure why he felt unsure, Corydon stumbled into the clothes she held out – warm, handwoven breeches, leather leggings, a shirt she had woven herself; the pattern on it was red and white, like the flowers on her skirt. It tugged at his memory like a chewing puppy tugs on an old sandal, but he shook off the feeling. The clothes felt warm, reassuring and, even more, comfortable, like a pair of arms around him.

He looked down at his feet – two perfectly normal, bare, brown feet – and he began putting on and lacing his sandals. He shook his head. Why was he staring at his own feet? Two perfectly normal feet.

Corydon's mother gave him a warm, lingering hug, kissed him, smoothed back his hair. A place inside Corydon that he had hardly known was cold and empty was suddenly full and warm. He gave his mother a friendly smile, then clattered down the stairs and out of the door.

His father, a tall man with a welcoming smile, was waiting for Corydon. 'We'd better go if we want to take the goats up to the high pasture,' he said, and something about his gentle, rumbling voice awoke Corydon's uncertainty; had someone else had a voice like that? For no reason on this bright sunny morning, he thought of snow and icy winds.

'Will it be cold up there, Father?' he asked, thinking, 'Perhaps that's the reason, perhaps I'm remembering mountains.'

'Not today,' said his father, looking a little surprised. Corydon shrugged, grinned, and his father ruffled his hair. They set off in the bright golden sunlight.

Corydon's life was nearly perfect. Every day he helped

his kind father with the work of the farm, and every day his mother held him, sang to him, told him stories of the Olympian gods, their home in the clouds, and their goodness to mortals. The whole village was friendly to him; he played every day with his friends. He was one of a group of boys recruited by the headman to stop the kleptis gangs from stealing sheep; he felt proud when he managed to help capture one in the act. The boy had been thrown into the well, or something . . . anyway, it served him right. And also served Zeus's justice. Like everyone else, he always looked forward to the festivals of the Olympians; the great feast of Zeus was coming soon, and his father had prepared a calf for the sacrifice.

Only one thing was wrong. And that was Corydon's dreams. Every night, he would tumble into bed, his cheek still warm with his mother's kiss, and every night he dreamed of terror – himself running, pursued by the angry villagers; great clashing bronze wings around him; sleeping next to a woman whose hair was made of snakes. That was all he could remember when he woke, time after time, screaming, sweating, feeling his mother's hands soothing him, as she whispered, 'Corydon, shhh, it's just a bad dream.' And Corydon was always glad to wake, and glad to go back to sleep, but the dreams always returned. What made it worse was that he felt sure the dreams were somehow important, that there was a message in them; it was like the nagging half-memory of a forgotten name.

After several weeks of this, Corydon's mother became so worried about him that she decided to take him to the temple of Asklepios, the healer-god. After a delicious supper of tunnyfish in oil, rich berried cheese-cake and his favourite barley bread, they walked through the darkened village. The stars burned bright overhead, and Corydon could see the families inside the houses, their hearth-fires vivid gold and red. His own heart was warm with the thought that he too had a family. Why did he feel so strongly about it? He wasn't sure.

Asklepios's temple was on the crest of a steep and rocky hill, open to the winds. As Corydon and his mother came up the path, a shadowy figure appeared in the doorway of the colonnade.

'Greetings,' the priest said. 'You are troubled by dreams. Come in and sleep. Then tell me what you dream here. Fear nothing; here Asklepios protects you.'

Corydon entered the temple. The priest handed him a bowl containing something that smelled heavy, like spices. He hesitated. His mother kissed him, quickly. 'Darling,' she said. 'I'll stay the night. I'll be close by. Not in your room, but close by. I'll hear you if you call me.' Reassured, Corydon drank, and almost at once sank into sleep.

In his dream, he lay on a smooth green hillside. Ahead of him, he saw a creature unlike any he had seen before. It had a lion's heavy body and legs, but also huge wings, and its head was the head of a human, a woman.

It was beckoning to him. Cautiously, he came nearer.

'You have forgotten, Corydon,' said the creature. 'You have chosen to forget. I am here to help you remember, if you want to remember.'

'Remember what?' Corydon asked, cautiously.

'Everything that is not a dream,' the creature replied.

'But *this* is the dream!' Corydon protested. '*You* are a dream.'

'No,' said the creature. 'The world has turned upside down. You are mistaken.'

Corydon felt a painful struggle beginning in his mind. The creature's name came back to him. It was called Sphinx.

'Yes, you have remembered my name,' she said. 'It is a beginning.'

And it was. Like unwelcome light streaming through the smallest gap in a broken shutter, the Sphinx's name seemed to illuminate Corydon's reluctant mind. Images from other dreams, images that had made no sense, suddenly became coherent. He had once been a monster. He had once been a thief. He had once had monster-friends. The gorgons, the Minotaur, the pirates' show. Being caged. Exiled from his village and left to die because of what he was. Who he was.

His foot. One of his feet was monstrous. Hoofed, goat-furred. He felt sick at the sight.

He wanted to run. From himself. From what he was.

'But I don't want to be him!' he cried. 'I want to be me! With my mother.'

'But you *are* you,' said the Sphinx. 'And in your dreams you know you are.'

Beside the Sphinx, someone else appeared. It was the monster with snakes for hair. It was Medusa.

'Oh, Corydon,' she said. 'You were so wise, the wisest of us all, the one who knew himself best, and so we didn't see that you were in great danger.'

Corydon wanted to hide. But there was something about her that he couldn't run from. Something that held him, held him close.

'Corydon, think.' She stretched out her hands. 'This world, with your mother – how *can* it be real? Nothing is *ever* this perfect. More than anyone, you *know* that. No mother is as nice, as pretty, as loving as this mother.

'You've seen me! You know it, Corydon. You know I get angry and sulky. And Sthenno is nervy and odd, and Euryale is greedy and practical, and the Minotaur is solitary, and we're all *real*! This is how things are!

'You know that, Corydon. You know it. Come back to us. I want you to love Gorgoliskos, to love him the way you've loved me. To teach him real love.' Her eyes were full of tears. 'Corydon, if everyone was perfect there'd be nothing special about love. Love is when we go on with each other even though we're not perfect.

'Corydon,' she pleaded. 'Come back. I never even told you that I love you. But it's true.'

Corydon's head was spinning. He knew now who he was. He knew, perfectly, what was real.

But for one moment, he wanted it to be otherwise, with all his heart.

For one terrible moment of betrayal, his heart was full of rage. He wanted his pretty mother, his funny father. He wanted his perfect life. He wanted the golden light on the floorboards, the hugs and stories and food.

And then, as he looked at Medusa's tear-stained face and remembered her songs, her jokes, he knew that he couldn't abandon her, couldn't abandon Gorgoliskos. He had to go back. He had to save them.

'How do I come back to you?' he said, trying to keep the anger and the tears out of his voice, wanting to protect her from her own monstrousness, though he knew that she knew all about herself, and all about him.

Medusa stretched out a hand to him, smiling with an amazed joy that told him that she had been afraid he would stay in what he now knew to be a dream.

The Sphinx smiled too, her smile cool and small like a sickle moon.

Corydon tried to return their smiles. His own felt watery.

'It is simple,' said the Sphinx. 'Say, three times, "This is the dream of a shadow".'

As she said this the vision began to ripple, to flow into the flooding waters of sleep, the blackness of deep dreamless night.

When Corydon woke, there were tears on his cheek. He knew by the pallet he lay on that he was in the temple, though the white sleeping-chamber was very like his room.

His mother sat beside him in the temple, holding out his breakfast cup, as usual. He wondered sleepily where it had come from. 'Another bad night?' she asked, softly, sweetly. 'Darling, you called me in your sleep, and I came at once.'

Corydon looked at his mother.

Was she real?

He thought about it. She looked familiar. But she didn't look real, somehow. He could see the force of what his dream had taught him. She was too good to be true, too much the mother he had always wanted.

He thought about the way every day here was essentially the same. The same love and food and even good weather.

That was it.

It never rained. But the flowers grew and the grass was green.

Now he felt certain.

None of it was real.

His mother – no, not his mother, his longing dream of a mother – was holding out the cup, puzzled. 'Corydon?' she said. And in a breath, Corydon felt almost impatient. A real person would be exasperated with someone who took five minutes to decide whether or not to take a cup they were holding out. He must be a very weedy person, he thought, to have dreamed a mother so sugary.

He remembered the words he should say. And for the first time, he said them. 'This is the dream of a shadow.'

And as he said it, her face changed. A look of horror came over her, followed by a look of cunning.

'Yes, it is,' she said, 'but that is the lot of mortal men.'

She drew in a breath. Her face, her voice were urgent. Pleading. 'And for mortal men this *is* paradise, the true paradise of the Olympians. You will never grow old here, and you will never die.'

'The Olympians are my enemies,' Corydon said. 'And if I stay here I will never grow old because I will never grow or change at all. I will be a child for ever. I do not want that.'

'But do you want to die?' she asked, in tones that chilled his blood. 'If you stay, you will never be adrift on those freezing winds, longing for blood. But if you go back, to the monsters, be very sure: war is here, and they cannot win. You too may fall, and be nothing but a squeaking bat-like ghost. Is that truly what you want? Or you can stay here, with me, and be loved every day of your life, Corydon.'

He felt oddly sorry for her. He couldn't quite say that she had no idea of what love was truly like.

'What are you?' he asked instead, knowing now that she had never been his mother.

'It doesn't matter,' she said. 'I can still be your mother if you are willing to forget.'

'I will never forget,' Corydon said. 'This is the dream of a shadow.'

She shrank back, and her face twisted with anger. She called loudly, and the man Corydon knew as his father came running, his face white and his eyes blazing with something like anger. 'Corydon!' he said, firm and clear. 'How can you hurt your mother so? She wants to help you, and you insult her. All mothers want the best for their children.'

'She's not my mother,' said Corydon, his own eyes angry slits. 'And you are both liars. And this whole place, this whole life is a lie.'

'We only want to protect you,' they said. 'We only want to help you. We only want to help. You. Help! Help!' As they spoke, their voices grew more whining, more shrill, and their faces began to fade to whiteness. Corydon saw with horror that they were shades. He pitied them; perhaps they too had suffered, had wanted a good life, a child. But his pity for them didn't change what he had to do.

'This is the dream of a shadow!' he cried, and taking the cup from her hand, he flung it furiously to the ground. As it shattered into a million shards, the scene began to unravel like a woven rug, then to shred into a dance of millions of snowflakes that hovered around him, whipped by an icy wind.

If he tried, he could still make out the shadow of the fountain-garden on the snow, as if someone had hung a painting of a garden in front of a howling winter wasteland.

So that had not been real, either.

'Here, drink this,' said a familiar, rumbly voice.

Corydon took the cup from the Minotaur and drained it. Its contents were bitter, and they stung his mouth and tongue. It was like drinking tears.

'What is this?' he asked, wiping his mouth.

'The waters of *alethe*, the waters of remembrance. Or truth. Yes, I have drunk it too. It comes from there.' He pointed to a slender, cold stream, half hidden by ice.

Corydon sighed.

Then he remembered Medusa's words, and stood up. 'Come on,' he said. 'We'd better get going.' He knew that they must hurry if they were to save Medusa and the others in time. 'Persephone,' he thought, clutching the Staff

268

tightly. Odd that it had been absent from his dream. 'Persephone, Persephone.'

He began beating his way through the snow.

But when they reached the bridge across the Styx, something had changed. The bitter old man no longer stood guard over it. Instead, a cloaked figure awaited them, his head cowled.

He looked familiar. And the cloak . . . At first Corydon thought it was black, but now he saw that it was dark green, so dark it was like winter ice – or, perhaps, like the trees whose leaves cannot be killed by ice and snow . . . Something else tugged at his memory, the image of a giant in the courtyard of the castle . . . the one in green . . . But the dancing snowflakes confused the images.

Still, he recognised the figure.

It was the priest of Asklepios. Corydon was sure. The one who had helped him.

'How can you be here?' he blurted. 'You are just a dream!'

'Am I?' said the figure. He threw back his hood.

Corydon looked into the face of Pan.

The god smiled his mocking smile. 'I too am a guardian,' he said, 'and I guard the ways of truth, and the ways of my sons. I can bridge the worlds. Even the worlds of dreaming and truth. I stole into this world like a thief' – he smiled slyly – 'but I also belong here.'

'Th-thank you, I suppose,' said Corydon. He wasn't sure how grateful he really felt.

Pan smiled again, this time sympathetically. 'Go, Corydon Panfoot. You can be victorious. As you have been here. But when you have won your war, you will return to the underworld, and you will redeem it.'

Corydon waved, then plodded forward, accompanied by the Minotaur. He tried not to think of all he still had to do; how could he, when it was all he could do to keep putting one foot after another? All he wanted now was to get home. Even if he was sure he would never feel at home again, anywhere.

They were almost there. Corydon could feel the wind's icy power lessening after they had crossed the Styx.

He began to relax. Soon he would be with Medusa, with the others. The Minotaur was happy too, and even hummed a little song to himself as he swung forward.

Suddenly, though, he stopped humming. 'Something is coming,' he said. 'Something is here.'

The snow ahead of them was churned up, as if beasts had been rolling in it. And there were hoofprints leading away.

But there were no animals in the underworld . . .

As Corydon thought this, he smelled a hot stink he half-recognised. Only a few feet away stood a heavy-set wild boar. It was covered in thick whitish-yellow bristles that glowed buttery and sickly against the pure snow. Sharp tusks protruded from its lower jaw. On one of the tusks there was a trace of scarlet, perhaps blood. Its eyes were blood-coloured too, set in deep wrinkly folds, and filled to the brim with rage and hunger. It moved its head from side to side to get a better view.

'Don't move,' breathed the Minotaur. 'He hasn't winded us yet – he's upwind from us. It's one of the goddess's sacred beasts of the chase. We cannot kill it.'

As he hissed all this, there was a small grunt from the left. Corydon turned his head slowly to see another boar coming towards the first.

The first boar, the nearer one, turned with a great snort to face the second. They both lowered their heads to charge each other. With a great churning, tearing and pawing of the ground, they attacked. Corydon gasped as the impact shook the ground. 'Come on,' hissed the Minotaur, and Corydon moved forwards, trying to use the beasts' preoccupation with each other to get away from both.

But as they began to move, the boars caught their scent.

And with a grunt, both swung away from each other and charged, heads down, hoofs flying, making a cloud of snowy dust around themselves.

As Corydon took this in, he saw something else break from the thicket of thorns behind them.

It was a vast white sow, and twenty squealing piglings, each one fully tusked and armoured.

Corydon and the Minotaur ran for the only shelter nearby. It was a single gaunt tree. Corydon swung himself into it and the Minotaur swarmed up behind him. They had just got themselves high enough when one boar crashed into the tree. The tree swayed, but did not fall. The boar squealed angrily. They circled the tree, squabbling, but also trying to root it up. The tree swayed but Corydon and the Minotaur clung on.

'Can't – hold – on . . .' gasped Corydon.

With a huge effort, the Minotaur boosted Corydon higher into the tree, but in doing so he lost his own grip on its bark, and tumbled into the snow. The oldest and fiercest of the boars wasted no time. He charged, headlong and furious, and caught the Minotaur in the thigh. At once, blood gushed onto the snow, and the minotaur sank to the ground.

Corydon drew the Staff from his robe; he knew it was the wrong time to use it, that he might spoil everything, but he felt he had no choice.

But suddenly there was a new sound, the rich sound of a hunting horn. Slower, darker, heavier than the horns of Artemis. And a group of dark-cloaked riders burst on to the plain, all on black horses, surrounded by their black, belling hounds. They sighted the boars, and the boars saw them too, and scuttled off, their legs flying. The huge black dogs began a pursuit that promised to chase the boars to the ends of underearth. And as they sped by, Corydon noticed that the lead dog had three heads, three lolling tongues. It was also taller than some of the horses.

'Kerberos,' he breathed. Hastily, he put the Staff back under his cloak.

He looked again at the hound-pack as they flew by. They were no normal dogs. They had no eyes, only blank skin where their eyes should be, but the centre of their foreheads glowed red.

The hunters were almost as frightening. All in black, with hoods over their faces, they could not be properly seen, even at close range. After they had gone by, he didn't know quite what he had seen, but he did remember that the last of them, the tallest, had a red flame flickering over his brow, as if he were a god of fire. Corydon held absolutely still. Somehow that tall hunter filled him with fear. And yet he had *felt* the tall rider notice him and notice the Minotaur. And do nothing to harm them.

The music of the hounds and the quick hoofbeats of the horses died away. Corydon leaped from the tree into the snowdrift where the Minotaur lay.

The Minotaur tried to sit up. But blood was still pouring from his thigh. Corydon stripped off his shirt and tore the fabric into ribbons to bandage the wound. But the blood kept coming.

He reflected that it was lucky that they were beyond Styx, or the shades would have gathered in millions to drink it. A few shades did drift over, crying 'Haima!', but they seemed to sense the passing of the hunt, and blew away quickly.

Corydon tried again to staunch the bleeding, this time with snow. But it didn't work.

The Minotaur was growing weaker. His brown face was pale under the soft fur.

Corydon had no idea what to do. He had none of the herbs he used on his sheep when they hurt themselves. But thinking of his sheep gave him an idea.

'Father!' he cried. 'Great Pan!'

He fumbled in his belt-pouch; he still had it, the shepherd-pipe. And he had been fasting, since there had been nothing to eat once he had drunk the waters of truth. Also he had seen his noble father here, so there was a chance that the summoning ritual might work. He played a shaky tune, his frozen fingers barely able to find the right holes.

But with a rush of warmth, and the scent of herbs, and of fur warmed by sunlight, Pan came.

And he simply took the Minotaur in his arms and strode off with him.

Corydon followed, still playing.

'Yes, play, my son,' said the god. 'Play for me and for yourself. Play all you remember.'

Corydon began to find tunes he had forgotten coming out of the pipe, tunes about living happy and free on the open mountain, about birds singing softly to delicate nymphs, about girls melting into fountains and the tears of mermaids that had once loved shaggy monsters. He played songs about his favourite ewe, the rich chalkiness of her milk. He played a song about rescuing a goat that had slipped down a cliff and lay on a ledge between sea and sky.

And those tunes began a magic which amazed Corydon, for as he played, the music seemed to run ahead and mark out a golden path on the snow, a path to the real world, to the world he knew. His father followed the golden path, and after only a little distance, it led into a cave that was thick with moisture, though it was not misty, only cold and damp. They had to splash through many pools. The pools were slippery with moss, and moss fringed the shelves and roof of the cave too. As the light grew stronger, Corydon saw more and more gaps in the cave roof, with plants protruding from them; they made his heart leap with joy, for he had seen nothing green and growing for many – was it days? months?

At last they reached the opening, floating on the golden thread of Corydon's music.

And Corydon looked out on the sleeping village where he had been born. He could see the light of the heroes' campfire.

His father carried the Minotaur still, and he began to move uphill from the mossed and fringed cave entrance, away from the village, towards Lady Nagaina's stronghold.

'Is everyone still alive?' he asked. He was surprised by the sound of his own voice; he had been piping for so long that it felt almost wrong to speak. The sudden absence of music was odd, too.

'It is all as you left it, for your journey has taken only the time you spent making your way to the dark door. The minions of the Olympians are still here.'

Corydon, to his surprise, felt his father's huge arms holding him closely, warmly, just for one second. 'This is a war between the gods, Corydon. As I foretold. You are our champion. Do not fail us at the last.'

Perseus had been having a much more difficult time than he had expected. The baby had squalled unceasingly ever since he had picked it up, as if it knew that he was not its father or mother.

But it had seemed at first that he had scored. When he brought the infant down and held it up to the army of heroes, the demoralised, miserable men cheered. At one stroke he had raised the army's morale, at a low ebb since the Minotaur had triumphed over Pirithoos. The baby, frightened by this noise, screamed even louder. 'Er – where is the mother?' asked Perseus, holding the baby nervously.

He had doubts about it, and he thought, too, that he could smell something.

The villagers had to struggle to shoulder their way to the front of the seething crowd, but at last they managed it. Those whose houses had been destroyed in the fire had expressions of sullen uncooperativeness. Some of the women and children had begun to look afraid of the heroes.

'Where is Sylvia?' asked Perseus. 'For I have something for her, something she has long missed.'

'Here I am, great lord.' The woman pushed her way to the front of the crowd. Perseus signalled, and Talos lifted her up beside him. Perseus handed her the screaming baby. She cradled it softly in her arms.

A silence fell. Men watched, and even grizzled veterans wiped their streaming eyes.

And then the beautiful picture was shattered.

'This – this is not my baby!' shouted Sylvia. 'This is not mine! Where is my baby? Where is he? Oh, why do you keep him from me? Why?' She broke into hysterical sobs, though she still clutched Gorgoliskos tightly. Another village woman, a strong-looking woman with a wide peasant face and body, came up beside her, took Gorgoliskos, and patted Sylvia on the shoulder.

'There, there,' she was heard to murmur. 'Tried to tell him, my daughter did, but he took no notice. It's been years since she lost her baby,' she said, confidently, to the heroes. 'You are all deceived. And no one else in the village has lost a baby.'

'These things can fly,' said Jason. 'Perhaps, on the mainland – could it come from somewhere else?'

'Well whoever owns him, he's hungry,' said the village woman. 'Let's find him a good wet-nurse.'

And they tried. But the village women with small babies were unwilling to take the strange baby in. 'You don't know where it's been,' said one, eyeing Gorgoliskos.

'I do know where it's been,' said the other, a fat woman with beady eyes. 'It's been with those monsters up there on the crag, that's where it's been. For all we know, it might be under a spell.'

None of it was what Perseus had hoped, but the entire army was looking to him to solve the problem. He couldn't simply abandon the waif – somehow he couldn't help remembering the way he had been lost himself, the stories his mother had told him before she had gone completely mad, of the two of them floating on the bosom of Great Poseidon's ocean in a giant chest, left to welter up and down until they died. He couldn't do that to another baby. Perhaps this child, too, was a son of Zeus, in which case it would be kinslaughter and the Kindly Ones would follow him to the ends of the earth.

But the baby would die if no one fed it. Its cries were getting weaker.

Perseus knew that he had only one chance to settle this little creature's fate.

'Father!' he shouted, into the unanswering sky. Hastily, he called for a sacrifice, slit the beast's throat, and called again. No answer. He made a fire, and roasted the skin and the fat, and at last his father came, looking harassed.

'What is it?' he asked testily. From all the perfume that hung about him in clouds, Perseus could see that he had been busy with a nymph.

'It's this baby,' Perseus said, holding it out. He felt an idiot. He held the baby as far away from him as possible.

Zeus didn't even bother to look at it. 'You want it fed, do you? I suppose I could ask my wife.' He paused for a moment, and Perseus heard some whispering, then an undignified rustling as the nymph evidently fled. The air cleared.

Then Zeus shouted, 'Hera!' and with a thump, a tall, beautiful woman landed in front of Perseus. She had the most perfectly arranged hair he had ever seen; it wasn't even like hair, but like some kind of helmet, and she was wearing elegant silk and sandals so light and slender that they made the winged sandals seem almost clumsy. Her face was set in an expression of murderous fury.

'Oh, not another baby!' she groaned. Timidly, Perseus handed over the crying bundle. The goddess pulled down her dress and gave the infant her breast, muttering all the while.

Gorgoliskos drank and drank and drank. His belly was as round as an egg. His eyes closed, he gurgled blissfully, then drank some more.

Hera put him on her shoulder and rubbed his back.

He vomited on her silk robe. Hera mopped and cursed. But Gorgoliskos didn't care. He had drunk the milk of paradise.

'There!' said Hera. 'Take him,' she called to the village woman, who came quickly forward. 'That milk will last him for weeks, it's strong stuff, and you may find it has other effects on him, some kind of destiny, when—' She stopped, staring at the baby's hand, splayed in pleasure.

'Oh, you fool of a man!' she said, her eyes meeting Perseus's bewildered gaze. 'You stupid, stupid man! You stupid, little man!' And she began to laugh, cruel and loud, like stones rattling in a drum. Still laughing that grating, tearing laugh, she vanished.

Perseus was baffled. 'Why am I fool? Why am I stupid?' he thought. 'It must be something to do with the baby's ha—' He looked at it closely for the first time.

It was a beautifully pudgy small hand, and there were six fingers on it.

He's part monster, he's part monster, he's part monster, said Perseus's brain, spinning its wheels like a chariot caught in a sand drift.

His first impulse was to pick the monster-child and dash its brains out.

But he couldn't kill what looked like a harmless baby without admitting to the army that he'd been wrong all along, that the baby was not a human but the child of the very monster who had been carrying it.

And yet at any moment the village woman might look down and see—

Just as Perseus's frantic thoughts reached this point in their rat-like running, something happened to distract everyone.

A brazen-winged gorgon appeared in the sky.

She was carrying an olive branch.

The heroes' mouths dropped open.

They had never expected the monsters to try to make peace. Or even a truce. What was going on?

Perseus strode forward. Now he must be truly cunning, or the creature in the air would blurt everything out.

'Begone, foul gorgon!' he cried. 'We do not speak with hellspawn like you!'

The ten-foot creature hovered – or hung – overhead. She showed no sign of going away.

'I have come with a challenge!' she cried. Her voice rang out like bronze cymbals.

'What challenge?' It was Jason speaking, pushing his way to the front.

'A challenge for Perseus. Single combat with one of us. The winner will be given the child you stole from us.'

Perseus was torn. He was happy because this looked like a way to get rid of the baby before the army found out what an idiot he had been. But he did not want to fight a gorgon, however many magic weapons he had.

'Which of you,' he asked, 'is the challenger?'

'Her name is Medusa,' said the hovering clashing voice, 'and she is a mortal like you.'

'She is,' said Euryale, smiling a little, 'the one with the snaky hair.'

Perseus went white. Then he bit his lip in indecision. Euryale saw that he was wavering. Her great bronze voice rang out. 'Perseus,' she said, 'are you a coward?'

A few of Perseus's soldiers whistled. Some of Kharmides' friends snickered softly. Perseus whipped round, but failed to spot the offenders. He turned back to the huge bronze creature.

'Go on!' shouted the soldiers. 'Go on, Perseus!' Their barracking grew louder. Perseus's cheeks grew scarlet. Finally, he managed to make himself speak.

He shouted up to the monster, 'I accept the challenge!'

The monster turned in midair to go.

And Perseus heard a voice behind him.

'Perseus, you son of a greasy kitchen-maid!'

Perseus turned.

A man stood there, covered in blood and ash from

head to foot except where the tracks of his tears had left white stripes on his face.

It was Kharmides.

'Do you know,' he gasped, through clenched teeth, 'do you know, Perseus, where my brother is?'

'How should I know?' Perseus replied, as smoothly as he could. He had always feared this man; now it looked as if he might be about to run mad.

'Yes, how should you?' Kharmides said, bitterly. 'For he is in Elysium, with the heroes, whereas you will sink to the blackest pit of Tartaros, and your journey begins now!'

Perseus shouted quickly, 'But, my friend, why do you blame me? I too have lost a friend today, the noble Pirithoos.' Kharmides gave a faint hoot of derision. 'There overhead lies one of the creatures who slew your brother. And you waste energy accusing me, your leader and companion?'

Kharmides looked up. 'It was not her,' he said, dully. 'And yet I want no more of them. No more!'

'Just what I was about to say!' Perseus beamed, holding out a hand. Kharmides ignored it. His gaze was fixed on Perseus's face, but he wasn't really seeing the hero. He was seeing the soft boyish face of Lysias, alight with devotion to this man in front of him.

'You know,' said Perseus, 'I can't help thinking that Lysias himself would want us to go on with our jobs here.'

Quite true, reflected Kharmides, annoyed.

'And you can help me,' Perseus continued, smiling persuasively. 'I have to fight this creature, this snaky-headed hag Medusa. You can help me find ways to defeat her.' He put a hand on Kharmides' shoulder.

Kharmides allowed himself to be led away. 'All right,' he said, uncertainly. 'The monsters. Let us sweep them away together.' He felt dazed, he hardly knew what he was saying, but he knew that this, at least, was what Lysias would have wanted.

On wings that felt as if they were made of lead instead of bronze, Euryale flew back to the tower. She wasn't sure this challenge was a good idea after all. The hollow feeling had come back to her chest and belly. She knew she should hurry back with the news, but she thought she'd do a little hunting first.

ΰψιλον

TWENTY

Medusa leaned out of one of the stronghold's windows. She had woken from an uneasy, tossing sleep, full of strange dreams. A few campfires dotted the plain below. From the stars' position, she thought it must be about midnight, or a little after.

Medusa was trying, hopelessly, to catch a tiny glimpse of Gorgoliskos. Just to know he was still alive.

Of course, Euryale had said that he was; she'd seen him when she offered Perseus the challenge.

But that was hours ago, and Medusa still couldn't see how Perseus was feeding him.

In the dim twilight, she could see nothing in the village except the giant of bronze, who stood sentinel on the outskirts, his head erect.

'At least I don't have to fight *him*,' she thought, 'though we must think of a way to deal with him afterwards. If there is an afterwards,' she thought, and grinned. She believed she could defeat Perseus; he was a coward and a lightweight and she had no faith in him. And she knew Gorgoliskos needed her. So did Corydon – but how long would he be this time?

Exactly as she thought this, she saw a faint light on the hillside. It was a marsh-glow, no more, but she saw that it illuminated dark figures moving up the slope. Were there two of them? Three? She wasn't sure.

At first she thought it was the heroes, trying a night assault.

Then she saw the immense figure in front, his head heavy with horns, saw the burden he carried. Her heart seemed to stop beating.

And she noticed that the small figure at the back was limping.

Her heart gave a great bound – it was Corydon.

He was back from the land of many. Back the same night he had left. Had something gone wrong?

A second later she was skimming down the stairs and out of the stronghold, running down the steep incline towards them, and catching Corydon in her arms, almost crushing him with the ferocity of her hug. They stood like that for a while.

'Did you find it?' she asked, urgently, and at the same moment, Corydon asked, 'Is everyone safe?' Then they both answered at once, 'Yes, but the Minotaur is hurt,' and,

'They still have him,' – a tangle of words, a tangle of arms and feelings. Each was glad to see the other, but Corydon was also made instantly miserable by her misery, and she was worried by the Minotaur's limp dangling limbs and head. By common consent, without a word spoken, both turned and followed the great horned god back to the stronghold, where they could talk by a warm fire.

Corydon sipped the hot game soup Euryale had prepared – she had brought back a goat and two deer – and watched the Minotaur weakly drinking his on a bed of skins. As Corydon had expected, his great father had vanished after helping the wounded monster inside.

Corydon had been assailed by question after question, which he had patiently answered. Now the monsters knew everything he knew except the weaver's name. They had been amazed and horrified to hear of the wounding of the underworld, of the shades, and of the wild white boar who had injured the Minotaur. Corydon was tired with talking, and he was glad to sit quietly now.

Medusa came and sat down beside him. She too held a bowl of Euryale's goat, but she wasn't drinking it.

'It was my fault,' she said, her head drooping, the snakes hanging limp and listless.

Sthenno spoke, her voice unusually sharp, even for Sthenno: 'You left him to go and fight, not to go to market. You sensibly thought that a battle was no place for a baby. And while you were fighting, that sneak-thief who calls himself a hero came and took him.'

Corydon winced. He was a kleptis himself . . . was he really like Perseus? He began wondering if he might steal Gorgoliskos back, like a lost lamb.

Corydon tried to sound more confident than he felt.

'Medusa doesn't need to fight now,' he said very loudly. 'In the realm of the dead – yes, that is what I shall call it – I learned how to use the Staff's powers to defeat Talos, and without Talos this army will collapse.'

Euryale's deep voice rang out. 'That may have been true yesterday,' she said, 'but it is not true today. For now that rabble have found a true leader, one who has every reason – even every right – to want us all dead. He is strong. He will fight well. And they will follow him. But he does not know this yet, and they do not know it either. We must strike before he can take command, or we are all doomed, without the giant or with him.'

'What do you mean?' It came from all of them, Corydon included.

'Kharmides is his name,' said Euryale. 'And I know a true hero when I see one. His brother was killed in the last battle.'

Suddenly, the Nemean Lion spoke.

'I think I know him,' he said softly, 'for I killed his brother. It is my fault.'

'If anyone else in the room says it is their fault, I will kill them myself,' said Lady Nagaina suddenly and fiercely, with a hiss. 'None of us is at fault. They came here; they try to kill us. How can we defend ourselves? As best we can. Why not try every way? Corydon's way, then Medusa's way. And if neither works, my way.'

'And what is that?' Corydon was not sure he really wanted to know the answer. He had a sudden memory of his lungs burning and rasping, filled with her green cloud.

Lady Nagaina smiled. In her mind a picture formed, of heroes gasping like beached fish as the green air around them became impossible to breathe. She said nothing, however, and Corydon forgot his question.

'I can use the Staff.' he said. 'That way Medusa doesn't have to fight.' His heart was black with dread at the thought of her fighting.

'Corydon,' she said. 'I have given my word. And if I defeat Perseus, I will get my child back.'

He saw that she was desperate to act, to do something, anything, to bring Gorgoliskos home to her arms, and that as long as he was gone she would not listen. He had been sustained in the underworld by the thought that he could save her and also her tiny baby. Now he saw that it had been useless, the whole quest. She would go her own way, and he could do nothing to stop her. Unless . . .

Corydon suddenly had an idea. If they could defeat

the heroes *before* the single combat, if he could destroy Talos, he might be able to steal Gorgoliskos in the confusion and smuggle him out of the area – and then Medusa would follow. And he would be safe, and she would be safe, and all would be well.

'Why not another battle?' he asked, his mouth full of soup and bread.

'We are willing,' said the Sphinx. 'But Corydon, last time we fought, one of us was killed. We cannot keep losing one of our number in every battle. We are so few, and they are so many.'

There was a silence as absolute as falling snow. Everyone thought of the Harpy.

'It is strange,' said the Nemean Lion. 'The Harpy was only annoying while she lived. But now I would give anything for her to return and annoy me again.'

There was another silence.

Then the soft, rough voice of the Minotaur was heard.

'Will you let me help?' he rumbled. 'For if you will, I believe I have thought of a way to help manage the heroes, though it will require all our efforts. That leaves Corydon to manage Talos – and he can, my friends.'

While he had been listening to the conversation, he had been drawing a diagram in the dust.

It showed a strange series of stick-like shapes, joined together oddly, with a curving cup at the end of one stick.

'What is it?' asked Medusa, fascinated.

'It will throw large rocks at the heroes as they run up the hill.'

'By itself? How?'

'We place the stones inside it and it will fling them when we pull a rope.'

'How big will the stones be?' All the monsters pressed eagerly around the Minotaur.

'They can be as big as we like, for each one of those sticks is a tree.'

'Then we must start at once,' said Euryale briskly. 'There are still many hours until dawn. Those of us who can fly will go and bring back – how many? – six – pine trees and lay them behind the stronghold, hidden by the peak and the dome from the heroes.' Inwardly, she thought that there would be many chances to grab the odd boar or deer once she was out of the stronghold.

'Get what rest you may, for work must start as soon as we have the trees,' said the Minotaur. Sthenno, Euryale and the Sphinx took off at once to search for wood.

Medusa took the Minotaur's hand in hers. 'You are doing this to spare me,' she said, 'and I am grateful indeed.'

'I am doing this because I want to save you. So does Corydon. And he loves you,' he said, softly, holding her hand tightly and looking into her face. To her own surprise, Medusa found herself blushing. The snakes on her head writhed, embarrassed. The Minotaur looked earnestly into her face. 'You know,' he said, 'while I was in the land of many guests, I could not remember exactly what you looked like.'

'That must have been a blessing,' said Medusa, with a shrill laugh. The Minotaur did not let go of her hand.

'You are beautiful to me,' he said, his voice a little fiercer than usual. 'I like to see you with Corydon and with Gorgoliskos.'

Medusa hardly knew how to believe him; she so hated the way she looked herself. But she knew he never lied, and his great dark eyes were honest. Amazing herself, she kissed him quickly on the forehead. The snakes stood on end with pleasure and excitement.

Then, scooping up the drowsy Corydon for warmth in the cold desert of her empty room, she went to bed, but the soft breathing of the sleeping boy could not lull her. He had lived through so much that he was not disturbed even by the snakes, but she tossed and turned, trying not to imagine what might be happening to her tiny son. She was glad when it was time to join the others in building what she had to hope might defend them.

ϕι

TWENTY-ONE

The heroes on watch were surprised to see the vague shapes of monsters flying overhead several times in the long night. One watchman saw a gorgon outlined against the stars, her dark wings covering and eclipsing them. He could see that she was carrying something huge in her claws. But he decided not to alert the leaders, who had gone drunkenly to bed after a victory *komos* lasting several hours, in which the village's whole annual supply of wine had been consumed.

On the other side of the hill, the monsters were busy. The Minotaur had been brought out and propped up to supervise the work; Lady Nagaina had unearthed a surprisingly large collection of rusty tools that she had built up, and with these the monsters set about shaping the trees as the Minotaur instructed. After hours of frantic work, with everyone helping, two machines were completed. The final machine was not yet finished.

It had been Medusa's part to gather up stones as ammunition. She was just as strong as Sthenno and Euryale, though she could not fly. She had collected an immense pile of them, working until her hands bled. She was glad to have something to do.

Corydon's hands were bleeding, too; he had made the rope pulleys for the machines, from goats' hair and hemp that the flyers had brought in. He felt exhausted.

'Well done,' rumbled the Minotaur softly. The monsters were impressed by their own achievements, though surprised. They had never worked so hard in their lives before, and they had never before worked with each other. All of them stood hot and dirty in the dawn light, unable to stop smiling at each other.

'We must hurry,' said the Minotaur. 'We must move the machines to the front of the stronghold, ready for the battle.' With many grunts and groans, all the monsters pushed and pulled the two huge machines to face the village. 'What about the third one?' asked Corydon.

'We do not need it yet,' said the Minotaur.

'Corydon, you must rest now,' said Medusa softly. 'It's still at least an hour until dawn, maybe more. Go and sleep. We need you in the morning.'

'I can help move the machines,' said Corydon weakly. The truth was that he felt grey with weariness.

'Go on,' said Medusa, sounding sterner. Corydon gave her an awkward hug and began the slow climb back to the stronghold. As he walked he seemed to see lengths of rope dancing before his eyes.

He was exhausted, but he couldn't sleep. His mind twisted and turned like the woven ropes, searching for a way out, a way to help.

Finally, he had an idea, an old kleptis-idea. The boys had often used koumos-traps when being pursued on thieving raids. If he built a koumos, there was a chance that it might trip Talos up, and if it did, that might give the Persephone magic a better chance – it might give the monsters a better chance too. It might catch a few heroes, as well!

Pulling his sheepskin around him, he rushed out into the chilly darkness just before dawn. With tired and bleeding hands, he scrabbled out the hole, making it as big as he could, between the stronghold and the village. He was grateful when the Nemean Lion came to help him, scratching fiercely at the earth with his claws. Then Corydon covered it, carefully, in bracken, so it would not be visible.

Now he had done all he could, he suddenly felt he could sleep. He went back to the stronghold and fell onto the bed.

Meanwhile, the other monsters were not idle. They dispersed, eager for breakfast, except Lady Nagaina, who hated food anyway. She stood looking at the unfinished third catapult with a thoughtful expression. Little hisses came from all her heads. Then she too went inside, where Euryale was handing out roast bird, snacking on it herself as she did so, and Sthenno had made bread on the hearthstone. The snake-girl kept watch on the topmost tower. As breakfast was finishing, she reported that the heroes' camp was seething with activity, and that the men were on the move.

'Treacherous swine,' grunted Euryale crossly. 'Bet heroic little Perseus has been up all night trying to think of a way out of single combat.'

But Perseus was hardly thinking at all; instead, he was suffering from a head that seemed to have become as big as a melon and as frail as a fine pottery jar. The sunlight hurt his eyes, and the men's voices seemed to echo in his brain like bats swooping in a cave. Perseus's only consolation was that some of the others were even sicker, so sick that they hadn't appeared at all. To make matters worse, Kharmides walked beside him, obviously fresh and rested despite the deep drinking he had done, and full of ideas.

'We can't just leave them alone till the single combat can be resolved,' he said. 'Let's try a morning raid on their stronghold. No one – no matter how heroic – could want to go up against a creature like that gorgon. No one.

Let's see if we can't settle this by good old-fashioned methods.'

Jason came around to Perseus's other side. Perseus was glad to see that he, at least, looked red-eyed and headachy, but he spoke out clearly: 'Perseus, we know how heroic you are, but plain battle is better. Let's at least try it.'

Perseus tried desperately to hide the great swelling wave of relief that possessed him, but he could see that Jason, at least, knew what he was feeling. He could also see that Jason didn't want him to kill the worst of the gorgons and go home with all the glory. He could see, too, that Kharmides only wanted to begin killing the monsters as soon as he could. He decided to agree, but he made a cautious show of reluctance.

'My friends,' he cried, taking both men by the arm, 'you are both thinking of everyone's good. I will do as you advise, but will fight and kill this creature myself if no other way can be found. Agreed?'

His heroic language and tone moved the others to admiration. Even Jason thought, 'He does do it well.' Then he thought, 'He talks well anyway,' and grinned secretly.

Kharmides had still not washed or changed his armour since Lysias's death; being coated in black ash was his way of showing how deeply he mourned. He had cut off all his hair, almost to the scalp. He welcomed the idea of

297

battle because it let him stop thinking for a moment about what his family would say when he came home without Lysias.

'What is your plan?' Perseus asked.

'There are thousands of us,' said Kharmides, in the same dead voice as before, 'and there are only nine of them – unless there are some small ones we have failed to notice. Direct assault. We must conquer eventually by weight of numbers.'

'Up that hill? It's a perfect field of fire. What about the gorgon's glance? What about the greenish smoke that paralysed the men in the last battle? We lost hundreds of men yesterday, and we killed only one monster.'

'Yes,' said Kharmides, 'there will be losses. Heavy ones. But we will conquer by weight of numbers.'

Jason was intimidated by Kharmides' certainty. 'Perhaps,' he said, trying a more cunning method of persuasion, 'but how will we motivate the men? They are – not exactly an army. They are frightened of the monsters after the last battle – have you not heard them? I saw one big strong fellow throw down his figurines and jump up and down on them.'

Kharmides grinned, for the first time since the death of Lysias. 'Find him and promote him,' he suggested. 'He shows good sense and good taste.'

Perseus took umbrage. Kharmides added, 'Well, he was at least focused on important things instead of trivia.

Perseus, you brought all these men here looking for treasure. I suggest we point out that little domed tower on the cliff, where the monsters are lurking, and tell everyone that they keep the treasure in there.'

'But how do you know they do?' asked Jason, baffled.

'The same way Perseus here knew the monsters had huge heaps of treasure in the first place. Right, Perseus?'

Perseus smiled weakly, wondering if there was a way to have this man killed in the night. Still, his logic was good.

'I think you are right,' he said. 'Where better for the monsters to keep their vast ill-gotten hoard than in a tower?' He avoided Jason's eye as he said this. 'We must rid Hellas of this menace, and we must do it now. Call your men together. We begin the assault as soon as the army is assembled. And don't forget – we have my father's gift.' His head throbbed; he wished he could lie down, but he could see that the day was going to be one of frenzied activity. At best.

From the stronghold, the monsters saw the lines of men approaching, the sunlight glinting on their armour, on their shields. Their spears stuck out in front of them, slender and deadly like the spines of a sea urchin.

'Get ready!' cried Euryale. The monsters ran lightly down to their war machines. To their surprise, Lady Nagaina had pulled the third, unfinished thrower into line with the others, and had done something to its throwing arm that made it glisten faintly, as if a huge snail had been there.

'On my signal!' said the Minotaur. He had made himself a crutch, and stood firm on the steps of the stronghold. 'Hold! Hold! Wait until they are in range! Now – fire!'

The monsters pulled on the ropes. Rocks shot from both catapults, arced through the air, and fell slowly and crushingly to earth. They began to roll down the slope, smashing through the heroes, carving pathways through the lines like a knife carves through bread. Men were crushed beneath them; some rocks bounced off the hillside and flew at other men. The slope was already littered with shattered bodies.

'Fire again!' cried the Minotaur. More rocks poured out of the machines, and rolled onto the hapless heroes, who were already struggling with a slope now slippery with blood.

Now, Lady Nagaina stepped forward to the machine she had altered. She gave a soft hiss.

Something flew through the air towards the oncoming heroes.

It was black and shining at first.

Then it began to grow transparent, until it looked like a large, soft crystal.

When it was poised above the heroes, it burst into flame.

And it fell onto a group of warriors marching together. They caught fire at once, and began to scream.

One, with great presence of mind, leaped into a stream on the hillside, but the fire only burned more fiercely.

The men had ignited the grass on the hillside as they lurched about in agony. The wind rolled a wall of grass-fire down the hill towards the next line of advancing heroes. They screamed and broke. Some older men tried to beat out the fire with their feet, but it was stubborn and strong. As they got it extinguished, Lady Nagaina gave another, longer hiss, and launched another missile at the oncoming men. This globe was milky-coloured. As it rose into the air, it began to grow and swell. When it reached the apex of its arc above the men of Hellas, they looked up at it, terrified, as men look up to see an eagle hovering.

Then it burst, expanding like a rose, with petals made of white-hot fire.

Fire poured down on the heads of the heroes.

Fire fell in fragments so tiny that they worked into armour, under breastplates and corselets. The men tore off their armour to get rid of the burning agony. But it seeped into every crevice, and they were helpless.

Lady Nagaina smiled.

But Corydon was beginning to feel sickened by the carnage. He stared at one man whose arm was now a mass of burnt flesh. The man was looking down at his own arm, wonderingly, as if he didn't know how it had happened. He wasn't screaming. He was just looking at his own ruin, without crying or fuss.

'Call – Talos!' Perseus was almost choking on the smoke. 'Our – only – hope!' He had wanted the heroes themselves to carry the day, increasing his glory. But it was clear that only Talos could prevail against such ferocious creatures.

Then pressing through the gasping, dying men came Kharmides, leading those most loyal to him, friends and brothers in arms. 'On to the stronghold!' he cried, his powerful legs making light of the slope. 'Come on!' And he gave a savage war cry: 'Oi, euoi, ehoi!' All the men took it up. The mountains rang with howls of fury. Dodging the flights of stones with surefooted ease, Kharmides ran on, his grotesquely blackened face set in an expression of fury and determination.

The snake-girl stood waiting.

In her hand, she held a huge krater-bowl of her own blood.

Then she spat in it and the blood began to solidify into stripes, and the stripes began to wriggle and change. They took form as snakes, green as poison, green as moss. Each one was armed with venom as fiery as Lady Nagaina's weapons. But the snakes' fire would burn inside a man, and send him reeling senseless to the Styx.

The snake-girl took up the jars she had brought from Lady Nagaina's collection of old pots. Into the mouth of each jar, she stuffed handfuls of writhing green.

Then, as Kharmides and his men ran up, she began throwing them.

At first the heroes laughed.

'A girl is throwing jars!' said one soldier with a grin. 'They must be desperate!' Heartened, the men ran faster.

But as the jars crashed against their shields and armour, their laughter turned to screams of horror as the jars' deadly contents spilled out. Snakes climbed into men's shirts. Snakes wreathed their helmets like victory laurels. Snakes wriggled down their shields. The snakes, maddened by their treatment, bit the men savagely, their venom acting instantly. Men fell to the ground with foam on their lips, thrashing wildly, their blood seeming to boil. Then they would jump up again, shout war cries, and in their delirium attack their friends, who had become monstrous to them.

In this way the grass was soon dappled with blood and scattered with writhing bodies. Kharmides pressed on, but was felled at last by a blow from one of the Minotaur's stone-throwers. He lay senseless on the hillside.

His attack had failed.

Now there was only Talos left.

XL
TWENTY-TWO

Perseus called the metal giant, and he came, his feet plashing in among the bodies of the slain as if he were treading grapes at harvest time. The shields of the dead broke under his feet.

Desperately, the monsters launched new attacks. But rocks simply bounced off the giant, as if they were hitting a wall, and even Lady Nagaina's strange missiles had no effect on the huge metal body. In fact, Lady Nagaina's missiles made him move faster and his eyes grow brighter. As for the snakes, he simply crushed them in his huge gleaming fists.

The snake-girl was upset; she loved her pets. All the monsters began to think of retreat. Lady Nagaina was already edging away.

'Wait,' shouted Corydon. 'I know what to do! But he must be closer! Don't try to stop him!'

The giant came on. Soon he was so close that Corydon could see the rivets in his metal flanks.

Corydon saw that it was time.

As the giant's shadow, black and enormous, covered the hillside, Corydon drew out the Staff, its ruby shining like a coal fire in the darkness of Talos.

'Come here! Now!' he shouted to the monsters.

Quickly, yet without error, trembling, he drew the circle, writing the name he had learned, the name Persephone. The letters enclosed them in a perfect circle.

Talos grew nearer. As he did, he began to give off a darkness, like smoke or airborne ash, as the fires within him grew hotter. Heavy clouds of his darkness blotted out the sun completely. There was terrible, flaming heat, and a stench like a blacksmith's forge.

He was almost within reach of the circle.

'Persephone!' Corydon cried, trying to make his voice strong. 'Persephone! Persephone!' And he drove the Staff hard into the ground.

The letters around the monsters began to glow ruby red in the Talos-darkness. The monsters could suddenly see one another well in the eerie light.

Beyond Talos, there was a faint rippling in the air. A whitening on the face of the dark. The rippling grew stronger. The air itself appeared to be growing white and solid.

Then came a cry that Corydon knew: 'Haima! Haima!'

The voices of millions of shades, billions, as countless as the stars. They burst out of everywhere, white and wraith-like. They beat against the circle, but they could not break through.

Then they smelled the giant.

And all of them descended on him; they could smell the warmth and life in him, the life that kept him moving and going.

His body was soon thick with them; they landed on his eyes so that he could not see and on his mouth, so that he could not shout. They were thick on his legs and arms. Talos was maddened; he tried, helplessly, to brush them away, then to strike at them, but nothing he did made a difference. They were in a hunting frenzy now. 'Haima! Haima! Haima!' they chanted, faster and faster and faster.

But the shades did the metal giant no harm. They swarmed over him, but could find no way to his blood through the thick metal skin. They increased his frenzy, made him more dangerous. The shades had also smelled the blood from the wounded heroes; they began to drift off in pursuit now of this man, now of that.

Corydon felt desperate. It wasn't working. The huge creature blundered forward; at any moment he would be upon them. There was only the koumos-trap left to stop him, and who knew if he'd ever come near it?

With a sinking heart, Corydon knew why it wasn't

working. The shades always needed a fresh wound to drain someone; they'd drunk his own blood only after he'd stupidly cut himself. It was hopeless; how could anyone break Talos's skin?

Suddenly, he remembered what he'd seen.

The rivets on the giant's foot.

Kronos had shown him that picture, of a fountain coming from the ankle-bone of a giant statue. He must have done it for a reason. His brain whirring, Corydon thought: perhaps if he took the metal plug out, the foot would spurt . . . like a fountain . . . and the shades . . . would they drink, then?

But he would have to get the stud out. It was so hard he knew he could only do it if he didn't think about it at all, if he let his kleptis-trained body lunge forward, by itself almost. And the shades . . . if he left the circle, they might easily get him. His hands were ragged from weaving rope. But if he was quick he would have a chance. The last chance.

He forced himself to wait. The giant's foot was almost at the koumos-trap. One more step . . .

Talos's foot plunged down into the pit Corydon had made. The giant was thrown off-balance. He faltered, stumbled to one knee.

Now! Setting his teeth, Corydon sprang out of the circle.

His mind refused to watch as he hurled himself forwards. He knew he'd only have one opportunity. He grabbed the huge foot. With his monster-strong fingers, he hung on, then brought up the other hand in a swift grab at the stud. Nothing happened. Corydon was battered against the lower part of the great heel as Talos took another step, but he managed to cling on. Now, now! He made another desperate grab. The stud was too tight. Breathing a short prayer to his great father, Corydon summoned all his strength. He flung himself at the rivet. This time, to his amazement, it came free. Corydon rolled swiftly aside as lava-hot gold blood gushed out. He sprang back into the circle.

One shade saw the golden blood pouring out.

'Haima!' it cried gleefully. It was stuck to Talos's foot, like a limpet on a ship, and as it drank it began to swell, to grow golden. Soon it was joined by millions more. The shades sucked on Talos's ankle, and as they did their white papery wraith-bodies grew solid and golden.

Talos began to sink.

Like a ship holed below the waterline, he dipped at one end. The magical ichor that had run through him began to ebb out of his body.

His fires went out. The monsters felt the air clearing of smoke.

Soon he could no longer lift his right arm. He looked at it in surprise. Then his right leg began to give way too, so that he was forced onto both knees. The shades gathered in more closely, the full-bodied ones standing aside for other white wraiths. As they drank, Talos's head began to loll. His head fell forward on his mighty, deadly chest, so fatal to the Harpy.

Then his great back began to bend, so that he crumpled forward, looking like an old man asleep in the sun. Finally, as the shades drained the last of the ichor-pouch that they had found, he rolled over and fell backwards. He lay at full length, staring up at a sky that was now clear and blue. He was still alive, but soon his eyelids closed, for the last time.

He had never noticed the sky before, and would never see it again.

The dead gathered around the circle. Full of haima, they were ample with personality.

Corydon and the monsters saw old friends and old enemies among them: the pirates they had slain, men who had fallen in battle. The Harpy was there, batting thick golden wings, and grinning as she aimed a little swipe at the Minotaur's head. But even she could not cross the circle of glowing red letters.

Corydon wondered what on earth would happen now.

Then he heard it: the dim, heavy sound of hunting horns and the belling of the hounds of underearth.

With a cry, the black hunters he had seen once before burst from the hillside. The blind black hounds scented the dead, and the dead – even the solid ones – began to run from them. The dogs, acting like sheepdogs, rounded up the flitting, fleeing shades, and drove them back the way they had themselves come, towards the cave entrance to underearth.

Onto the hillside in their wake, came the dark-cloaked riders on their coal-black horses.

As they passed Corydon and the astonished monsters, the last rider of all threw back his hood.

And Corydon knew him; it was the man who had made the Staff.

And the rider knew *him*, too. Their eyes met in the ruby light. And more than anything he had seen, the man's burning gaze seemed to sear Corydon's soul, for it held a depth of pain and desolation unlike anything he had ever known.

Then the rider turned and galloped away, after the others.

As he did so, Corydon noticed a drop of blood fall from the rider's thigh.

He watched, his mouth open with amazement. As the rider disappeared, the drop of blood blossomed into a whole hillside of dark, fragrant purple narcissus that smothered the metal remnants of Talos and filled the air with the rich perfume of offerings for the dead.

And the circle of words, also, transformed itself into white flowers, delicate, tiny, but piercingly sweet.

Inside it, the monsters united in a huge, grimy, sweaty, relieved hug. Medusa almost crushed Corydon with her embrace, Euryale tossed him high in the air, and the Minotaur and Medusa did a kind of dance around the snake-girl, who had begun to search for her beloved pets. The Nemean Lion rolled kitten-like on the grass, playing with the Sphinx's tail; she didn't mind. Even Lady Nagaina threw back her head and laughed.

But it was different in the heroes' camp.

The camp was full of the wounded. Men writhed in charred agony; they lay on stretchers with limbs smashed and mangled by stones. But the worst injuries were those done by the snakes. Those who had been bitten were still running mad on the mountains; their strange cries could be heard ringing from the cliffs. Others had been captured by friends, and locked into village houses, where their deafening howls split the night air.

The dead still lay unburied.

By now, the few survivors could see that they had been fools to come on the quest.

There was no treasure.

It had all been a pirate's lie.

They had journeyed to ruin, ash and desolation.

Kharmides was the only one of his party to have returned. Somewhere on the hillside lay all the men who had followed his lead to their deaths. His eyes held an

312

enormous emptiness. He knew it had been his fault that the attack had been so costly. He had thought of revenge; he had not thought of the men.

Perseus had watched Talos's destruction, transfixed with horror. The only faithful friend he had ever had lay in a jumbled heap of metal on the hillside. Having wasted his father's greatest gift – without more than one dead harpy to show for it – Perseus was humiliated. How could he ever face Almighty Zeus now?

He went to consult Kharmides. The man was a nuisance, but he had useful ideas that Perseus could borrow. It was already late, so he took a beaker of warm wine and some cheese as gifts. The village had already been picked clean by the hungry heroes, and supplies were running short.

Kharmides looked up as the golden hero entered the circle of firelight. The man's face was like the face of a hero-god. But Kharmides knew that the man's heart was so tiny and shrivelled that you would not find it with a pin.

Perseus sat down and handed Kharmides the wine, without speaking.

Kharmides felt a surge of malice. It felt a little like life, anyway.

'Well,' he said, 'now you are our best hope, my *friend*.'

Perseus was so startled that he dropped the cheese in the dust.

'What do you mean?' he asked, unable to keep the fright out of his voice.

'I mean your single combat with the creature. Kill her, and then we can turn her face on the monsters themselves.'

Perseus swallowed. Hard. 'Marvellous plan,' he said, suppressing the obvious retort that her face hadn't harmed the others so far. 'But after today, perhaps a bit of a tall order, you know.'

'Oh, nonsense,' said Kharmides ferociously. 'You're *too* modest, Perseus. Isn't he, Jason?' The other leaders had come up behind Kharmides and now they ranged themselves around him. Suddenly the scene felt like treachery, subversion.

'Yes,' said Jason, 'you really mustn't think so badly of yourself, Perseus. After all, you've told us often that you are the son of Zeus. And you have those wonderful gifts, too. That sword. It was a sword, wasn't it?'

'No,' said Perseus sulkily. 'Just the sandals and the shield.'

'Well, borrow mine, then,' said Kharmides. 'And Perseus – did you fix a time for the combat?'

'No,' said Perseus. He refused to say another word.

Jason spoke. 'Well, Perseus, I suggest we send a herald with olive branches to tell the gorgon that we expect her at noon tomorrow. High noon. Let me have the honour of sending my own serving boy.' He whistled and an

314

eager boy came to his side, then raced off into the darkness with the message.

'And meanwhile, Perseus, try to get some sleep,' Kharmides added. 'We've agreed to – er – stand guard all night – in case the monsters try a stealth attack, of course.'

Perseus was trapped. He thought of the hideous writhing snakes on the gorgon's head, her purple skin, her face at which no man could dare to look. He was sure that this was his last night on earth.

The messenger boy raced up the narrow track, stopping only once to give his skin water bottle to a man dying of burns. He was not afraid, but glad to serve his lord.

Averting his eyes, he shouted: 'gorgon! Perseus expects you at noon tomorrow!'

At the stronghold window, a face appeared. The boy hid his face in his cloak. But he heard a high, shrill voice reply, 'I will be there, never fear!'

Medusa turned away from the window and saw stricken faces all around her.

Corydon was the first to speak. 'Medusa,' he said, earnestly, taking her cold hand, 'you don't have to fight him now. I still have the Staff, and we can use it to get Gorgoliskos back from them. You wait and see. We'll start before dawn – all of us will go – and—'

'Yes,' she interrupted savagely, 'and how many of us

315

will die? And will one of them be my son? And will another be you, as dear as my son? Or will it only be the Minotaur, who journeyed through the realm of the dead for me? Or will it be Sthenno, or Euryale, my sisters? Or just a gentle little snake-girl? Or maybe Lady Nagaina, who has let us all live here in her tower, though she hates having us? Or the Sphinx, who has saved us all countless times?

'Any or all of us.'

She paused, and drew a ragged breath. 'Or perhaps things will go well, and it will just be a few more mortal men, a few more of those fathers and sons and brothers and lovers who lie outside our windows crying with pain. We can't help them. I can't even look at them. But they are dying because of us.'

Corydon was silenced for a moment. He could see what she was arguing very clearly. He had seen, too, how miserable the dead were. He felt worse and worse, though, at the thought of losing her. Hearing her argue and fight made him love her more, because that was her, how she was.

'But, Medusa,' he blurted, 'we cannot spare you. Not because you are powerful, but because – because . . .'

'You helped to get everyone to work together,' said the Sphinx.

'You were the one who made all the plans,' said Euryale.

316

'You were the one who was always kind to me even though I'm soft and not very clever,' said the snake-girl.

'You always hugged me,' said the Nemean Lion in a soft rumbling growl.

The Minotaur just looked at her with great, liquid eyes.

'. . . because we all love you,' said Corydon in a shy, embarrassed rush.

'And I love all of you, too,' said Medusa fiercely, 'and that's why I can't let another battle happen. The worst thing that can happen if I fight him is that I'll die. So many, many worse things than that could happen in a battle, and I might still die.' She turned and looked at Sthenno. 'And you haven't tried to tell me not to go, Sthenno, and I know what that means.'

Sthenno's eyes met hers. She nodded reluctantly.

'What have you seen?' asked Corydon.

Sthenno looked nervously around the room. 'Corydon,' she said, urgently, gently, 'you can never be sure, with the stars. Never.'

'But what did you see?' Corydon asked.

Sthenno sighed. 'It is better not to know, sometimes.'

'Sthenno,' said Corydon. 'I need to know this. What did you see?'

Sthenno put her head in her hands and spoke in a tiny voice, a voice hard and bleak. 'I saw Medusa guarding the gates of the kingdom of the many,' she said.

Corydon stopped arguing, then, and ran to Medusa for

317

a hard hug, for he saw that what he did or said would make no difference. It was all already spun on the distaff, as Sthenno would have said. All that remained was for Atropos to cut the thread that bound Medusa to the world.

Perseus tossed restlessly, asleep, but still afraid.

Suddenly, he was no longer in camp. He thought he was dreaming, but in his dream he was asking urgently the whole time for help in the battle on the morrow.

And in the dream, help seemed to come.

He stood on thick snow, drifted into piles that glittered in the bright sharp moonlight of a winter night.

A hand that looked very like his father's was stretched out to his. Yet the hand was not, he felt sure, the hand of Zeus.

It belonged to a figure wearing a heavy black cloak, velvet and dark like night itself.

In his other hand, which he was holding away from Perseus, was a cap made of grey fur.

The dark figure put on the cap and vanished. Vanished completely. Perseus could not see him. But he could see that he had not gone away, for his feet had left marks in the snow where he stood, and no marks led away.

Then he reappeared, the cap in his hand.

He held out the cap to Perseus. Perseus smelled flowers, the same flowers that had erupted on to the hillside that day.

Perseus took the cap, and the figure turned away. Not a word spoken. But when Perseus woke, he held in his hands what he knew to be a magical gift, the gift he needed – the gift of invisibility. And he turned it over and over in his hands, wondering, fearing the one who had sent it. He knew the name of its owner. He would not say it aloud.

He arose, and went to sacrifice a goat to the gods of the underworld. And then he began the slow process of preparation; he did his exercises, called his squires and wrestled them, ran a stade-race distance, was oiled, had his hair combed and his arms and armour polished. All this he did as if still dreaming of the Lord of Many.

Perseus had known all along that he could not fight Medusa in front of his army. He had no real wish to do so, and her power made it impossible; spectators would rapidly become statues. He had found the perfect place: the village threshing floor, a wide room that would prevent her from hiding in corners and turning her deadly gaze on him unexpectedly. Polishing his shield to mirror brightness, he went over and over his battle plans. He knew he could win, if only he was lucky enough.

Corydon oiled Medusa's mauve skin, as if she were a real warrior. But he knew she wasn't. It was all a pretence, like some silly game of dressing-up that had gone much too far. Like the shepherds' plays, where they acted out the deaths of great kings in the past.

Corydon knew that he was afraid, more afraid than he had been in the underworld, more afraid that he had been in his dream of Kronos, more afraid than he had been in the pirate show, more afraid than he had been as the pharmakos-boy that long-ago morning.

He wanted to beg her not to go. But he understood and loved her reasons. So he kept on with his oiling.

Euryale and Sthenno came in. Euryale bore a sword, which she had taken from the dead body of a slain warrior. Sthenno carried a spear, which she had taken gingerly from the dead hand of a boy so young he looked as if school and not the battlefield was the right place for him.

'Which one, Medusa? Sword, or spear?' said Euryale. Her face was stern, even for a gorgon. Corydon dared to think that she, too, was sad in her way.

Medusa thought for a moment. Then she said, 'Sword.' Euryale handed her the bright bronze weapon. Medusa took it, held it aloft. It caught the firelight, shone golden. Medusa kissed the blade.

'We could . . .' Lady Nagaina hesitated. 'There are things we could put on the blade . . .'

'No, thank you,' Medusa said, trying to make her voice kind, instead of shrill. 'Then I would truly be the monster he thinks me. If I fight him, honestly, perhaps he at least will see that I am not as he imagines.'

Corydon went to the window and looked at the sun. It was more than halfway up the sky.

'Medusa, it is almost time,' said the Sphinx.

The Minotaur limped in. He took her lilac-coloured hand in his great brown ones.

'I have been sacrificing for you,' he said. 'To the powers of underearth. Hecate. The Lady of Flowers. The Lord of Many. And now I have come to say goodbye.' His voice did not break, but he had to steady it. Medusa smiled at him, and brushed his shoulder with her other hand. For a moment their eyes locked, and each thought, 'Tomorrow. If there is a tomorrow.' Then the moment was over, gone, borne away like a shade in the Styx.

'Good luck,' said Lady Nagaina, casually. At least, she tried to sound casual, and then turned her heads suddenly away. The Nemean Lion shambled in and bent low to rub his head against Medusa's knee, like a dog. The snake-girl came and put a timid hand on Medusa's lap. 'Here,' she said. 'I have made a sword belt for you.' It was made of snakeskin; the snake-girl had sacrificed one of her beloved pets to do it. Medusa put it on, grateful and humble. 'After all,' said the snake-girl, 'you are a snake-girl too!' And she patted the wild vipers of Medusa's hair.

'We will accompany you,' said Sthenno and Euryale, firmly.

'No need,' said Medusa, getting to her feet.

'Yes, there is,' said the other gorgons.

'After all,' said Sthenno, 'you are one of the only things on which we have ever agreed.'

Euryale was having a quick venison snack. With her mouth full, she said, 'Nothing will ever be the same, anyway. Let us go, and go together, three of us facing the world of men.'

'So it was meant to be,' said Sthenno.

'I shall come too,' said Corydon firmly. 'And I shall bring the Staff. That will make sure there can be no treachery.' Medusa began to protest, but Corydon took her arm urgently. 'Don't you see?' he said. 'It's Gorgoliskos I'm thinking of. Suppose they've found out he's one of us? They might try to kill him.' Medusa could see that he was trying to persuade her, but she let herself be persuaded. And so the four of them walked out into the brilliant sunlight.

ΨΩ

TWENTY-THREE

Perseus walked down the alley towards the threshing floor. He couldn't shake off the feeling that all this was happening in a dream. Trying to sound alert, he said, as crisply as he could, 'Go. Fetch the baby.' His serving boy ran off.

The threshing floor was dark and shuttered. Perseus wanted it that way; the less light there was, the less chance of catching a glimpse of the gorgon's face. But he had asked the villagers to put four pine torches in the cressets, and they burned with steady orange flame. Jason and Kharmides were to watch the combat 'to make sure there is no treachery,' they said, Jason barely able to repress a grin. They had provided themselves with mirror-shields, too – not as brilliant as Perseus's, but good enough to let them look at the combat.

Perseus's serving boy came running back. 'Lord, Lord,'

he panted. 'There is something you must see. Something is wrong – with the – baby.'

Perseus gasped. Had they found out? If they had, he must act as surprised as anyone.

'What is it?' he asked.

His squire said, simply, 'Behold.'

The village matron who had been looking after Gorgoliskos entered the threshing floor, accompanied by a boy of about seven. A boy with dark, lovely skin, with a sheen on it like ripened olives. With blue-black curling hair. With enormous eyes, dark as well, eyes with a hint of grape-purple in their black depths.

A boy with six fingers on each hand.

Perseus could hardly believe his eyes.

'Are – who – how?' he stammered. His dream was rapidly becoming stranger still.

The woman spoke. 'He cannot speak well, lord, though he is learning all the time. It's Hera's milk, my lord. It has given him the short infancy of the gods.'

Perseus decided to test this. Turning to the boy, he said, 'Do you understand me?' The boy nodded.

'Pick up my shield,' the hero ordered. The boy turned, picked up Perseus's shield, tossed it lightly in the air, caught it, and handed it to the hero, who could not have done such a thing himself. Perseus began to see that this boy could be a real and terrible new danger.

As he was thinking this, the three gorgons entered the

threshing floor, conducted by an extremely nervous villager who ran as soon as he had brought them there. Corydon followed, unnoticed. Everyone immediately hid their eyes and picked up their shields – except Gorgoliskos.

Who saw his mother.

And ran, like an arrow flying straight at the target, flinging himself into Medusa's arms.

And she knew him at once, though his babyhood had been stolen from him, stolen from her too. 'My Gorgoliskos,' she said, stroking his curling hair. 'My Gorgos, for you are not so little, now.' Her voice shook. 'What have they done to you?' she whispered.

The village woman, who was not afraid of her but who kept her eyes hooded, said, softly, 'He was fed on the milk of paradise, my lady. The breast milk of Hera. He's half-god, now. And half-monster, if I may make so bold. I noticed his fingers at once.'

Medusa replied, 'Then I thank you for your care of him. And if I should fall, I charge you, with my dying will, to take him from here with these my sisters and to keep him safe from such as these.' She pointed at Perseus, and at the flabbergasted Jason and Kharmides.

Kissing her son for the last time, she said, 'Go, darling. Go with this good woman. I will see you again, whatever comes next.' Gorgoliskos clung around her neck for a few more precious moments, and she had to struggle to disentangle him. 'Go,' she said. 'Go.' And they parted, with difficulty; it was like when ivy has to be pulled away from the warm stone that has sustained it.

Medusa drew her sword. 'And now,' she said, in her highest, angriest, most hissing voice, 'where is this great hero?'

Perseus also drew, though he stood at an angle. His face was white and his knees shaking, but he knew he had to go through with it.

Kharmides watched, dark and sardonic. Jason smiled openly.

Without further ado, the two combatants began to circle each other, warily. Perseus looked in his shield, and saw all the writhing snakes atop her head. His goal was to try to get far enough away from her to put on the cap he had been given, and then to stalk her with the aid of invisibility and flight. He had oiled the sandals carefully, and they were in a good and willing mood.

'Come on!' whispered his shield. 'Make a break for it!'

Distracted for a crucial second, Perseus failed to parry Medusa's thrust. She had cut his shield-arm and blood was beginning to pour down it, blurring the shield-image. The monsters cheered; Corydon, his hands balled into fists, hoped, and hoped, and hoped that the wound might disable the hero enough to end it: *let it be over, let it be over* . . .

Perseus knew he had to act quickly, before he lost more blood. Cunningly, he aimed a slash at Medusa's head, soaring up into the air, beyond her reach. While she was distracted, he shot across the room and pulled on the cap.

Now he was in his dream-world, and everything was slow, slow as honey dropping peacefully from the comb.

But for Medusa, it was nightmare. She couldn't see him. Where was he? Where *was* he?

All the monsters were puzzled. Then fear slammed into them. He could be anywhere.

And as they felt it, they also heard the faint rustle of bird-wings. 'There!' screamed Euryale. 'The sandals!'

But it was too late for Medusa, then or ever. She did not have time to turn.

Perseus flew in behind her, and with his sword, stabbed her in the back.

He did not even need to use his bloodstained shield.

Purple blood flowed in a river across the floor, as Medusa tilted slowly forward. Perseus freed his sword with a jerk, and she toppled, face down.

Corydon ran forward, uncaring. He reached her side just as Perseus, triumphant, roaring, brought his sword down on Medusa's neck and severed her head from her body. Corydon heard someone give a great wailing cry, as if the world itself were breaking. Later, he realised he had made the sound himself.

Perseus held the severed head aloft, and laughed, cruelly, as Jason and Kharmides ducked. 'Now,' he said,

'I have something to show to both the men I call father!'
Wrapping the head in his bloodstained cloak, Perseus
headed for the door. He could hardly wait to tell the
world. He was, he was truly, a hero at last.

Jason, quickly spotting the winning side, followed him,
his mouth full of praise.

Only Kharmides hesitated by the broken body of the
monster, the boy sitting still by it as if it might spring
back to life with watching and tending. He saw that the
boy was too distraught even to cry; instead his face
looked like someone who had reached the end of everything. The purple blood swirled over the floor.

Surely there was too much of that blood? Her body
was only woman-sized, and yet there was a river, a lake.

The blood slowly began to rise. Like a fountain, it
forced its way upward. And from the blood, something –
or two somethings – began to take shape.

Wondering, Kharmides crept closer. The mourning boy
turned his head, and he, too, saw what was happening.

As the blood reared higher, grew more solid, the two
shapes became identifiable.

One was a horse, but no ordinary horse. A horse with
wings.

The other was an armed man.

Kharmides had seen wonders on the isle, but this was
the greatest.

While he stood, amazed, colour began to run over both

new bodies, dispelling the purple of the blood. The horse was lit white like the winter moon. The warrior man flushed golden, the gold of armour and the gold of skin.

Kharmides suddenly wondered whether standing here was a good idea. Neither horse nor man looked very manageable.

As he thought this, he was proved right. The horse and man burst the building open, the horse by flying at the ceiling, which crumpled away and gave him passage, the man by knocking down a wall. Sunlight streamed in, illuminating the body lying like a felled purple flower on the floor.

Kharmides went over to it and to the boy. Beside him, now, were the other two gorgons, and around them a silence thicker than the snows of winter.

He drew off his helmet, and raised his sword above his head in a salute to the fallen. 'You,' he said, aloud, to the dead monster, 'you are the truest hero I have seen.' Turning, he walked away.

They bore her body back up to the stronghold.

The monsters came out to meet them. They had seen the party coming. They knew.

The blueness and gold of the afternoon were insults. It should be dark for ever.

Already at the stronghold were Gorgoliskos and the woman who had cared for him.

Gorgoliskos saw his mother's body. But without a head, he hardly knew who it was. He was puzzled. He turned, uncertain, to the village woman.

'Mummy?'

'Now, darling,' she said, 'your mummy is dead.' Gorgoliskos gave a great gasp.

The woman laid a finger on his lips. 'Yes,' she said. 'Your mummy died. She died because she was brave. You have to be brave, like she was.'

'I can't be that brave,' said Corydon. 'How can he?'

'You'll help him along,' said the woman. 'You all will.'

'I will,' said Sthenno. She held out her arms to Gorgoliskos and he leaped down and ran into them. The village woman smiled.

'I know,' she said. 'It seems like it will hurt for ever. I won't deceive you; no one knows better than I how much it will hurt. I've been hurt myself, and so has my daughter. But this one knows all about that, this little one here.' She patted Corydon on the head. 'He knows my daughter. He knows her name.'

'I've given you a present,' she added, lightly, to Gorgoliskos. 'A present I tried once to give another boy, only his mother wouldn't have it. You'll find not much will hurt this lad.' She pointed proudly at Gorgoliskos. 'Only one or two things and I'll be back to tell you about those. Truth is, I've never really been away. A village woman, that's all I am, grinding the corn.'

330

But as she spoke, Corydon and the others could see the radiance of an immortal creeping out from her plain black robes, her plain brown skin.

'You have unfinished business in the realm of the many,' she said to Corydon, with a faint trace of sternness underlying the tone, warm as bread, that had lulled them all. 'I'll see you there, and you'll see me.'

And with that, she drifted away down the hillside. Where her feet fell, swathes of red poppies sprang up, pied daisies and fresh rose bushes shrouded the unburied dead of the battle. Laurel sprang, and ivy. A light came from her. And her veil slipped back, laying bare a train of hair as gold as corn.

Then Corydon knew her: the Lady of the Corn, the goddess, Demeter. Mother of all.

Corydon sighed. He went over to Sthenno and knelt before Gorgoliskos. 'Gorgos,' he said, 'I must leave you now to finish the work that your mother began. But I will not be gone long, and when I am back, we will make a song for her together.'

Gorgos didn't cry, or whimper. He held out his hand, Corydon took it, and they were friends, brothers.

'Now, I go to the realm of Hades!'

'And I go with you,' said a deep voice. Beside Corydon stood Kharmides.

Corydon found that he was not surprised, though he had no idea how Kharmides could have known of his need.

Perhaps Kharmides himself could not have explained. He was still grim, still in battle array. He was still streaked with the ash of mourning.

'I lost my brother,' he said, 'and you have found one. But you, I think, have lost a mother. Of a kind. We two know what death is; it is pain and the rending of hearts, the sundering of people who love each other. It is desolation. But perhaps if we travel in hope, we can change what it means.'

Corydon nodded, strangely shy. 'Let us go together,' he said. Holding the Staff aloft, its red light warm and fierce in the dying light of the day, they walked steadily towards the underearth.

ὠμέγα

TWENTY-FOUR

Back amidst the torments of ice and wind, Corydon simply let the Staff show them the way. It knew where it came from, and that was where they had to go.

They followed a path unlike the one Corydon remembered, though it led into equally wintry landscapes, through a frozen marshland, then over icy lakes and swamps. The wind began to smell of salt.

And at last they burst out on the edge of a cliff, a great white bluff of chalk, glowing whiter than the snow. At its base, thousands of feet below them, was a great city made of wood that gleamed with pale moonlight. The sea lapped the shores of the city. Ghostly white ships rested in its harbour. The city was proud, domed, delicate.

The most visible building in the city was larger than any temple or palace in Hellas, larger than a cave or forest even, with a clear ice dome blue as the winter sky at night, studded with stars, capped by a full moon. Was it really the moon? Corydon didn't see how it could be, because on the isle the moon was still dark, but here it was full again. And yet it looked like the moon to him.

'The Hall of Poesis,' breathed Corydon.

'What is it?' Kharmides asked. It was the first time he had spoken. He had not complained, but the toil of pushing through ice and snow had taxed his mortal body far more than it had the monster-bodies of Corydon or the Minotaur.

'The place where the dead go to be reborn,' Corydon explained.

'Is that where we have to go?' asked Kharmides.

'The Staff is taking us to the city,' Corydon answered.

Kharmides looked at the sheer cliff face.

'Well, I don't see how we're going to get down,' he said.

'I'm going to jump,' said Corydon.

'You can't be serious,' said Kharmides. 'It's Zeus knows how many hundred feet down. And at the bottom it's ice.'

'Watch,' said Corydon patiently. As he spoke, a rivulet of ice-white shades poured over the edge of the cliff and eddied towards the dome of the Hall, like snowflakes borne on blizzard winds.

'Those are the dead, I take it,' said Kharmides, after a

pause. 'Which explains why they can jump over a cliff and not be killed.'

Corydon thought it over. 'Maybe,' he said. 'So what's your plan?'

Kharmides hesitated. 'I don't have one,' he admitted.

'Well, then, let's at least give my idea a try,' suggested Corydon in a reasonable tone, as if jumping over a cliff were quite a normal idea.

The truth was that he didn't very much care if he died or not. Perhaps Kharmides felt the same, for after a moment he said, 'The terrible thing is that if you're wrong I won't be able to give you the thrashing you deserve because we'll both be dead.' He gave Corydon a shaky grin, and held out his hand.

'Come on, then,' said Corydon, and hand in hand they ran for the edge.

The last step took them over.

They began to fall, going faster and faster. The wind of their speed pushed the breath from their lungs. It was icy. And yet somehow Corydon found himself roaring with delight. It wasn't like flying. It was falling. Soon they reached a speed where they could hardly breathe. Their hair froze.

And the ground rushed towards them like a stampeding bull.

Corydon shut his eyes. So did Kharmides.

They both felt like the gods themselves, because they

were going to die; their bodies knew it and told them so, yet they were not afraid.

With terrible, bone-shaking thuds, they hit something. Something that was not the ground.

Something warm, silky, furred.

Something that was itself alive.

Corydon's eyes opened.

He was on the back of a horse. A horse with wings. Kharmides was clinging to it too.

The horse swung gently down to the ground, shook them off, then mounted, swift and agile as a seabird, over the white-maned waves.

'It is he who was born this morning,' said Kharmides, his voice full of awe. Corydon said nothing. But for the first time, he knew that Medusa was not far away.

They found themselves on a causeway that approached the city. At the end of it stood a great gate, made of some light metal that glinted, luminous and soft. But it was all rusted, and broken in places, its filigree decaying and chipped.

In front of it stood a dog so big that it had to be part-wolf.

Kharmides tried to draw his sword, but the blade had long since frozen in the scabbard. While he tugged, the dog approached. Corydon looked into its burning white eyes, and a knowledge passed from them into his mind.

'It wants us to say its name,' Corydon said. 'Just its name.'

'And how are we supposed to know it?'

'We must ask it,' said Corydon, sensibly. 'What is your name, my friend?' he asked. 'You guard your city well.'

The wolf-dog wagged its tail, once, then somehow Corydon knew to say, 'Loxias.'

The wolf stood aside.

The gates opened, and they entered.

The city was beautiful. It was light, with delicate pillars, intricate ornaments, domes as airy as bubbles. But it was also a city of the dead, and it was itself dying. A stench of decay emerged from it. Dust mixed with the light flakes of snow in the streets. Everywhere, groups of shades rushed past, speeding towards the Hall of Poesis, but there were no other inhabitants; it was very truly a ghost city.

They stayed on the widest street, the Staff pulling them forward; its glow was the only warm thing in the city.

Or so they thought, for suddenly, into their path sprang another dog, this one the size of a small horse, with reddish fur like a fox.

'Do we have to say its name again?' said Kharmides wearily.

'I suppose so,' said Corydon, but the dog nosed his hand friendlily, and seemed inclined to let them both go past.

'Maybe this one doesn't have a name yet, and we have to think of one,' suggested Kharmides, a little tongue-in-cheek.

'Iakhos!' said Corydon at once. 'You can see, he's a mystagogue, a follower of fun. And he's laughing at us, too.'

'All right,' said Kharmides, laughing himself. But mirth was somehow stilled by the emptiness of the streets, the fleeting shades, the damp and decay and cold.

At the end of the street stood great heavy copper doors, grown jade-green with verdigris in the damp salt air. Above them rose a great high roof, its paint peeling to reveal stone, supported only by cracked pillars. The building was enormous, but its walls were fragile frost; the wind soughed through them.

In front of the doors stood a creature Corydon knew, a dog, black as midnight, with three huge blind heads. It was vigilant; its blind eyes, always sealed, could never mislead its keen sense of smell. It knew they were there, and it knew they didn't belong.

One of its heads growled.

'What do we do now?'

'Everyone knows his name,' Corydon said. 'I'll say it, but it can't be that simple.'

'Kerberos,' he said, carefully sounding the first syllable. 'Kerberos, Kerberos.' The great dog did not move.

'Look,' breathed Kharmides.

Next to the dog was a bowl of bloody scraps of torn meat. Some of them looked like human tongues, bits of liver – was that a pair of lips, a brain? An eyeball? A nose?

Corydon wasn't a squeamish person, but he didn't want to touch those fragments. Still, they were obviously there for a reason.

He put his hand into the bowl.

He tried to use only the tips of his fingers, but the stuff was so spongy and slippery that his hand somehow slithered in. He felt the soft textures close over his fingers. The meaty smell sickened him.

He grabbed a fragment and pulled it out. Then another. Then a third.

The big dog's mouths opened. The tongues began to loll, and drool.

Corydon took a deep breath. He placed the first titbit on the tongue of the first head. It vanished. Then he gave something white and wobbly to the second head. Then the third head actually began nosing for the miserable lump of decaying purple he still held.

Kerberos licked his chops – all three of them – with satisfaction. Kharmides was open-mouthed.

The huge dog stepped almost daintily aside from the great doors, which swung open.

Corydon and Kharmides walked through into a wide hallway.

At the end were two dark hooded figures. Corydon

339

recognised them as two of those who had hunted the wild boar, and later the shades.

'Be welcome,' said one, in a cold voice, 'to the palace of the king of underearth.'

'He has been expecting you,' said the other. His voice was hard as frost.

'Do you wish to see him?' asked the first. 'We will take you to the throne room if you wish it.'

'I wish to see him,' said Corydon firmly. The Staff was pulsing, pointing towards the dark guards, and beyond them. It pulsed more and more as they approached the place where it belonged. Corydon knew they were very near now. Kharmides shuddered. There was a coldness here that pierced the stoutest heart.

They followed the dark guards into a room so big, so cold, so delicate, so decayed that they knew it must be the throne room.

Its walls were so frail that they let in snarling gusts of wind. Flurries of snow eddied around the vast room. The floor was slippery with thick rime.

At one end, a dark-hooded man slumped in a chair, one leg propped up before him.

Corydon had no idea what to do.

As he stood, wondering, he could smell the wound in the man's leg even from where he was. It was putrid; his whole leg must be infected.

Then, suddenly, it came to him.

Running down the room, the Staff held before him like a lance, sliding to the dark king like a skater on hard ice, he plunged the ruby into the king's leg, as if he was trying to spear him.

There was a crimson explosion. In its light, Corydon knew what to do next. He remembered the words of the scroll in Kronos's library.

In front of the wounded king was a small square of earth, with a few dead plants in it. Corydon hastily scrabbled a hole in the dry dust. Then he pulled the glowing, pulsing ruby from the Staff and flung it into the hole.

As he did so, everything began to change.

The first thing Corydon noticed was the light and the silence. It was silent because the wind dropped. Without the shrieking, pitiless wind, the cold weakened, as when a fire is lit in a room in the morning. The light, meanwhile, grew stronger, and the cold and desolate palace began to blink, to shimmer, then to fade from sight, like a cloud in sunlight.

The king was still there, but his clothes were no longer black; they were brilliant blue, like lake-water, and ripe crimson, like fruit. A golden band encircled his head.

Where the walls of the palace had been, green grass began to spread out.

And where the ruby had sunk into the ground, a huge tree sprang up in seconds. It was twenty, thirty, forty feet tall. It had leaves, suddenly, all over. It bore fruit, huge, ripe, heavy fruit that hung rich and red and scented from the branches.

'Pomegranates!' breathed Corydon, amazed.

Then a small flower pushed its way up beside him. Then another, nearer the tree. And another, and another, until the entire place was covered in rich purple and dark red narcissus. Their heavenly scent filled the air. Beyond them, whole rose bushes flung pink and white and crimson petals that hurled more perfume about, heady and almost choking. A small bird flew past, beginning to build a nest, a green twig dangling from its beak. A small herd of deer ran by.

Everywhere, everything was green, and growing. And alive.

'Is there no more death?' asked Kharmides, in a whisper.

Corydon looked at Kharmides and said honestly, 'I don't know. But I think perhaps death is different now.'

As if to confirm his words, the dead began to be visible.

No longer white and wraithlike.

Corydon turned in a slow circle, taking in the new life all around. A girl wandered past, reading a scroll; she laughed aloud at something in the story. A group of men walked under the pomegranate tree, talking. Ahead, a group of children were dancing together on the distant seashore, while others picked up shells.

The king stood hand-in-hand with a girl so beautiful that light and flowers sprang out all around her; it was the weaving girl, the Lady of Flowers. Persephone. Violets sprang up in their footprints.

And there was one man, tall solitary, smiling, swinging a hazel stick at the blossoming hedges.

It was Lysias.

'Brother!' he cried. 'Are you one of us too?'

'No,' said Kharmides. 'I came not to trouble you, but to say I am sorry. I crushed your dreams too often.'

'It doesn't matter any more,' said Lysias. 'Come and see.'

'I will one day,' Kharmides responded.

Lysias smiled understandingly. 'I'm sorry, too,' he said. 'But I can't seem to mind much about it.'

'No,' said Kharmides. 'There will be no more rebirths needed, now. Corydon has released you all from the wheel of life.'

Corydon himself was taken aback, but it was true. The Hall of Poesis had vanished; in its place were trees, flowers, mountains. And instead of the wailing souls, there were people dancing and birds singing.

Lysias smiled at Corydon. 'We all thank you, my friend,' he said. 'And a reward awaits you. Go. Follow the path over that hillside. And greet the doorkeeper from me!' He hugged his brother, hard, and ran off.

Together, Corydon and Kharmides followed the spiral

path. The landscape was so changed that they hardly knew where they were.

Along the way, they passed what looked like a market garden: serried rows of vegetables, leeks as tall as a man's arm is long, cabbages bigger than helmets, all neat and severe. An old man with a tanned face was hoeing the rows. He suddenly looked familiar as he bent to his task. Corydon gasped. It was Kharon, who had once guarded the Styx. He waved, uncertainly, and the man waved back.

Corydon saw that the River Styx itself, running by the old man's garden was altered. It meandered along as if it loved to delay. Floating on it were lily pads as large as an opened scroll, with the pointed petals of white flowers above them. Frogs and dragonflies swarmed over the languid river. Here there was no rickety bridge, but a marvellous archway of gleaming marble, delicately carved by what looked like the same artist who had made Persephone's castle. Honeybees drifted by, buzzing lazily.

The path took them up a hill to a pair of bright copper gates that glinted in the bright light. They were the gates of the underworld itself, made new like all else.

By the gates was a small cottage, with an orange-tiled roof and a climbing rose. This rose was dark and heavy with petals, so richly scented that it made the air around it seem heavy. And Corydon could see its brilliant red thorns, long and hooked.

One look at the rose, and his heart knew. He knew who lived there. He could not have said how, but the rose was like her; it refused gentleness to be more intense. His heart bursting, he ran forward to the door and flung it open. And she was there, Medusa, just as he remembered.

He'd half-expected her to have been transformed into something prettier, something like her old self, but she was lilac and green and snaky-haired, as he had known her. He hugged her and hugged her, and she hugged him back, and the snakes twined themselves into comfortable knots of writhing pleasure.

'I thought you might have changed too,' he said.

'No, this turns out to be who I want to be,' she said. 'The Olympians were right.'

'Were they?' said Corydon, in surprise.

'Well, only about this. Otherwise I think they are the tyrants I have always thought them to be. And I shall never, no, never forgive Almighty Sky-Thunderer for taking me from you, Corydon, and from my son. You must go on fighting them. We've won a great victory – two victories. Against the heroes, and against the wounded land here. You are Corydon the Renewer.

'Don't you see?' she went on. 'Persephone's people, as she calls them – we're all monsters, in our way, carried below before our time, not living out what was proper to us. Deformed by death itself. Reduced. But what we've learned is that we have to accept that and also hate it.

Both at once. If we only accept, we are weak and wailing. But if we only hate, we know no peace. You have brought us both. Strength and peace. Because you've always had both yourself. Tell Gorgos.'

Corydon didn't pretend to understand all she said; he never had. But he knew what she meant in his heart. He gave her a bunch of violets he had picked. He knew he had to speak. And that he said could never be enough.

'Medusa,' he faltered. 'I do not have any strength without you . . .' His heart thundered in his ears. He was not equal to what she asked: to go on, to care for Gorgos and the others, without her . . . For once, he could think of no words.

She seemed to understand, for she flung her arms around him in a last warm hug. Her snakes twined themselves painfully in his hair, as if reluctant to let him go away. He winced. And she released him. He saw that her eyes were full of unshed tears, but her voice was hopeful.

'I foresee great contests at my funeral games,' she smiled. 'And a visitor.' She twinkled at him, and refused to explain. She was just as she had always been.

Corydon could not cry. But he thought his heart would break.

'We will meet in eternity,' she said. 'And now you have seen it, you will not be afraid.'

With a last hug, she gave him a gentle push. And to his

346

surprise, Corydon saw that Kharmides was waiting outside the cottage with a familiar figure; it was Demeter,
with the black cloak. Come to lead them home. She
opened the bright doors, and they passed out onto the
hillside of the earth.

EPILOGUE

The heroes left the island, except for Kharmides, who went up into the mountains and made a small hermitage, to serve the black-cloaked goddess, Demeter. It seemed as if the old life was unreachable for Kharmides too.

Perseus used Medusa's head to get rid of his stepfather, who became a famous statue. Perseus became king, and head of a huge shipping and trading company. It is true that his father Zeus said, 'You're a hopeless failure, Philotas,' but Zeus also set him up with a good portfolio of part-shares in silver mines and pine plantations.

Perseus preserved the head of Medusa in a special myrrh-filled tank in his main palace. It became a much-visited work of art, bringing tourists flocking to Seriphos, and allowed Perseus to found a sculpture collection, and later a further successful venture in garden sculpture.

This gave Perseus the opportunity to sell the leftover Golden Hoard figurines as gallery souvenirs.

The villagers went back to scratching a hard living from the hard land.

And the monsters?

They held an enormous party for Medusa's funeral, the best party ever held on the island.

Corydon and Gorgos presided over the funeral games. There were krater-and-snake races, with snakes provided by the snake-girl; you had to hold a krater full of snakes out in front of you and run with it, without dropping any of the snakes. The snake-girl won this herself, by singing a calming song as she ran. The Minotaur organised a missile-firing contest with the old war equipment. Corydon won a singing contest, and the Minotaur, to general surprise, won a storytelling contest with a tale of a man who made a labyrinth and became trapped in it himself. There were three-legged races – or in some cases five- or seven-legged – which the Sphinx and the Nemean Lion won. There were games of blindman's buff, in which everyone laughed and fell down a lot.

And there were prizes for all the winners: snakeskins, meat from Euryale, cheeses from Corydon, wooden figures of Medusa carved by the Minotaur, Lady Nagaina's prized parasols stolen from her stronghold by the gorgons, a few rocks the Nemean Lion picked up and hoped might be useful.

Finally, there was a great feast. There were honey cakes and honeycombs, fresh cheese, barley porridge, glowing golden globes with sweet insides (brought by the Sphinx), pomegranates heaped high in great piles, olives, olive oil, and many, many wineskins. The monsters had sacrificed a brace of milk-white deer to the old gods, and an ear of grain to Demeter, and a fish to Hecate, so there was also plenty of fresh and tender meat to eat. Enough, even, for Euryale, who for the first time in her life, felt full.

Well, almost. Because everyone knew they were trying to fill an aching void inside, as they looked around and saw that Medusa wasn't with them any more.

As they were feasting, however, a stranger slipped in amongst them.

At first they didn't notice her. She was a tiny and bent old woman in a dark-blue cloak. She sat down at the end of the long trestle table the Minotaur had made. It was Corydon who sat next to her, and he didn't even notice her until she suddenly made him jump by asking him for bread. He passed it to her absently. Then she asked Gorgos for wine, which he also handed her willingly and politely. The old woman smiled.

'This is a terrible day,' she said, 'though you have won a great victory. You will be needed soon, for another land requires the kind of help that you gave to underearth. Will you serve?'

351

As she spoke, Corydon could see that this was no simple village woman.

'I will gladly help those who fight for freedom,' he said, 'but I will never lift a hand to help those who oppose it.'

The old woman smiled. 'I believe I am answered,' she said softly. 'We will meet again, Corydon Panfoot. Be well, Gorgos. And bear your loss as you may.' Patting him once on the shoulder, she left. Gorgos and Corydon stared at each other; they could see that new adventures might be beginning just when they had expected months of idleness and grief.

And then Corydon rose to perform his last act for Medusa. He sang her the song he and Gorgos had made.

Her body lay on a pyre of pitch-pine, quick-burning wood that would consume her.

Lady Nagaina had added some resins and gums, so when Corydon threw a torch at the pyre in a great arc, the wood roared into dazzling life; blue flames, red flames, green flames, hot gold burning flames. It was like Medusa herself: beautiful, strange, and yet you couldn't look at it for long without being dazzled.

As the fire grew higher and higher, Corydon watched the sparks fly upwards like flocks of birds, through the dazzle of his tears. He held on tightly to that last moment with Medusa in the underworld. It would sustain him in whatever dangers might lie ahead.

GLOSSARY

Olympian gods and heroes

Olympian, Olympos. (OH-**LIMP**-E-AN). The most powerful Greek gods formed a kind of bossy multinational corporation (a bit like McDonalds?), by moving to Mount Olympos, from where they could look down on humans and human life. In modern terms, the Olympians are like a football team that buys all the good players so it can win everything and no one else can even score. (Some people think this is cool, but it's boring for everyone else.) The Olympians are bullies. Their chief competitors include the chthonic gods (see p. 365).

Agamemnon (AG-A-**MEM**-NON). High King of Mycenae. Brother of Menelaus and leader of the expedition to Troy. Bossy.

Akhilleus (AH-**KILL**-EE-US). The strongest and the fastest and the scariest and the most beautiful of all heroes. Not really liked by the Olympians, because he's half-god himself.

Aphrodite (**AF**-ROE-DI-TEE). The Goddess of Love. Sounds nice? It's not. It's not cosy. It's the kind of love where you suddenly spend all your time hanging around someone you don't even LIKE just because they look fit. Some say Aphrodite is the most powerful of all the gods, because insane, silly love can kill reason and wisdom and intellect and friendship and skill.

Ares (**AH**-REES). Greek god of war, but the simple kind of war; the sudden longing to punch someone's head in. Or the mood in which you might sing 'Ere we go, 'ere we go, 'ere we go'. A macho man. A spoilt brat, though. And not, in fact, a very good fighter.

Artemis, also called Lucina, or sometimes the Maiden (**AH**-TEM-IS). Goddess of hunting, wild animals, young girls before marriage, wild nature (woods, mountains). Virgin, but also a midwife and goddess of birth. Some links with the chthonic gods.

Athene (AH-**THEE**-NEE). One of the twelve Olympians. Extremely powerful goddess, who represents cunning (inherited from her mother, Metis – whose name means cunning) and also warrior skills, but also weaving, olive trees and the city of Athens. Virgin, and doesn't like sex or babies much. Likes cunning, clever heroes like Odysseus.

Atropos (**ATT**-ROE-POSS). One of the three Fates. One is Clotho, the one who spins the thread of a human life. Another is Lachesis, who winds the thread on the spindle. And then there is Atropos, who cuts the thread with her shears. Shakespeare turned the three Fates into the three witches in his play *Macbeth*.

Epaminondas (EP-AM–IN–ON-DAS – emphasis wherever you like, really). Historical, not mythological; led the Thebans in war to be Top City State.

Hera (**HEAR**-RAH). Zeus's wife. Definitely *doesn't* like nymphs *or* parties. Likes having her hair done. Likes some carefully selected heroes.

Hermes (**HER**-MEES). Cunning Olympian, patron of thieves. Robs his brother Apollo when he is only a toddler. Helps souls find their way to the land of the dead.

Jason (**JAY**-son). A hero who acquired the Golden Fleece; brave, but also famous for treachery.

Menelaus (MEN-E-**LAY**-US). King of Sparta. Married to the most beautiful woman in the world, Helen of Troy. Pretty annoyed when she left him for a Trojan prince called Paris, and pretty keen to get her back. Not a brilliant fighter or speaker or a brilliant anything, but determined and brave. Learn more about him in the third book in this series, *Corydon and the Siege of Troy*.

Odysseus (Oh-**DEE**-SEE-US). The cleverest of all the heroes, and especially admired by Athene.

Oidipous (**EE**-dee-pos). A hero who guessed the Sphinx's riddle, but then accidentally killed his father and married his mother. His daughter was his sister and his son was his brother. Ugh.

Perseus (**PER**-SEE-US). A really famous hero. Son of Zeus and the mortal woman Danae, to whom Zeus appeared in a shower of gold. Unpopular with his stepfather. Popular with his real father, Zeus.

Philip and Alexander. Alexander the Great and his father Philip, the greatest military leaders of all the Hellenes. The Sphinx has seen them only in visions, because they come thousands of years after the Age of Heroes. But Alexander, at least, loves heroes and hero stories, and tries to be like his favourite hero, Akhilleus.

Pirithoos (**PIR**-I-THOOS). Theseus's best friend. Like most heroes' best friends, not as competent. A pirate. Likes a good fight.

Theseus (**THEE**-SEE-US). Exceedingly famous Athenian king of legend. Mainly famous for killing the minotaur.

Zeus (ZOOS). King of the Olympian gods, or in modern terms, headmaster, gang leader, king, emperor, pope, prime minster, all rolled into one. Likes nymphs and parties. Doesn't like monsters or being disobeyed. Easily bored. Doesn't get on with his wife, Hera. Has a huge number of sons.

Monsters and chthonic gods

Chthonic gods (OK, this is *really* hard to say without spitting a lot, but it's pronounced just as it's written – K-TH-**ON**-ICK). It means earth-gods, or underworld gods. Among those that appear in this story are Hades, Artemis, Persephone, Pan, Demeter, Hecate (although some of these also count as Olympians, which makes it confusing).

Demeter (**DEM**-ET-ER). Goddess of seed brought to life as plants; without her blessing, nothing can grow. Also a mother first and last.

Dionysos (DY-OH-NY-SOS). God of everything about ourselves that's fun and that we can't control – running around yelling and driving our mums mad, for instance, or if you are adult, wine and being very drunk. A very powerful god. See *Corydon and the Fall of Atlantis* for much more on him.

Euryale (YOO-REE-**AH**-LAY). One of the two immortal gorgons.

Gorgo (GOR-GOH). The Greek word for gorgon. Also means anything scary, and means fright itself.

Hades (**HAY**-DEES). Zeus's brother, but much sadder. King of the underworld.

Hecate (Shakespeare said **HEK**-AT, but this is wrong; it's **HEK**-AH-TEE). Goddess of the dark of the moon, witchcraft, and women too old to have babies.

Kerberos (**KER**-BER-OSS). Three-headed dog who guards the gates to the city of Dis. Possibly an embodiment of Hecate.

Kindly Ones. The Furies, who pursue and drive mad anyone who kills their blood kin. You say 'the Kindly Ones' or 'Eumenides' (YOO-**MEN**-EE-DEES), because saying their real names might call them to you.

Lamia (**LAY**-ME-AH). Snaky monster below the waist, beautiful woman above. Can sometimes seem human all over.

Medusa (ME-**DOO**-SA). The third gorgon and the only mortal woman, transformed after violating Athene's temple.

Mormoluke (MOR-MO-**LOO**-KAY). Mormo-demon. Greek children used to play a game where one of them dabbed black ash on his face and jumped at other children; the scary faces were mormo-faces. Greek mothers also played a game like peekaboo, called mormo-bites. Greek demons can often be recognised because there's something wrong with one of their legs. Some people think Mormo is the same as Hermes.

Pan (pronounced to rhyme with ban). Goat-legged god of wild nature, shepherds, pipe-playing, wild hillsides, and being alone. His name is the origin of the word 'panic' because he can either make people very afraid (especially in lonely places) or make them very brave. One of the chthonic deities. Usually opposed to the Olympians.

Persephone (PER-**SEF**-OH-NEE). Daughter of Zeus and the goddess Demeter. Abducted by her uncle, Hades, when she was picking flowers with the nymphs. Hades attracted her with a purple narcissus. Before her abduction there were no seasons and flowers bloomed all year round. Her name was a secret of the Mysteries at Eleusis, and she was always called simply Kore (which just means 'the girl'). The Queen of Flowers. She has hundreds of names.

Sphinx. She wasn't a Greek monster; the Egyptians drew the first pictures of her. She guards territory, and often does it by asking riddles. She asks the hero Oedipus this one: 'What goes first on four legs, the on two legs and then on three legs?' The right answer is 'a man'.

Sthenno (Z-TH-EN-OH – sounds impossible to say, but it's quite easy if you try). The other immortal gorgon.

Other beings/things

Haima (**HAY**-MA). The Greek word for blood. In the *Odyssey*, Odysseus has to make the shades speak by giving them blood to drink.

Hall of Poesis (POE-EE-SIS). Poesis just means 'making' in Greek; that's the origin of our word 'poetry'.

Helios (HEE-LEE-OSS). The sun. Later on, people decided he was really Apollo.

Hellas (HELL-ASS). The ancient Greeks didn't call themselves 'Greeks', but Hellenes, and they came from Hellas, which is the word for the lands where the Greek language is spoken. There was no such country as 'Greece' until modern times.

Kharon (**KA**-RON). In our story, once one of Persephone's gardeners. Usually described as the man who helps the dead cross the River Styx (pronounced STICKS).

Lethe (**LEE**-THEE). The waters of 'forgetting'. In Greek lethe means 'forgetting', but alethe means 'truth'.

Nymphs (NIMFS). The Greeks thought that nature was full of gods who were groups of girls, and these were called nymphs. Every fountain, cave and tree has its own nymph. They're quite powerful and their anger can be dangerous, but they are weak compared with the

Olympians and the chthonic gods, both of whom prey on them. Syrinx was one. Some goddesses have a group of nymphs that hang out with them; Artemis, for instance.

Pasiphae (**PASS**-EE-FAY). The minotaur's mother. She's seriously ashamed of him.

Pharmakos (**FAR**-MA-KOS). Means scapegoat. This really happened; people would choose the ugliest person in a village and drive them out into the desert to carry away bad luck and disease. People still use the word 'scapegoat' to describe an innocent victim blamed for something many people have done wrong. The word 'pharmakos' also means 'medicine' and 'poison'.

Polydectes (POL-EE-**DECK**-TEES). Perseus's stepfather.

Sappho (probably pronounced very oddly, like P-**SAPP**-O, but most people now say SAF-OH). The greatest woman singer and poet. Ever.

Syrinx (**SI**-RINKS). A nymph whom Pan loved. He chased her, but she didn't like him and fled. Her father helped her escape by turning her into reeds by the river; Pan made them into a pipe so she would always be with him.

Excerpt from Kronos's Library Catalogue

Books:

Robert Graves, *The Greek Myths*.

Robert Graves, *The Golden Fleece*.

Homer, *The Iliad* and *The Odyssey* in Robert Fagles' translation, published by Penguin.

Virgil's *Eclogues*.

Theocritus, *Idylls*, translated by Robert Wells.

Sylvia Plath, *Ariel*.

Shelley, *Prometheus Unbound*.

Gavino Ledda, *Padre Padrone: The Education of a Shepherd*, and the film based on it.

Michael Herzfeld, *The Poetics of Manhood: Contest and Identity in a Cretan Mountain Village*.

The Oxford Companion to Classical Myth and Religion.

Andrew Dalby, *The Classical Cookbook*, British Museum publications

Other media:

Time Commanders, BBC TV series.

Hitler: The Rise of Evil, C4 TV series.

Gladiator, feature film.

Age of Empires II: The Age of Kings, PS2 game.

Age of Mythology and *Age of Mythology: The Titans Expansion Pack*, PC game.

Gettysburg, Sid Meier, PC game.

Wagner, Gtterdammerung.

Giambologna, garden scupture of *Apennino*, at Pratolino, 1579.

If you enjoyed

CORYDON AND THE ISLAND OF MONSTERS,

read on for a taster of the next adventure – on Atlantis!

They could see the minotaur's hut now, on the coast. Almost at once, Euryale felt that something wasn't right. It took her a moment to work out what it was. Then she knew. There was no smoke coming from the chimney. She tried to reassure herself. Perhaps the minotaur had gone to pay a visit to the other monsters, just as *they* were visiting *him*. But it felt unlikely. The minotaur was even more solitary than she and Sthenno were, even more unwilling to go beyond the boundaries of the small and ordered world he had made for himself. And it was just too much of a coincidence.

'Sthenno,' she shouted. 'He's not there.'

'I know,' Sthenno called back in her high bird-voice. 'There's something wrong.'

Euryale landed, claws outstretched to steady herself, panting from the flight. 'Could he just be away? On a visit?'

Sthenno was beside her. 'No,' she said, her voice stern. 'Look.'

The minotaur's tiny garden had been trampled by many feet, the crushed plants turning brown in the harsh island sun. Two of the beehives had been knocked over and were lying on their sides, looking almost comical, like abandoned hats. The door of the hut stood open. Inside, Sthenno and Euryale could see that the minotaur's simple wooden table was broken in two, his hearth-fire scattered across the room, his plain benches smashed, as if by a giant hand.

Sthenno pricked herself on a shard of pottery. 'This happened days ago,' she said grimly. 'Look at the plants. And the bees have fled, too. It could have happened as long as a week ago.'

Euryale was studying the marks on the ground, in the soft earth of the vegetable patch. She lifted her head. 'Men!' she almost spat. 'The heroes! Could they have returned? And yet these marks aren't quite the same – a narrower heel, see, and more pointed toes ... and the men not quite so heavy ...' A picture of them began to form in her hunter's mind.

Sthenno was looking around too. 'Which way did they go?' she asked. 'To the sea?' She pointed to one heavily booted print. 'This one might have been carrying something heavy ...'

Euryale took a quick glance, agreed. 'The thing is to get after them immediately,' she pointed out. 'We can't waste any more time.' Both sisters were just about to spring into the air again, when they felt the ground judder, like a ship turned too fast into the wind. There was a rumble like thunder in the rocks.

'What was that?' asked Euryale, startled.

Sthenno didn't have time to answer. 'Look out!' she shouted. Euryale sprang into the air. A huge pine tree crashed to the ground where Euryale had been standing only a minute ago. But, twenty feet up in the air, Euryale was safe.

'Hurry up, Sthenno,' she shouted. 'We have to hunt!'

Not a word of thanks. Sthenno grunted irritably, and leaped for the sky. This was no time to quarrel. The minotaur needed them.

When Corydon finds out that his friend, the minotaur, has been kidnapped by the Atlanteans, he must set out on a perilous journey through strange seas to rescue him. With Corydon is Medusa's son, Gorgos, whose thoughtlessness exasperates Corydon but whose courage and strength save him. For Gorgos is determined to avenge his mother – by attacking the Olympians directly . . .